I0629897

CORONACYDE
The Charaka Adventures

CORONACYDE
The Charaka Adventures

L&M PAYTON

First Edition: January 2022

Cover Art: Rafael Andres

ISBN: 979-8-9852808-1-4

www.payton-books.com

DEDICATION

To my late son, Brian. I will always love and miss you!
—Dad

ACKNOWLEDGMENT

I would like to thank my dear wife, Mandy, for teaching me to appreciate literature and then encouraging and supporting me as I endeavored to write this book. Without you, The Charaka Adventures would never have come to fruition. But most of all, I'd like to thank you for being the perfect partner for me in every facet of our lives. I could never imagine a finer wife. You are the woman of my dreams and the answer to my prayers! I will love you forever!!!

PROLOGUE — PART 1

The glow of the sun began to encroach upon the night sky as Tinzhe walked with his two boys, Mingli and Minzhe, to the dock. Like always, he was on his way to board his boat for a day out fishing in the South China Sea. Every day, the boys would wave goodbye and watch their father's boat get smaller and smaller until it disappeared over the horizon. When the boat finally vanished, Mingli and Minzhe would walk the half mile from the dock to their school.

Tinzhe had married his beautiful wife, Biyu, when they were both very young. They had four children: Mingli was the oldest at ten; Minzhe was six; their daughter Chenric was three; and their baby girl, Chen, was just eleven months.

Tinzhe made a decent living and was happy being his own boss while providing relatively well for his family. He considered himself most fortunate to have enjoyable work with his two best friends as his fishing partners.

After he'd left his sons, the day started out just as any other, with Tinzhe and his small crew baiting hooks on the fishing lines. Each line had hundreds of hooks, so that task alone took them from the time they left the dock until they reached their favorite fishing waters.

As they started tying the buoys to the lines and dropping

them overboard, Tinzhe noticed a large boat in the distance. That didn't surprise him because the fishing industry in China was the largest in the world. With over seventeen percent of the world's fish caught by thousands of Chinese fishing vessels each day, it wasn't out of the ordinary to see another boat or two. However, the boat Tinzhe saw was much larger than most—a commercial fishing vessel, perhaps—and it caught his eye because the waters weren't very conducive to that kind of fishing.

Nevertheless, Tinzhe and his two buddies continued throwing their lines overboard, setting a circular trail of fishing hooks a half mile wide. As he and his crew finished throwing in the last of the lines to complete the large circle, he noticed the commercial fishing vessel was headed in their direction. He became more apprehensive. If the bulky ship were to run through his lines, it would cost him thousands of dollars in fishing equipment, not to mention the fish they could've caught.

Tinzhe stood and waved his arms to make sure the pilot of the ship could see him. "Stop!" he cried, straining his voice.

The water splashing around his small fishing boat seemed almost violent as the large commercial vessel continued its direct path toward him.

"Stop! Stop!" he repeated over and over with sweat beading on his forehead and dampening his clothes.

As the vessel neared, Tinzhe waved his arms more and more frantically, screaming as loud as he could, but the ship sustained its course toward his boat. The vessel's hull was made of steel, and it looked monstrous compared to Tinzhe's twenty-six-foot wooden fishing boat. He realized the large vessel wasn't going to be able to steer clear of his fishing line, so Tinzhe focused his thoughts on self-preservation. A collision would be unavoidable if he didn't take evasive action.

"It's going to hit us!" one of Tinzhe's companions shouted.

"Let's get out of here!" the other crew member screamed.

"I'm trying, I'm trying," Tinzhe's frantic voice shrieked as he rushed to the tiller and gunned the motor to move out of the oncoming ship's path, heedless of the attached fishing lines.

But as he moved his boat perpendicular to the approaching vessel, the large ship changed its course to match Tinzhe's. It was only a couple hundred feet away, so in a last-ditch effort, Tinzhe turned his boat 180 degrees to avoid the bow of the huge ship slicing his boat in half. The ship grew closer, just a few feet from slamming into Tinzhe's boat. He threw his engine into full throttle as he raced to maneuver his boat out of the vessel's path yet again. He didn't quite make it, and the ship grazed the corner of his stern, swinging Tinzhe's little fishing boat 90 degrees and forcing it parallel to the ship. Fortunately, minimal damage was done other than the loss of his fishing lines, and at least Tinzhe and his crew were safe.

"Whew, that was a close call," one of his buddies said.

"Nice maneuvering!" his other friend said.

Just then, the three men caught a glimpse of a large object hurtling from the deck of the vessel before it slammed through the hull of their boat, virtually cutting it in two. Tinzhe and his companions were thrown into the air and landed in the water as the bow and the stern were thrust upward, submerging the center of their little fishing boat.

The men hadn't realized just how big the ship was until they were helplessly floating beside it; it must've been over two hundred feet long. The suction of the ship pulled Tinzhe, his companions, and the remains of their boat in toward the hull as it motored along, unconcerned for their lives. Eventually, they were pulled underwater, the ship's undertow dragging them along the bottom of the hull until they reached the massive propellers.

Then, nothing.

* * *

After school, Mingli and his brother headed to the dock to meet their father. There was always something to do down by the water's edge, and they never tired of waiting for their dad. But on that day, the afternoon turned to evening without any sign of him. Once in a while, Tinzhe was late and even came in after dark a few times whenever he'd encountered engine trouble, but as the sun ducked under the horizon and the stars rotated in the darkness, they began to worry and ran home to tell their mother.

Days later, after many unsuccessful rescue attempts, the China Coast Guard Bureau called off the search and declared Tinzhe and his two crew members officially lost at sea. Persistent urging from her family and friends finally persuaded Biyu to give up hope, and she reluctantly agreed to a funeral for her missing husband a week later.

Biyu worried about how she'd care for her children since she and Tinzhe didn't have any savings or life insurance and she was a stay-at-home mom. Her only skills were cooking and cleaning, but she wasn't as youthful as she used to be and couldn't scrub other people's floors or stand over a hot stove all day. Biyu recalled how, before Mingli was born, she'd worked as a housekeeper for a wealthy businessman and his wife in Beijing, but she'd been much younger then, and that made her reflect on how very naïve she'd been.

During that time, she'd worked for Mr. Wu. He was a forceful man who was used to getting his way, and he'd had his way with young Biyu. After Biyu had summoned up the courage to tell Mr. Wu of her condition, he was happy to pay her to leave and keep her pregnancy a secret from his wife. Biyu married Tinzhe soon after she'd realized she was pregnant, and she'd kept the secret of the baby's father just as she'd promised. Mrs. Wu never knew Biyu was pregnant, and Tinzhe never knew Mingli wasn't his.

When Tinzhe and Biyu combined their savings, they were able to put a down payment on a modest three-bedroom house, and they bought a simple twenty-six-foot used fishing boat with the rest of their money. They were a young couple living a humble but happy life with their first child on the way. Over the years, as their family grew, they continued to live modestly, but they were happy raising their children in a loving and comfortable environment. After the loss of Tinzhe, however, that all changed.

* * *

A few weeks after the funeral, there was a knock at the door late one night. The children were all in bed, and Biyu was hesitant to answer. When she did, she was shocked to see Mr. Wu standing in front of her, dressed in an expensive three-piece suit as always.

"Hello, Biyu. I'm sorry to hear about your husband."

"Thank you. What are you doing here?" she responded, her countenance darkening as her eyes drew together.

"May I come in so that we can discuss why I am here, privately?"

Glancing behind her, she hesitantly said, "My children are in bed, and I don't want to disturb them."

Mr. Wu disregarded her words and entered the house. Biyu, because of her submissive nature, simply stepped aside and allowed him in.

"My wife died from cancer a few years ago," Mr. Wu started as he presumptuously sat down on the sofa. "Since then, I've been alone."

"I'm very sorry to hear that," Biyu replied with genuine empathy. "I liked her. She always treated me kindly."

"I know your situation and that it will be difficult to support your family without your husband now. I have a proposition for you that will make your life much easier." He sighed dramatically and took his glasses off to wipe a spot from them on his handkerchief. Replacing them, he looked at Biyu intently. "I would like to take custody of my son."

"No!" Biyu shouted forcefully, startling even herself with her outburst.

Mr. Wu gestured soothingly to her, keen to keep her from getting even more agitated. "Just hear me out. I will give you a monthly stipend that will allow you to live comfortably and take care of your other children."

"No, I'll manage somehow," Biyu said, biting her bottom lip anxiously.

"This arrangement will be good for you, me, and all of your children. Mingli will have the *best* of everything. You will be able to provide very well for the rest of your children." He waved his hand around the room, gesturing to the pictures of her children tacked up all around. "You will never have financial worries again. As for me, I won't be alone anymore," Mr. Wu appealed.

A thousand memories flashed through her mind as she glanced at the photos. "I just can't." Her words were barely audible as tears streamed down her cheeks.

"You can come and see Mingli anytime you want. You will always be welcome at my house—you and all of your children."

"But Beijing is so far from Shanwei," Biyu said.

"I can arrange for my plane to take you. It's only a three-and-a-half-hour flight."

"I just can't imagine ever letting him go. You are asking too much of me." But even as she tried to convince Mr. Wu, Biyu was reluctantly starting to consider his overwhelming proposition.

Mr. Wu began to get a bit indignant at her persistent refusal; how dare someone question his ideas or plans? When he spoke again, his voice was tipped with irritation. "How are you going to survive? How are you going to take care of Mingli and his siblings?"

"I don't know."

"Do you have a job?"

"No."

"There's no sense in making the children suffer. I'm

offering a comfortable life for your kids. Isn't that what you want for your family?"

"Yes, but…"

"You have to. Don't make your kids suffer a deprived life. They shouldn't have to. If you just say yes, you and your children will have a good life."

"But—my baby."

"Here are the papers," the master negotiator said, sensing her weakening state of mind. Pulling them out of his pocket, he placed them on the coffee table and said, "Here, take this pen and sign right here. Secure your future, and more importantly, safeguard your children."

Biyu reluctantly took the pen from Mr. Wu. With swollen and blurry eyes, she signed the papers, her steady stream of salty tears smearing one of her signatures.

"You have to give me some time to say goodbye and explain to him what's happening," Biyu demanded.

"Of course. I'll come back in two weeks to pick him up. Don't worry about packing for him—he won't need to bring anything. I'll get him the best new clothes and whatever else he wants."

Having accomplished his mission, Mr. Wu took his half of the papers, folded them, and returned them to his coat pocket. Without another word, he turned and walked out the door.

During those last two weeks with Mingli, Biyu revealed to her son the shocking truth about his real father. She tried her best to reassure him that although she had to let him live with Mr. Wu, she loved him and would miss him very much and would visit him as often as she possibly could. Mingli was heartbroken, scared, and confused. Ever since that fateful day when he last saw his dad, his whole world had been turned upside down. Nothing made sense to him anymore.

* * *

Mr. Wu didn't really have a sense of how to show love and compassion to a child, which contrasted sharply with how openly Mingli's mom and dad had always expressed affection. He may not have been warm, but he did have lots of money and knew the secret for success in the business world. He took Mingli to his home in Beijing and introduced his son to his new surroundings. Mingli was in awe of his new bedroom, which was almost as big as the house he had grown up in. He had his own personal bathroom and a living room with a couch and two recliners, a big-screen television, and an entertainment center complete with a stereo, two gaming consoles, and more games than Mingli had ever known existed. He wouldn't ever want for anything, but he couldn't help but think about how much fun it would have been to have his brother there with him and how much he missed his mom, dad, and sisters.

Mingli only saw his mom a few more times. The first was about six months after he'd moved in with Mr. Wu. During that visit, Biyu and her daughters stayed in one of the guest rooms, while Minzhe stayed in Mingli's room. The boys had such a good time enjoying Mingli's new games, and they made memories that Mingli would cherish for years to come.

The next visit was about a year later, when Biyu came to tell Mingli she was going to remarry. From the beginning of their arrangement, Biyu had had a standing invitation to visit and stay at Mr. Wu's house anytime she'd wanted. On that visit, however, she stayed in a hotel to placate her possessive fiancé. She'd been so excited to take Mingli and his siblings to an amusement park, something the children had seen advertised on television and always dreamed of doing. It was a joyous occasion that would be forever etched in each of their memories, but none of them knew it'd be the last occasion they'd see one another for a number of years.

After she'd remarried, Biyu began to realize her new husband was profoundly insecure and didn't like her visiting her son at Mr. Wu's. She began to feel like her affection was divided between her new husband and her firstborn son. Her husband eventually made it unbearable for her to see Mingli. For the sake of her whole family, Biyu stopped her visits to Mingli entirely, although her heart longed to see her eldest son each and every day.

* * *

Mr. Wu may not have been a loving father to Mingli, but he continuously made sure Mingli had the best things money could buy. He enrolled Mingli in the finest schools and made sure he went to the most prestigious university in China, where Mingli earned a master's degree in business. Along the way, Mr. Wu indoctrinated Mingli with the mentality of superiority and the "correct" way to manage their servants.

Mr. Wu never remarried. He taught Mingli it was best to remain single and hire servants who could also serve as companions to be discarded on a whim. Mingli matured in an emotionally sterile atmosphere, becoming callous and indifferent toward anyone he viewed as inferior to himself.

Mr. Wu had initially made his fortune from a gasket company he'd started as a young man. He'd supplied the automotive industry first, then grew larger and began to supply the China National Space Administration. As the years passed, Mr. Wu acquired many more businesses, including a pharmaceutical company. He became one of the wealthiest men in the world and was well respected as one of the most influential people in all of China.

Unbeknownst to most, Mr. Wu had also been involved in less-than-honorable business practices for some time. His pharmaceutical company frequently cut corners and even tested drugs on poor people. Of course, they'd offer their unsuspecting victims a few dollars, but the side effects were often lifelong afflictions and sometimes even death. He'd also been involved with some unsavory individuals who'd engaged in terroristic activities and much worse. At a certain point, Mr. Wu began to have little regard for the lives of others, especially those who had subservient roles in *his* life.

When Mingli was in his mid-twenties and had graduated from Tsinghua University, Mr. Wu introduced him to his business world. At that point, Mingli was groomed to take over his father's empire. Wu had been thinking of retiring, as he was getting older and slower, and Mingli was a quick learner. That, combined with the years of Mr. Wu desensitizing him from feeling any sort of compassion for others, put Mingli on course to become more ruthless and power-hungry than Mr. Wu had ever been.

When it came time for Mingli to completely take over operations from his father, he took the initiative to buy Mr. Wu a 310-foot yacht complete with every imaginable amenity. He hired a crew to care for his father's every need and desire. Mingli eventually persuaded his father to just relax and enjoy his remaining days sailing around the world in the lap of luxury. Mr. Wu accepted his new role graciously, but he still wielded a measure of power, as he consulted with Mingli often and frequently advised him on business matters. As time passed and Mingli's confidence grew, he required less and less assistance from the old man, his father. Hui fang Wu reluctantly relinquished his powerful position and passed the wand to Mingli, the new Mr. Wu.

PROLOGUE — PART 2

A little after midnight on June 18, 2015, Malaysia Airlines Flight 818 took off from Kuala Lumpur International Airport and climbed to an altitude of thirty-five thousand feet before leveling off for the six-hour flight to Beijing Capital International Airport. Although the Boeing 777-200 aircraft was thirteen years old, it was still one of the most sophisticated aircrafts in the world and could practically fly itself from takeoff to landing. The captain, Najah Rahman, was a fifty-two-year-old man from Langkawi, Kedah, Malaysia. He'd been flying for thirty-two years, the last sixteen in command of the Boeing aircraft, and had amassed a total of 19,670 hours of flight time in his career. He'd made the flight hundreds of times and expected to make it many more.

His copilot for the flight was Zikri Attar, a twenty-eight-year-old first officer who was born in Tehran but raised in Abu Dhabi. He had joined Malaysia Airlines six years earlier. Najah was used to working with younger, less-experienced pilots since he'd been a flight instructor and examiner for the past seven years, training the company's up-and-coming pilots. It was Zikri's final training flight, and he was scheduled to be examined during his next. He'd accumulated 2,846 hours of flying time and was, according to Najah, an excellent pilot with a promising future at Malaysia Airlines.

After successfully taking off and reaching cruising altitude, Zikri excused himself to use the bathroom. He told Najah his stomach didn't feel quite right. Zikri exited the cockpit but then bypassed the lavatories and instead snuck into the food-preparation area, unnoticed by any of the crew. In that area, he had access to the door leading into the avionics bay below, and from there, he could enter into the plane's other compartments. Zikri quickly slipped down the hatch and closed the door behind him, allowing himself complete privacy as he got to work.

A wooden crate with eight compressed air tanks that looked very much like scuba diving tanks had been loaded into one of the cargo bays along with a large metal suitcase for Zikri. It didn't take him long to find the crate and the suitcase since they both were very different from the luggage and packages that were normally transported in the cargo holds. The suitcase contained a crescent wrench, a small crowbar, and an electronic manifold with nine hoses attached to it. Eight of the hoses were the same size with ends made to screw onto each of the pressurized air tanks. The ninth hose had a larger diameter, sized to screw onto the service port of the air-conditioning duct feeding the aircraft. Zikri took the crowbar and pried open the crate, exposing the valve ends of the air tanks. Then, he joined the hoses to the air tanks and tightened the connections with the crescent wrench. He removed the cap from the service port on the air-conditioning duct and attached the ninth hose, resized his wrench, and tightened it. Zikri flipped the toggle switch on the manifold, causing a green light to glow bright. He took his iPhone out of his pocket and opened the app that controlled the chamber. He needed to make sure the Bluetooth was connected—it was.

With his task complete, Zikri returned to the access hatch and peeked out to see if the food-preparation area was clear. He didn't see anyone, so he propped the door open and climbed out, only to find a flight attendant rounding the corner. She looked at him with her eyes wide and mouth open in disbelief. Zikri still had the crowbar in his hand, and before the flight attendant could do or say anything, he impulsively swung the tool and hit her on the side of her head, knocking her out. He grabbed her by the legs and dragged her to the access hatch, where he dumped her limp body down below. He tossed the crowbar down with her, then closed the hatch before anyone else noticed anything out of the ordinary. With adrenaline pumping, he returned to the cockpit. Right before opening the door, he pulled out his phone and pressed the initiate button on his app. He tucked his phone away and entered the cockpit, closing the door behind him.

Zikri had been informed that the methoxypropane in the air tanks wouldn't take effect on the 239 passengers and crew members for seven to nine minutes once administered. Within a minute or two of taking effect, everyone on the plane would succumb to the oneirogenic anesthetic, so Zikri didn't want to initiate the fumigation until he was ready to put on his mask, just in case the methoxypropane worked more quickly than expected.

"I still don't feel quite right," he told Najah. "Maybe a few minutes of oxygen will help."

"Sure," Najah said, as it was a common practice for pilots to put on their face mask and breathe oxygen for a few minutes to cure whatever ailed them.

Just then, the radio came to life and told Flight 818 that they'd be transitioning from Kuala Lumpur Radar to Ho Chi Minh Area Control Center. Captain Rahman confirmed the change, which would be his last verbal transmission.

A few minutes later, Najah felt dizzy. When he turned to Zikri to tell him, the captain failed to utter any words and lost consciousness, slumping down in his seat. The program controlling the air tanks released the gas in steady increments to ensure that the passengers stayed unconscious for the duration of the flight, while Zikri breathed through an oxygen mask that was on a separate system from the rest of the aircraft.

With the captain unconscious, Zikri turned the plane's transponder off and banked the aircraft hard to the left, turning it to a westward heading with a final destination 870 miles northwest—the deepest region in the Bay of Bengal.

As Zikri continued his flight path across the Andaman Sea, he couldn't help imagining what he'd do with his three-million-dollar reward. Although he loved flying, it was worth giving up his career if it meant being able to enjoy life without a care in the world. His uncle in Iran who had set him up with the opportunity was himself a powerful man with many connections. He'd promised Zikri a new identity and a fresh start in life. Zikri could eventually fly again if he wanted to, but it'd taken him six years to get as far as he had, and he didn't know whether or not he'd go through all of that training again. He had many options and plenty of time to make up his mind.

After crossing over the Bay of Bengal, Zikri began his descent toward his destination's prearranged coordinates: a location in the middle of the bay and northeast of Sri Lanka. At ten thousand feet, Zikri saw the row of lights floating on the water and breathed a sigh of relief. He continued his descent directly toward them. He was to land the plane on the water and open the exit door if everything went as planned.

That night, the conditions were perfect. The sea was calm, almost as smooth as glass, and there was very little wind. Despite the ideal circumstances, landing on the sea wasn't going to be easy, as any number of things could go wrong—especially because Zikri had never landed on water outside of a flight simulator. A slight wing dip could catch the sea and catapult the plane, or a slightly downward attitude could cause the nose to burrow into the water and flip the plane. If the landing was even just a bit rough, there was the possibility of seriously injuring or killing himself.

There were a lot of risks, but Zikri was an excellent pilot, and in his youthful arrogance, he knew he could pull it off.

As the plane struck the water and every alarm in the cockpit sounded, the aircraft skipped on the sea like a rock thrown just right on a pond, *skip, skip, skip, skip, skip*, until it finally slowed and settled on the water.

"Textbook," Zikri thought out loud as he unbuckled himself. Holding his breath, he removed his mask and hurried to his suitcase stored in the pilot's locker. Zikri grabbed the miniature oxygen bottle out of the bag and put on the face mask attached to it, then threw the bottle's strap around his neck and shoulder. Before opening the exit door, he mused about what a fantastic pilot he really was and the incredible feat he'd just pulled off. Then, the door opened, and two men wearing their own oxygen bottles and face masks climbed out of a rigid inflatable boat, or RIB, and entered the plane.

"Great job!" one of the men exclaimed. Then, in a flash and before Zikri could reply, the man pulled out a pistol, stuck it to Zikri's forehead, and pulled the trigger in one smooth motion.

Both men knew exactly who they were looking for as they walked down the aisle of the slowly sinking plane in search of seat 22A. One of the men pulled out his phone and compared a photo on it to the passenger slumped against the window.

"That's Quon," one of the men said to the other.

The two men pulled the passenger out of the aisle seat and dumped him out of the way so they could get to their intended target. One of the men grabbed him by the feet, the other by the arms, and together they carried him to the exit door, where a third man was waiting for them in the RIB. One of the men took a canvas backpack, threw it into the open door of the plane, and they sped off. A few minutes later, there was an explosion in the distance, and all traces of Flight 818 quickly sank 15,400 feet to the bottom of the Bay of Bengal.

CHAPTER 1

They were cruising at twenty-five thousand feet when the light overhead turned from red to green.

Duke hollered, "Go, go, go!"

The four men took off running for the opening at the back of the V-22 Osprey and dove into the air once they'd reached the end of the ramp lowered for their departure. They drifted apart for sixty seconds before pulling their rip cords. The Mach III parachutes came to life, slowing their descent while they steered toward their target ten miles away. The men were all dressed in black, the same color as their parachutes. An observer looking up into the night sky from the ground would be hard-pressed to see anything. An astute onlooker might have noticed the stars blacked out for a moment as the parachutes blocked their line of sight. However, given they were traveling over the Gulf of Aden—an extremely remote location—no one would be down below looking up.

Their target was a Panamax oil tanker sitting a few miles off the coast of the northern tip of Somalia. Somali pirates had hijacked the ship and held it and its twelve crew members hostage, demanding ten million dollars for the vessel and everyone's safe return.

As Duke rapidly hurtled toward the ship, the air rushing past his ears, he flashed back to another very similar mission. During it, his team had also parachuted and landed on a ship with over forty well-trained militia who gave the impression that they had been waiting for them to arrive. Half of the gun battle had been waged while his men were still in the air, reloading as they hit the deck and ducking for cover as bullets flew everywhere. He still didn't know how they had made it through that unscathed—but visualizing a worst-case scenario seemed to stimulate his cognizance and prepared him for the imminent conflict that lay ahead.

At six foot two, Duke Snider had an intimidating presence, and he'd learned to use that to his advantage while spending most of his adult life in the military. Growing up in East Texas had not only ingrained in him a Southern drawl, but it had also introduced him to an assortment of guns and recreational vehicles. With his freckled white skin, green eyes, and auburn hair adorning his chiseled good looks and muscular frame, it was surprising to most that he had never found a woman to settle down with. Considering the dangers his way of life imposed, it was likely for the best.

As the four men approached the bow of the ship, they readied their silenced SIG P226 MK25 pistols and turned on their infrared laser sights, which were virtually invisible except for the red dots that illuminated their targets. There were only two pirates near the bow of the ship, and the men took them down quietly before they reached the deck. Duke was the first to touch down, followed by Steve, then Kabir, and Ali on their heels. They shed their parachutes and spread out, making their way between the pipes and tubes along the ship's deck and taking out every pirate they saw on their way to the bridge. Within ten minutes, they'd covered the thousand feet from the bow to the superstructure, encountering eleven pirates in total. But as they entered the main deck, they were surprised to find the level deserted. Duke made a motion with his hands that told his veteran crew to split up to cover more area—Duke and Steve took the stairs up to the next level while Kabir and Ali descended the stairs to the level below.

Duke and Steve stopped at the top of the stairs and listened—nothing. Then, Duke glanced around the corner and spotted a wide-open room with tables and chairs—obviously the dining area—but still no pirates. The two men entered the room and snuck to the nearest door, which lead to the galley and food-storage areas. A quick look around revealed no pirates there either.

They went back out and proceeded up the next stairway. Stopping again at the top of the stairs, they listened. That time, they heard the faint sound of someone snoring. As they crept into the main salon, they saw couches, recliners, and exercise equipment—the level where the crew most likely spent their downtime. They followed the snoring, which grew louder as they neared one of the couches. Steve put the red dot on the man's forehead and stopped his snoring forever. They searched the remainder of the level but found it empty of any more pirates.

Meanwhile, Kabir and Ali descended the companionway to the level below. There they found a long corridor with evenly spaced doors on each side. As they quickly peered around the corner, they saw two men lounging in tilted back metal chairs, supported by the chairs' rear legs with their backs resting on the wall behind them. Both men seemed to be napping and didn't notice Kabir or Ali spying on them. Two more men were sitting in the same kind of chairs further down the corridor and playing cards on a makeshift table between them, oblivious of the two men sighting them in with their silenced SIGs. Kabir and Ali didn't need to discuss their strategy—they each instinctively knew what to do. Just one shot apiece, and before the two card players' bodies thudded against the floor, a second shot exploded each head of the pirates who sat just a few yards away, leaving them reclining in their chairs.

They moved stealthily to the nearest door, and without a word, Kabir took his place in front of the door while Ali moved to a position beside it. He reached to his side and quickly turned the handle and flung it open. With his gun at the ready, Kabir swept the room as he stepped forward, only to find a man sitting on a bed with a bewildered look on his face.

Kabir Kumar was the Syndicate's weapons expert. He joined Duke's SEAL team as a lanky five-foot-eleven twenty-two-year-old. But after a couple of years, the black-haired, brown-eyed man had bulked up to tip the scales at two hundred pounds. He had proven that he could be counted on in any situation, and he had the amazing ability to handle any kind of weapon or fabricate one from whatever was available at the time.

"Who are you?" the man asked incredulously.

"Shh," Kabir said with a finger against his lips. "My name is Kabir. My team and I are here to rescue you," he whispered. "How many pirates are on board, and how many crew?"

Whispering in a halting accent, the bewildered man answered, "I don't know how many pirates; they come and go. I've been holed up here, in my cabin, since the first day. I don't have a clue what's going on outside of this room."

"Stay here. My partner and I will check the rest of this level and be back in a few minutes to get you," Kabir told him as Ali stood watch in the hallway.

The two men finished searching the rest of the rooms on that level and gathered the crew members as they headed back to the companionway to wait for Duke and Steve.

Continuing their search, Duke and Steve went up to the next level, which was full of electronics and other equipment, but still—not a soul in sight. As they ascended the last stairway up to the bridge deck, they heard voices. They held their breaths as they continued their ascent, each step calculated as if trying not to disturb a leaf on a forest floor, and Duke peered around the corner. A couple of men sat in two of the four captain's chairs overlooking the deck of the ship. They were carrying on a conversation in Somali when one of the pirates turned to face his companion and caught sight of Duke over his comrade's shoulder. He immediately leaped to his feet but didn't even have time to raise his machine gun before falling to the floor. His buddy immediately slumped out of the other chair and fell on top of him.

As the team reconvened on the ship, Kabir began, "We found these men locked in their sleeping quarters on the level below this one. There were only four pirates on watch in the hallway, and we took care of them before they could fire a shot. All the crew are accounted for except the captain. He was taken off the ship right after it was hijacked—the crew assumes he's being held captive onshore and is being used to communicate with the Exxon executives who own this oil tanker. We didn't search any of the lower levels because we already had all the hostages and didn't want to leave them unprotected."

"Good work," Duke said. "Ali, you stay here with the crew. The three of us will search the rest of the ship to make sure we're alone."

Abd al Bari Ali was one of the Syndicate's two information technology experts; the crew called him Ali for short. At twenty-six years old, his lanky physique and boyish good looks made the dark-haired, brown-eyed young man look even younger. Duke snatched him up as soon as he graduated at the top of his class from Carnegie. But despite his glasses and intelligence, he wasn't a nerd in any way. Ali could pilot the ship as well as anyone and was the master of its collection of electronics and weapons.

After finding the lower levels vacant, Duke, Steve, and Kabir ended their radio silence and began to chat about their situation.

"I'm surprised they didn't have more men guarding the ship," Steve said.

"They must have figured they wouldn't encounter any resistance or a rescue mission," Kabir responded.

"They probably figured Exxon would just pay the ransom and get their ship back underway as soon as possible," Duke stated, "but from what I understand, Exxon has had a number of ships hijacked lately, and it's causing them a substantial profit loss. They want to send a message to the pirates in these waters that they aren't going to continue taking this abuse."

As the three men reached the level where Ali and the ship's eleven crew members were still quietly waiting for them to return, Duke announced, "We didn't find anyone else. It looks like we're the only ones left. Steve, can you get this tub out of here?"

"Yes, sir. Give me thirty minutes, and we'll be underway," Steve replied.

"While Steve is preparing to raise the anchor, let's all gather the pirates and give them a proper sea burial," Duke said sarcastically.

Between the eleven tanker crew members and the three Syndicate men, it didn't take long to get the seven dead pirates from the superstructure and throw them overboard. The eleven pirates laying on the deck of the ship followed suit. By the time Steve was ready to go, the only thing remaining from the pirates was blood spatter that could be cleaned once the ship was underway.

"The sun won't be up for another couple of hours. We should be able to put some miles between this ship and the rest of the pirates before they realize it isn't anchored out here anymore," Duke said. "Ali, you and Kabir stay here and help Steve out. I'll have Diego pick me up in the Osprey. Steve, if the pirates pursue you, which I imagine they likely will, put a call in to Valerie. Between her and Kabir, I'm certain they can stop anything the pirates throw at you."

"Ten-four," Steve and Kabir said in unison.

As the Osprey began its descent to the deck of the oil tanker, Duke fought the prop wash of the massive thirty-eight-foot rotors and climbed into the copilot's seat once the aircraft was hovering a few feet from the deck. Diego pulled back on the yoke, and the Osprey began to rise above the ship. At one hundred feet, Diego rotated the nacelles forward 90 degrees, and the Osprey gained momentum in horizontal flight until it reached its cruising speed of 310 miles per hour, heading back to their base of operations aboard the *Charaka*.

Diego Alvarez was one of the Syndicate's two pilots. He'd flown fighter jets as a Navy pilot for years before Duke recruited him. Diego was a flying marvel, able to expertly fly anything: a plane, a helicopter, a drone, or anything else above or below the water. Three years older than Duke, the stocky Hispanic man was rarely utilized for anything but flying since just about every mission called for some type of aircraft.

After two hours of cruising at full power, or about eighteen knots, the sun was beginning to peer over the horizon. The tanker had traveled forty-one miles away from its anchorage and was about one hundred miles from the *Charaka*, which was sitting in the Gulf of Aden. As Kabir scanned the water for visitors, he spotted three motorboats about three miles from the oil tanker, approaching rapidly.

"Valerie, this is Kabir," he called out over his communication device: an earpiece concealed within his ear canal that acted as both speaker and microphone, something all the crew members wore on a mission. "We have three fast-movers closing in on us. Spin up the GLGP and take them out."

"I have them locked in on radar, and the GLGP is just about up," Valerie replied from her comfortable seat in the *Charaka*'s control room.

The GLGP, or gun-launched guided projectile, fires a twenty-three-pound hypervelocity projectile, or HVP, that travels at a speed of 5,400 miles per hour and is guided by microelectronics, sensors, and energetic systems directed from the *Charaka*'s control center. At such a high velocity, the HVP explodes upon impact with an object. The projectile fragments into millions of pieces and travels outward with proportionate force, causing the object it strikes to do the same.

"Okay, they're on the way," Valerie announced in her crisp British intonation.

Valerie Watkins was Ali's counterpart. A twenty-eight-year-old, blonde-haired, green-eyed woman from Manchester. Like Ali, she graduated at the top of her class from a top-notch information technology school, the University of Cambridge. With her perfectly proportioned athletic figure, she was just as pretty as she was smart. Along with Ali, she could control any function of the Charaka *and could be a valuable asset in the field if needed.*

Kabir watched the boats through his binoculars as they neared the tanker. Fifty seconds later—the time it took for the HVPs to travel one hundred miles—the first boat exploded, then the second and third at ten-second intervals.

Kabir heard Valerie in his earpiece say, "All clear. I don't see anything else on the radar near you."

Kabir let out a breath of relief, but he knew he couldn't relax just yet. The Syndicate knew very little about the pirates or their capabilities, even though they hadn't been especially impressive to that point, and it was hard to speculate about what they would try next. Regardless, their mission wouldn't be complete until they had the captain back—dead or alive.

CHAPTER 2

The *Charaka* wasn't your average, run-of-the-mill cargo ship. She was a 649-foot Ultramax dry-bulk cargo ship built in 2015 by a Chinese shipbuilding company and merely masqueraded as an ordinary well-maintained cargo transport. However, the *Charaka* wasn't like any other ship. The vessel had been heavily modified to make the five cargo holds considerably shallower. There was a second set of hydraulic bay doors installed at the five-foot level under four of the shortened cargo holds. When the cargo hold was empty, the secondary set of doors opened to reveal hidden bays containing many types of top-secret equipment the Syndicate used to carry out their extreme and varied missions. The fifth cargo bay was entirely dedicated to holding the iron ore pellets that were exclusively used as camouflage.

When the *Charaka* expected company, usually in the form of an inspection, the crew could distribute the supply of iron ore pellets between the other four visible cargo bays via a hidden conveyor system. Then, they could raise a platform in the fifth bay where the pellets were stored so if anyone was nosy enough to look, they'd see all the holds filled with iron ore.

While the ship was underway, if any of the Syndicate's toys were needed for a mission, the four cargo holds could be emptied into the dedicated pellet storage bay so that the secondary doors could be opened and the equipment could be deployed. Because it only took about twenty minutes to completely refill all the bays with iron ore pellets, they were never put back in place unless the *Charaka* approached a port. If an unplanned inspection was suddenly demanded, Duke was certain he could distract any inspector long enough to get the holds refilled to maintain the inconspicuous facade.

In bay number one, there was a weapons platform that housed the GLGP, a guided missile launching system, a Gatling-styled M134 Minigun, a Gatling-styled M61 Vulcan gun, a powerful laser, and two Metal Storm guns, all mounted on individual platforms that could be raised above the deck for the best trajectory.

The second bay housed a vertical-takeoff V-22 Osprey aircraft. It was strapped down to a platform that could be raised to the top of the deck via hydraulic rams, allowing the Osprey's wings to unfold so it could take off and land vertically on the platform.

The middle compartment was the storage bay for the iron ore pellets.

The fourth bay housed two helicopters: a Bell AH-1Z Viper attack helicopter and an older Bell 214 passenger helicopter.

In the fifth compartment, there were an assortment of shipping containers, which housed all sorts of vehicles. The compartment also held a variety of RIBs and other miscellaneous items.

An area in the bottommost center of the ship was dedicated to two submarines: a modified DSRV submarine, or deep-submergence rescue vehicle, and a customized mini combat submarine. They could be launched and retrieved through clamshell doors that opened at the hull centerline and folded down, creating a pool of seawater at the bottom of the ship. The massive straps cradling the stored submarines in place were designed to lower and set them afloat in the exposed sea pool, allowing the underwater crafts to easily submerge into the depths below.

The vessel's primary propulsion system was also hidden in the bottom of the ship. The magnetohydrodynamic drives, or MHD accelerators/generators, were the heart and soul of the *Charaka*. The system was powered by an unlimited supply of seawater utilizing the Lorentz force principle. The MHD accelerated an electrically conductive fluid, such as salty seawater, by applying an electric current between two electrodes with a perpendicular magnetic field. The Lorentz force accelerated the charged particles, both positive and negative, triggering them to travel in the same direction and causing the fluid to be dragged through the reactor. As the reactor starved for more charged-particle collisions, it drew more and more water through two forty-eight-inch tubes, one on either side of the bulbous bow, with each pipe feeding its own MHD. The water expelled from each reactor was ejected through forty-eight-inch pipes and exited the ship's stern, thereby producing a tremendous amount of thrust. Turbines within the reactors were able to produce unlimited amounts of electricity through four massive generators that powered the ship, and the reserves were stored in multiple lithium-ion battery banks.

The technology had been around since the 1960s, and after decades of research, the MHD accelerator was subsequently deemed impractical due to its low efficiency. That is, until Duke met Mandy Graham.

Mandy graduated as the "outstanding graduate" of her engineering class at MIT. But her intelligence wasn't the only thing that made her stand out; her five-foot-six frame carried her 120 pounds in just the right proportions. Mandy's blonde hair and blue eyes accentuated her pretty face, and when she spoke, her calming Southern accent captivated her listeners. But her looks could fool someone because she was an expert in martial arts, and any man who wouldn't take no for an answer could quickly find himself in a bad predicament if Mandy felt inclined to teach him a lesson.

With the Syndicate's backing, Mandy was able to resolve the issues preventing the MHD from reaching its full potential. She created a mechanism that was installed on either side of the reactor to enhance the electrical conductivity of the ions in the seawater by increasing the particles' current density vector. That allowed the electrolysis within the reactor to surge exponentially, creating a tremendously volatile response in the MHD accelerator's reaction chamber and thereby increasing the power output by more than one million times.

Mandy and the Syndicate had created an energy system second to none in the world. The two had agreed to indefinitely keep their little device a secret to prevent the technology from reaching the hands of those who could exploit it for destructive purposes.

As important as all the ship's modifications were to fulfilling the Syndicate's missions, none were more important than the crew's comfortable living quarters. The members of the Syndicate each had their own luxurious home aboard the ship, nicer than most houses on land. Each living compartment had a living room, a kitchen, a spacious bedroom with an en suite bathroom complete with a jetted tub, shower, toilet with a heated bidet, generous vanity, and spacious walk-in closet. There were twenty of those individual living quarters on board.

There was also a fine dining room that would rival any five-star restaurant as well as a gourmet galley for the ship's Michelin-starred chef to prepare world-class cuisine in. There were two hospital rooms and an operating room on board. A prop and makeup shop were also available, where Abe Lim could disguise anyone so thoroughly that their own mother wouldn't be able to recognize them. There was a state-of-the-art fitness center and an Olympic-sized swimming pool with a four-lane running track circling it.

The most impressive room on the ship, however, was

the control room, where everything on the ship could be operated. It was a substantial room with two rows of large-screen monitors spanning three walls and one extra-large monitor front and center. Under the extra-large monitor were two captain's chairs in front of a console with two computers and three monitors for each one. That was where Ali and Valerie usually sat. Elevated in the center of the room was the Picard chair, the crew's nickname for the captain's chair because Duke's favorite show was *Star Trek: The Next Generation*. The Picard chair was perfectly located for maximum visibility and could swivel for a perfect line of sight of the double row of big-screen monitors on all three walls.

There was a ready room, which resembled a small auditorium and could double as a theatre room, with twenty electric leather reclining theatre-style loungers—five chairs on each of the four rows of risers. That was where they prepared for their missions. In addition, there was also a conference room, which contained a twenty-four-foot-long table surrounded by sixteen luxurious office chairs and a large-screen monitor at one end of the room. There, the team had discussed everything from the best interrogation tactics to how they could prevent an impending nuclear war.

Other rooms included a firing range, a mechanical shop, and an interrogation room. At the bow and the stern of the ship were storage areas for the four torpedo tubes. However, none of those spaces would ever be seen by anyone outside the Syndicate. Only a select few outsiders had ever been below deck, and they had all been unconscious or were blindfolded and limited to a holding cell or the interrogation room.

The superstructure of the ship was where visitors and inspectors were allowed. The main bridge and engine room were fully functional, and the ship could be operated from the bridge if the control room below the deck allowed it, but it was mainly just a façade. The eleven levels of the superstructure had all the normal things you'd find aboard any other ship. The bottommost area was the engine room, taking up three of the eleven levels, and included the diesel engines, generators, water-makers, storage compartments, water-treatment plant, pumps, air-conditioning systems, and a host of other mechanical equipment.

The next level up was the 'tween deck, which had eight crew cabins and eight guest cabins, all with en suite bathrooms. Up another level was the main deck, featuring a repair shop, laundry facility, medical room, and more storage areas. The poop deck was above that, where the galley and mess hall were located as well as an exercise room, game room, and common area. The next level up was the A deck, which was a mirror image of the 'tween deck with eight crew cabins and eight guest cabins.

The only difference between a guest cabin and a crew cabin was a hidden door in the closet of the crew cabin that opened into a secret hallway leading to an elevator. From there, the crew could access each level of the ship, from the bottom level to the bridge. Under normal circumstances, the crew made their way to the bottom of the ship through a hidden elevator entrance on the main-deck level of the superstructure.

The next level, the B deck, contained eight officer cabins. One more level up, on the C deck, was the captain's quarters and office along with a semi-formal conference room and an electronics room. The top deck was dedicated to the bridge with wings on either side, where the crew could walk out and see the edges of the ship when docking. There were cameras throughout the ship that gave the control room below a clear shot of everything above the deck and beyond.

To an outsider boarding the vessel, it appeared to be a well-maintained, fully functioning cargo ship. But in reality, it could take on most naval warships and could most certainly outrun anything on the ocean.

CHAPTER 3

The Osprey slowly lowered onto a platform supported by hydraulic rams raising the stand above the deck of the number two bay. Duke got out, and Diego folded the wings back toward the tail, keeping the rotors in the helicopter position so it could be strapped in place and lowered back into the hull to be refueled and readied for its next flight.

Down in the control room, Duke climbed into the Picard chair and asked Valerie, "What's the status of the captain's location?"

"I spoke with the execs at Exxon," Valerie replied. "They said they'd talked to the captain fifteen minutes ago but weren't able to deduce exactly where he was being held. The pirates are trying to bluff them into thinking they still have the ship. So, under our direction, the execs told them they'd wire the ten million."

Duke asked, "Can you show a false wire transfer?"

"Yes, once I get the account number, I'll ghost the figures into the account, and as soon as we get the captain back, I can expunge it," Valerie said, her eyes sparkling with mischievousness.

"Perfect. Make sure the execs at Exxon insist on talking to the captain *before* the money is wired, and let's see if we can triangulate his position. I'm certain they'll be using a cell phone; these guys aren't the sharpest tools in the shed. How far out are we from the town where they're holding the captain?" Duke asked.

"We're one hundred fifty-seven nautical miles out at the moment."

"Power the MHD to forty percent, and let's park the *Charaka* within one hundred miles of the coast so we can use any weapon we need to." Duke raised his hand and moved it forward just as Jean-Luc would and then said, "Engage!"

Valerie swiveled her chair while rolling her eyes at his poor imitation. She quickly made the necessary preparations.

When Diego entered the control room a second later, Duke turned his attention to him. "Load the Osprey with two four-wheelers and two cargo parachutes. Bubba and I will be ready to drop in using a couple of Mach IIIs if needed."

"I'll have it ready to go in fifteen minutes," Diego said and hustled out of the control room.

Billy McIntosh, or "Bubba," was the Syndicate's mechanic. He was the only crew member without military experience or a formal education. He was a fit thirty-one-year-old man with brown hair and blue eyes. Born and raised in Georgia, he might be described as a typical Southern gentleman, and anyone who got to know him loved him, including the entire crew. What Duke valued in him was that not only was Bubba able to fix anything, but he could always be counted on in any situation. That's why Duke chose Bubba to help him rescue the captain.

By the time the Osprey approached land, Valerie had triangulated the captain's location from their last call to the pirates. He appeared to be located in a large house on a hillside, which made it impossible for them to approach by ground undetected.

"Looks like parachuting in will be our only option," Duke told Bubba as they readied themselves on the flight.

"Let's hope nobody looks up," Bubba said. "We'll be sitting ducks coming down in the middle of the day!"

"We will have our .300 Win Mag sniper rifles with silencers just in case we are spotted. We should be able to pick off three or four men each if they do spot us," Duke tried to reassure him.

"Well, at least we'll have a sporting chance," Bubba replied with a wink.

"Our plan is to eliminate everyone outside with our sniper rifles, then continue to the interior using our Sigs. Nobody should ever hear us coming." Duke hoped that would be true.

"When's the last time a mission went according to plan?" Bubba drawled.

"Touché!" Duke replied. "Well, if all else fails, we have our HK MP5s."

"You just never know when you might have to mow down a big cluster of pirates," Bubba told Duke with a smirk as they packed their weapons.

"Ready?"

"Ready as I'll ever be," Bubba said.

Diego circled the plane so Duke and Bubba could jump out over the uninhabited mountains to the north, and if they could catch a break, coast down unnoticed.

But things didn't go as well as they had with the oil tanker. As Duke and Bubba approached the house at an altitude of about a thousand feet, they noticed two men below pointing up at them. Duke and Bubba each sighted a pirate's head through the scopes on their silenced sniper rifles and fired. Both heads exploded almost simultaneously, and the noise from the explosions as well as the red flashes of blood splatter caught the attention of three other men standing nearby. They looked around with their rifles at the ready, not realizing the shots came from above. Duke and Bubba took aim again, and the other three men dropped to the ground. Duke and Bubba landed close to the fallen bodies on the north side of the house, hoping nobody would notice them.

But as they shed their parachutes, they heard a ruckus. Suddenly, a stampede of men rounded the east and west sides of the house. Duke and Bubba each swapped out their sniper rifles for their HK MP5s from their custom-designed, dual-back holsters and stood back-to-back with their sights set on the corners of the building. The MP5 submachine guns were loud, but the element of surprise had already come to an end. The pirates ran around the house without regard for their lives, and Duke and Bubba took them out one, two, three at a time. The compact MP5 machine guns held thirty-round clips, allowing the men to mow down the first round of pirates. The remaining pirates retreated, finally realizing that running around the corner of the building wasn't going to accomplish anything other than committing suicide.

Just as the pirates retreated, bullets started raining down on Duke and Bubba. Two men were firing from the roof, but they weren't very good marksmen. Duke quickly swung his MP5 up and returned fire, making the pirates duck behind the parapet and giving him and Bubba just enough time to head around to the west side of the house. Duke dove just before reaching the corner, rolled, came up on his knees, and fired, dropping four men hiding around the corner.

All the while, Bubba followed Duke's lead, both men silent and only using hand signals. They continued to the southwest corner of the house, and Duke peered around the corner while Bubba focused behind them—not an easy task when trying to keep a lookout for anyone who might be squinting over the edge of the parapet on the roof too. But Duke knew his life was safe with Bubba protecting his rear.

Three men rounded the corner Bubba was watching, and he dropped them. Six more men came out from the front of the house on the south side, and they looked around, trying to decide which way to go. That moment of hesitation cost them their lives, as Duke put bullets in each one of them before making a break for the front door.

A gabled roof sheltered the entrance from the men firing from above. The front door was wide open, so Duke stood with his back to the wall next to the doorway while Bubba kept an eye out for anyone coming from around either side of the building. With Bubba watching his back, Duke darted into the entry ready to fire, but it was empty. He entered the house with Bubba on his heels. They found themselves in a large round room with a curved staircase cascading down the right side. A balcony overlooking the floor below curled around half of the circular room. Duke looked up to see a man spring to the handrail above, aimed and ready to shoot, but Duke was too fast for him and shot him in the forehead with his silenced Sig sidearm. They may have easily rid the exterior of pirates, but they had no idea how many were still in the house. They also didn't know where the captain was or even if he was still alive, but it was their duty to find out.

Duke and Bubba advanced up the stairway—higher ground would give them the advantage if they encountered more pirates during their search. Duke noticed the fold-down attic stairs were slightly ajar and motioned to Bubba. As they walked along the balcony, Duke swiftly and quietly pushed up on the stairs to close them and then continued his search by opening the first door he saw. He assessed the room, swinging his MP5 around, but the space was empty. Bubba stood outside each door as Duke entered, keeping an eye on the attic access and for anyone approaching from behind.

They continued their strategy all the way around the balcony and down two corridors, but they still didn't find anyone. As they walked back toward the stairway, Duke noticed the attic door was cracked open about an inch, so he emptied his clip around the opening and straight down the center of the folded stairs. There was a thud, and then the attic stairway sprang open, the coils creaking loudly as a man fell to the floor. They heard footsteps above hurrying toward the center of the round room when all of a sudden, another man broke through the ceiling and dropped to the floor. Stunned, he staggered to his feet, but Bubba put a bullet in the back of his head before he could run.

Duke and Bubba began to descend the stairs, ready for someone to appear from anywhere in the house, but they were alone. They started opening doors like they had on the balcony, searching room after room until they'd checked all but one.

The last door opened inward, exposing a staircase leading to the basement. Other than the light radiating through the doorway and illuminating the first few steps, everything below was pitch black. Transitioning from the bright house to the underground room left Duke and Bubba virtually blinded to anything beyond the dim glow emanating from the open door. They looked at each other in silent consult, eyes searching for answers in the other's face. Then, silently and in unison, they each pulled out a flare and grinned. They lit their torches and flung them in opposite directions into the basement, where they burned bright. Anyone in the dark abyss would find themselves momentarily blinded as soon as they looked into the glowing flares.

Duke and Bubba quickly descended the stairs before anyone could adjust to the bright light. Duke's military training and the countless missions Bubba had experienced enabled them to move down the steps in seconds, and they knew exactly what to do when they reached the floor. Turning in opposite directions, Duke saw a man standing over another with a gun pressed to his temple. He recognized the man latched to the chair as the captain.

Duke couldn't see the entire basement from his vantage point, but Bubba had his MP5 trained on two pirates standing on the opposite side of the stairs from the captain, each with a rifle of his own trained on Duke.

With his gun holstered at his side, Duke placed his MP5 back in its holster and faced the captain with his hands up in a surrendering position. "Drop the gun, and step away," he told the pirate holding the gun to the man's head.

The pirate responded in Somali, one of the few languages Duke didn't understand. From the tone of the man's voice, Duke could tell he was threatening to shoot the captain in a vain attempt to gain control of the situation.

Duke spoke softly into his earpiece and told Valerie to call the kidnappers and tell them the money had been deposited into their account, and it was time to release the captain as they'd discussed. After an extremely long twenty seconds, the gunman's phone vibrated in his pocket. He pulled it out and began talking, nodding his head, and then he smiled. Suddenly, the gunman pointed his weapon at Duke—a fatal mistake. Quicker than a striking snake, Duke grabbed his Sig sidearm and shot the man in the forehead as a barrage of shots rang out from Bubba's MP5. The two other men dropped as well.

Duke untied the captain and said, "We need to get out of here." Then, into his earpiece, he said, "Valerie, we have the captain. Send Diego over with the four-wheelers."

After freeing the captain from the chair, Duke grabbed him by the arm, helped him up, and began pushing him up the stairs right behind Bubba, who was rushing toward the front door. Bubba stopped suddenly and ducked to the side of the open doorway. Taking the cue, Duke pushed the captain behind an interior wall, told him to hunker down, and then took position next to a window facing the front yard. As Duke and Bubba peered outside, they saw a dozen or so men riding up the long driveway in three military jeeps, each with a mounted machine gun on the roll bar.

Bubba traded the MP5 for his sniper rifle and sighted in the driver of the leading vehicle. The bullet penetrated the windshield and took the right half of the driver's head off, causing the jeep to veer from its path. Its momentum forced it to topple over and roll back onto the driveway, blocking the following two vehicles. The other drivers and passengers jumped out to take cover, leaving only two men with the vehicles to man the machine guns. They cut loose and shot up the house. Fifty-caliber bullets pierced the front walls as they traveled through the house, penetrating each partition they encountered until the projectiles exited the back of the building. Duke, Bubba, and the captain were trapped with nowhere to hide.

"Valerie, we're pinned down. Fire up the GLGP." Duke had his rangefinder out to help him pinpoint his latitude and longitude and relayed it to Valerie. "Hit them!"

About fifty seconds later, there was an explosion about twenty yards in front of the wrecked jeep.

"Valerie, I miscalculated. Make that thirty-yards farther to the south!" Duke called out.

By that point, the house was so riddled with holes that it was a wonder it was still standing. Duke and Bubba could see right through the wall. A few seconds later, the gunfire ceased as one of the jeeps took a direct hit that practically disintegrated it and sent the other jeep soaring into the air, landing on its top. It seemed unlikely that anyone had survived the second explosion, but Duke and Bubba still approached carefully while they told the captain to stay put in the house.

As they neared the burning and overturned jeeps, a shot rang out and knocked Bubba down. Duke saw that his partner had been hit in the arm, so he grabbed him by his good arm and dragged him to cover behind a large boulder at the yard's edge.

"Are you okay, Bubba?" Duke asked.

"I've been shot worse than this before. I'm fine. Just stings a little," Bubba replied through gritted teeth as they crouched behind the rock.

"Valerie!" Duke called to the *Charaka*. "Lay down four rounds at thirty-foot spacing around your last coordinates," Duke said as the bullets continued to pepper the large rock. Fifty seconds later, another blast rocked the location where the shot was fired from, followed by three more explosions—one every ten seconds, which was the fastest speed at which the GLGP could fire multiple shots.

Duke climbed out from behind the rock and was walking around the site to make sure there wouldn't be any more shots fired when he heard the Osprey flying overhead. Two parachutes opened up and floated to the ground in the front yard with a Polaris Sportsman XP 1000 four-wheeler hanging from each of them.

Duke shouted for the captain, who limped out of the house and winced while jumping on the back of Duke's four-wheeler. He held on for dear life as they tried to catch up with Bubba. The three men headed to their prearranged rendezvous point with the Osprey, six miles away.

As Duke and Bubba drove their four-wheelers through the rugged terrain, two more military jeeps sped up the drive. Blocked by the destroyed vehicles, they had to cross the berm beside the driveway to go around the house. When they located the four-wheeler tracks, they began their pursuit, but the jeeps couldn't travel as fast as the ATVs because they were bulky and less maneuverable. However, they weren't far behind.

The Osprey was on the ground in a secluded area between small mountain peaks on a plain three miles away from the nearest road or trail. The rotors were turning, and the rear ramp was down and ready for Duke and Bubba to drive up into the aircraft. Bubba was hurting, but he was tough and didn't let it show. The bullet had gone through his muscle and exited his arm the same size as it had entered—he was fortunate it wasn't an expandable bullet.

Navigating by GPS, Duke and Bubba crested the last hill and saw the Osprey sitting on the open plateau ready for takeoff. Breathing a sigh of relief, they sped along the plain, not even slowing for the ramp, and ran up into the back of the aircraft. They slammed on their brakes as they arrived safely in the cargo area, and the Osprey instantly rose while the ramp closed on its way up. Duke and Bubba got off and strapped the four-wheelers down as Diego rotated the rotors and moved forward. A minute later, bullets began whizzing by, but as the Osprey gained speed, they were soon out of range of the fifty-caliber machine guns and were safely on their way. Duke patched up Bubba's arm while the relieved captain sang their praises all the way back to the oil tanker.

CHAPTER 4

"Can you safely set us down on that oil tanker?" Duke asked Diego.

"I don't think so," Diego admitted. "But I can hover over the gangway and lower the ramp so that you and the captain can board the ship. Then I'll cruise around until you are ready to leave, and you guys can get back on the same way."

Duke crawled back to where the captain and Bubba were sitting. "Captain, how's the leg? Do you need medical care?"

"No, it's just a slight sprain. The pirates thought it was funny to give me a shove when I jumped from the boat to the dock when we arrived at their hideout."

"Well," Duke said, "I'm going to need you to jump again. This time from the plane to the ship. Do you think you can do it?"

"What?" the surprised captain exclaimed.

"I promise I won't shove you," Duke said with a grin, waving his hands in submission.

"You have got to be kidding me! I'll be lucky if all I end up with is two broken legs!"

"You aren't going to jump from here. We're going to get within a few feet of the gangway. It's not really a jump—

more like a hop."

"How many feet is a few feet?"

"Three, or maybe less if Diego holds her steady. The problem is that we can't land. Our exhaust from the engines is too hot, and there just isn't enough open space to set the plane down. But we're going to get as close as possible and climb down from the ramp. I can have my men do their best to catch you, so I don't think it will be too bad," Duke explained.

"I think I can do that. Let's give it a try."

Diego maneuvered the plane and lowered it within a few feet of the oil tanker before lowering the ramp. All the men remaining on the ship gathered around the open railing, ready to grasp their captain as he jumped a couple of feet from the Osprey's ramp to the ship's deck. Duke followed, and Diego took off, putting the plane into a holding pattern.

Handshakes, hugs, and laughter overflowed when the crew and their captain were reunited.

"They were going to kill me," the captain told the group.

"They were just waiting to get their money," Steve said.

"You guys showed up just in time. I can't believe so few of you were able to pull this off," the captain said in disbelief.

"We had help," Duke admitted.

One of the ship's crew spoke up and said, "From the stories we've heard, very rarely does a hijacking like this take place and the entire crew is able to return to the ship."

"Another ship was recently taken, and half the crew and the captain were killed even though the pirates received their ransom," another crew member added.

"Well, everyone on this ship is safe and sound," Kabir said, his pride beaming.

"We're going to keep an eye on your vessel until you're in safer waters," Duke reassured them.

"We can never express how thankful we are to you and your crew for saving our lives," the captain sincerely conveyed, and the rest of the crew echoed his sentiments.

After their final goodbyes, Diego positioned the aircraft and lowered the ramp so Duke and his men could jump aboard. Once the door closed on the plane and their mission was over, the Osprey began its short flight back to the *Charaka*. Twenty minutes later, Diego started his descent to the deck of the ship, where they were promptly greeted by the doctor.

As was custom after a mission, everyone was eager for a hot shower and a clean set of clothes. After getting themselves cleaned up, they reconvened in the ready room to review the mission while Ethan, the chef, prepared a much-anticipated celebratory meal in the galley. Duke started off the briefing by asking Dr. Cho Bai how Bubba's arm was, even though Bubba was sitting only a few chairs away and looked fine.

Doc Bai said, "Bubba will be alright. It was a through-and-through and did minimal damage."

Truth be known, most of the men on the ship would've taken a bullet just to get worked on by Dr. Cho Bai. She was a petite, five-foot-two thirty-nine-year-old Korean woman who could pass for twenty-something. She'd never do anything unethical, but her pretty face accentuated by her silky black hair and green eyes made many men wish she would.

The *Charaka* had an important rule: no dating fellow crew members. Duke worried the drama of relationships would diminish their ability to make tough decisions in the field when a situation called for it. Workplace relationships would increase the chances of someone getting killed, and their jobs were already dangerous enough.

"I figured Bubba would be okay," Duke said, "but let's keep an eye on him to make sure an infection doesn't present itself."

Duke knew Doc Bai would have done that anyway, and she nodded her head in agreement.

Duke continued, "Exxon wired our fees: five million dollars. I had your shares transferred into your personal accounts. Please make sure you each see a deposit of

$156,250."

The Syndicate's policy was to take the first 50 percent of the fees, and then each of the sixteen crew members split the remainder of the fees evenly, from Duke, the chief executive officer, to Ami Tanaka, the ship's housekeeper.

Ami Tanaka's title was deceptive. Although the thirty-year-old Japanese woman was responsible for the laundry and light housecleaning, her fluency in several languages and extreme proficiency in martial arts and gymnastics made Ami an invaluable asset to the Syndicate. On more than a few missions, the petite, five-foot, ninety-eight-pound fireball with shoulder-length black hair and dark eyes had proven her importance to Duke and the rest of the crew.

Everyone in the Syndicate was happy with their compensation arrangements, especially because nobody ever needed to spend much of their own money; all their needs were cared for by the company. All they had to do was give Rodney Dawson, the butler, a list of items they needed each month, and Rodney ordered everything: toiletries, snacks, and an endless variety of other requests.

Rodney was an Englishman who had been raised in London by a prominent family. He was a pudgy man, standing at five feet, ten inches tall. He had brown hair, brown eyes, and though rarely used on missions, Rodney was an excellent driver and marksman. But what set Rodney apart was his elegant personality and charm. He was a charismatic man with polish that everyone found to be very enchanting. He had found his niche aboard the Charaka.

The Syndicate purchased all of the crew's clothing, fed them, and provided housing aboard the *Charaka*. Each member had received $250,000 when they were hired to decorate their cabin any way they wished, and they would be hard-pressed to find another home as nice as the one they had on the *Charaka*.

It was a requirement for all members to practice weekly at the firing range on the ship in order to maintain their excellent shooting skills. The crew practiced headshots because hitting someone in the skull meant they would no longer pose a threat. Most were also proficient in martial arts and practiced their skills regularly in the gym. The exception was the chef and butler. Rodney occasionally went on assignments, primarily as a driver when the situation called for one. But Ethan, the chef, never left the ship because the crew's nutrition was of the utmost importance, and he didn't possess the same skills as the others.

Ethan Bernier was a Michelin-starred, world-class chef who had grown up and trained in France. Duke had persuaded the forty-six-year-old man to join the Syndicate with the promise of adventure and ever-changing scenery, and Ethan had never regretted his decision. The five-foot-ten, brown-haired, brown-eyed man had a hefty stature, which reassured those he prepared his culinary repasts for that they were in for a treat and gave credence to Duke's motto that you can't trust a skinny cook.

Duke told the crew sitting in the theatre seats of the ready room that he'd received a message from Johnathan Rosenthal, the president of the United States' imperceptible security advisor. He wasn't a member of the president's cabinet, nor had anybody heard of a Johnathan Rosenthal. He handled the sensitive matters the president couldn't convey to the heads of Homeland Security or the CIA. Plausible deniability was crucial to the president if something were to go wrong or if the media or another nation caught wind of an unsanctioned mission. Rosenthal always used the Syndicate because of their discretion, and in doing so, he never had to deal with blowback from a botched mission.

Duke went on to tell the crew that Rosenthal had offered them the opportunity to track down the source of the COVID-19 virus, which sounded like it would be simple. But very seldom did missions prove to be that straightforward, and they never went exactly as planned. However, the task did sound like easy money—do a little research, conduct some interviews, obtain the hard evidence, and collect ten million dollars. All fifteen crew members in the ready room unanimously agreed to accept the mission. Ethan was the only crew member not present, as he rarely attended any of the crew's mission meetings, but he never questioned their decisions. Duke required everyone to be united in agreement before he accepted any mission because each of them could potentially be putting their lives on the line with even the simplest task. Fortunately, the Syndicate had never lost a team member, and Duke intended to keep it that way.

"Doc, would you update the crew on what the virus is and how it originated?" Duke asked.

Cho Bai got out of her leather recliner and went to the podium as Duke took his seat in the front row. "The coronavirus," she began, "or COVID-19, which started the worldwide pandemic in 2019, is known to scientists as SARS-CoV-2. This means 'severe acute respiratory syndrome coronavirus two.' It's believed to have originated in animals and mutated to infect humans. Now, it's rapidly spreading from human to human. Scientists first identified the virus in 1965 and named it for its crown-like appearance under magnification. SARS was first discovered in Southern China in 2002. It causes fever, headache, and respiratory problems such as a cough and shortness of breath. Its effects on people can vary widely, with some experiencing no symptoms, some developing what is very much like a common cold, and others affected more severely, even succumbing to death. The latest outbreak is believed to have originated in an open-air wet market in Wuhan, Hubei, China, from some sort of exotic animal, but the evidence I've seen so far doesn't necessarily support that fact."

"That's why we're being called in to investigate," Duke said. "There's some suspicion that this virus was manufactured and released into the world, and we've been asked to find out who's behind this and why. We're going to sail to Hong Kong and begin there as our base of operations. Then, we'll see where that leads us. It'll take about a week to get there depending on weather conditions, so enjoy some R and R for the next few days. Any questions?"

Nobody had any. They all made small talk amongst themselves as they filtered out of the room until just Duke and Steve remained.

"How does the weather look for our cruise?" Duke asked.

"It looks fairly calm for the most part," Steve replied. "We should be able to make pretty good time. It's about fifty-seven-hundred nautical miles away, and I'm confident we can average forty knots. That'll put us there in six days."

Steve Taylor was Duke's longtime best friend. He was an ex-special operations commando in the Australian Defence Force whom Duke had met during a joint task-training exercise in South Korea. After leaving the military, Steve was finally able to let his blond hair grow out, and he looked much more like a surfer than the savate expert he really was. Steve, with his blue eyes and six-foot-one frame, could pilot any boat on the ocean no matter the size, but what made him so valuable to the Syndicate was his ability to take the lead in any situation.

The *Charaka* was capable of speeds up to sixty knots, or about seventy miles per hour, but such high speeds would make for a very bumpy ride, and the sea state had to be almost perfectly calm to comfortably maintain that pace. Averaging forty knots, or about forty-six miles per hour, was the maximum speed the ship could travel while still providing a relatively smooth ride for the crew.

The *Charaka* had a state-of-the-art autopilot system that maximized comfortable speeds when conditions allowed and automatically slowed back down when waves increased. The ship's software measured wave heights through a radar flowmeter velocity sensor, which used an algorithm and then interfaced that information with the autopilot system. It could control the ship more efficiently than any human and allowed the crew to relax without the ship lurching up and down.

A marine gyrostabilizer, a very large device comprised of spinning flywheels mounted in a gimbal frame, also kept the

Charaka from rocking back and forth. The angular momentum of the spinning flywheels combined with the flywheels' precession oscillation generated a large amount of stabilizing torque, which directly opposed the rolling motion of the ship.

A sonar system was also integrated into the autopilot so the ship could maneuver on its own around any object it detected floating in the sea. Despite its autonomy, the ship still sent out an alarm so whoever was on watch could verify that the ship was on a safe path whenever the autopilot deviated from its course. The *Charaka* was also equipped with a radar-jamming system that activated when another vessel's automatic identification system, or AIS, was detected, keeping the *Charaka* invisible to other ships and allowing the autopilot to reroute their course and prevent anyone searching the horizon from spotting them. At the ship's intense speeds, it would certainly arouse interest if anyone noticed how fast it was traveling—faster than what was possible for any other ship of its kind. Another Duke-ism went: "*Charaka* out of sight, *Charaka* out of mind."

* * *

Somewhere between Singapore and the Philippines, Duke called another meeting in the ready room to initiate the planning stage. Duke, Steve, Dr. Cho Bai, and Ami Tanaka would take a commercial flight to Wuhan as two happy couples enjoying a leisure trip in China, where they'd snoop around the open market to see what they could find out. The rest of the crew would be split into two groups— one on the ship for a few days, and the other enjoying some time in Hong Kong before trading off. Duke expected the crew's time in Hong Kong to amount to four days.

After checking in with the General Administration of Customs, Duke and Ami took a taxi from the dock to the airport, and Steve and Doc Bai followed in a taxi of their own. They were traveling as two couples who didn't know one another. Steve and Doc Bai made a nice-looking couple—Steve's charisma, plus the fact that he could speak fluent Mandarin, made him the perfect candidate for the mission, and with his Australian accent, he'd definitely amuse the locals. Doc Bai could also speak Mandarin and a few other dialects of the Chinese language. Although Steve towered almost a foot over Cho, they appeared to be the perfect couple, and the camaraderie between them solidified the ruse.

Duke, admittedly not as good-looking as Steve, was still a pretty handsome man in his own right. However, it was his charm that made him so appealing. Duke's features would surely make him stand out among the Chinese citizens. Ami's Asian features would allow her to blend in with the given environment, making it easier for Duke to attract less attention. Duke and Ami made an attractive pair, and like Steve and Cho, they could communicate in Chinese as well as any of the other multiple languages they were fluent in.

When the four of them arrived in Wuhan on the same flight, Steve and Cho took a taxi to the Westin Hotel while Duke and Ami rented a car from the airport and drove to the same place. Both couples checked into the rooms Valerie had booked for them. Each room was furnished with two queen-sized beds. Once they'd unpacked their suitcases and were settled, both couples went to the hotel bar for drinks and to get better acquainted with their surroundings. Because they'd taken a commercial flight, nobody had brought any weapons. Without weapons or the *Charaka*'s protection, they were quite literally on their own. But they didn't expect any trouble. They were merely on a fact-finding mission.

The next morning, each couple had a mediocre breakfast, but after eating regularly on the *Charaka*, any meal off the ship would be unexceptional at best. However, the view from the restaurant's balcony over the Yangtze River compensated for the average fare. Duke and Ami finished eating first, and as they rose from the table, Duke nonchalantly nodded to Steve from a couple of tables away. Then, Duke and Ami took their rental car and drove toward the busy market. By the time they found a parking spot, Steve and Cho had arrived as well and were getting out of their taxi. Thanks to their concealed ear communication devices, all four were interconnected, and they proceeded to mill around.

Nothing seemed out of the ordinary; it was just a regular market. It reminded them of Pike Place Market in Seattle, Washington, but with an international Eastern flair and a variety of items not typical at markets in the states. There were whole plucked chickens—everything except the feathers and innards, their beaks and feet still intact. There were all kinds of sea creatures and other animals, most of them identifiable. There was an array of different fruits and vegetables, jewelry, and clothing—just about anything a person could imagine and even some things a person couldn't.

By the end of the day, they'd made small talk with many locals. The coronavirus was easy to talk about since it was on everyone's mind, just as masks were on everyone's face. Ami's stomach was upset, probably from the lunch she'd eaten from a sidewalk cafe. Duke dined from a street cart vendor and felt fine, but then again, he could eat anything. His maxim, one of many, was that he would eat anything that didn't move faster than he did. Duke told Steve and Cho that he and Ami were heading back to the hotel room and would meet up with them there. Steve and Cho hailed a taxi and followed them.

The latter team returned to their room to change clothes, then got in the elevator and went up two floors to Duke and Ami's room so Doc Bai could check on Ami and the four of them could discuss the day.

Duke let Steve and Cho in and shut the door. Cho went over to the bed Ami was resting on, gave her a thorough once-over, and determined her digestive troubles stemmed from a spice she wasn't used to.

"You should be fine in a few hours," she told Ami.

"I already feel much better," Ami said as she reclined on her bed, sipping a glass of wine.

"Anyone want a drink?" Duke asked as he opened the minibar.

"I'll take a scotch on the rocks," Steve said. He sat back on the couch and propped his feet up on the coffee table. "Anyone find out anything about the virus? I heard a couple of locals say they thought it somehow escaped from the local lab complex, but nobody thought it originated from one of the animals at the market."

Cho spoke up and said, "Is there any more wine?" Then she added, "Everyone we spoke with said they didn't know of anyone selling sick animals. They told us the virus first affected a variety of businesses located close to one another, and the majority of people initially infected were their customers. I don't think it originated from the market vendors either."

"I agree," Steve said as he accepted a glass from Duke. "I think it originally spread to people at the market, but I think someone, maybe a customer, brought the virus there."

"I think you're right. Maybe one of the workers from the pharmaceutical lab was infected by a sample stored there, contracted the virus, and then went to the market?" Duke probed as he poured a miniature bottle of wine into a glass for Cho.

"The lab would have strict protocols in place to keep that kind of thing from happening. I find it difficult to imagine someone from the lab could contract the virus and carry it outside the complex without anyone knowing," Cho said.

"Perhaps someone made a mistake or didn't follow the rules?" Steve queried.

"Perhaps," Duke repeated. "But there's no way we can gain access to the complex to look around. I heard some locals say that right after suspicions arose about the lab being the source of the spread, a security fence and guarded gates were installed so only those with clearance could gain entry into the complex."

"Why don't we do a drive-by just to see the place for ourselves?" Steve suggested.

"Let's do that first thing in the morning," Duke said, then changed the subject. "What are you two doing for dinner?"

"How about Chinese food?" Steve said.

"That's kind of vague, Steve. Wouldn't even McDonald's be considered Chinese food here?" Duke countered.

Ami took a sip of her wine and said, "I really don't feel like going out tonight. Could we eat here at the hotel? It has a great view of the river and the city, and that way if my stomach acts up again, I'll be close to my room."

They all agreed, and Steve and Cho went down to the restaurant. Duke and Ami followed shortly thereafter, each couple getting a table out on the balcony overlooking the river.

As the two couples ate their dinner, they were able to carry on a conversation with each other through their earpieces, despite sitting several tables apart, without drawing attention to themselves. A bystander would've thought they were just talking to the person sitting across from them.

CHAPTER 5

Duke and his crew pulled up to the lab the next morning, refreshed and ready to find some answers. The pharmaceutical lab complex was made up of several large buildings that stood around two parallel lanes. At the very end, the lanes were connected by a half-circle driveway, and between them was a lavish botanical garden. The entrance and exit at the other end of each roadway consisted of two large wrought-iron gates, both just wide enough to allow a vehicle to enter or exit and controlled by a large security guardhouse between them. The entire complex was enclosed by a ten-foot-tall wrought-iron fence that matched the gates and was virtually impenetrable.

Duke and Ami had picked up Steve and Cho down the street from the Westin, then proceeded across town, where they drove around the block surrounding the complex several times. They weren't going to access the lab with their limited resources, so they returned to the hotel to brainstorm, dropping Steve and Cho off around the corner to avoid suspicion.

A quick internet search didn't reveal who owned the pharmaceutical company, so they made a call to Ali on the *Charaka*.

"We need some information," Duke said. "Find out who the owner of Wu International is and what they have going on at their lab here in Wuhan."

"No problem," Ali replied. "I'll get back with you shortly."

Ten minutes later, Duke's cell phone rang. On the other end, Ali reported, "The owner of the company is Hui fang Wu. Mr. Wu owns many companies all over China, not to mention the corporations he holds in six other countries." Between Ali and Valerie, there wasn't much information they couldn't track down. "I'm going to email you everything I have on Hui fang Wu. I'll try to get into their server to see what information is available there."

"That sounds good," Duke replied. "Try to find their employee list, possibly the areas of research they're currently working on, and whether they have coronavirus samples in-house."

"Okay. It may take me a while, but I'll start working on it right now. Valerie will be back in a little bit, and I'll have her help me when she returns," Ali said.

As Duke and the other three examined the material Ali had sent, Cho said, "Mr. Wu also owns, or at least is part owner of, another pharmaceutical company in Belarus. We should probably have Valerie and Ali see if they can find out more about it too."

As the four of them scrutinized what little information they had at their disposal and their observations from their trip to the market, they couldn't find any logical link to the virus or its origination.

A few hours later, Duke's phone began to ring. He answered and switched it over to speaker so everyone could hear. "Go ahead."

"Wu International has a very sophisticated firewall protecting their server at the pharmaceutical complex, and it took us longer to penetrate it than we would have thought," Valerie said. "However, we did finally breach their security measures and were able to get the information you were looking for. Nothing jumps out from their employee list, except that one employee was murdered a few months ago. They found him floating in the Yangtze River, but there was no motive, and so far, there aren't any suspects. There was nothing that indicated the coronavirus was located anywhere within the complex. However, they've been manufacturing a vaccine for the virus since about six months before the initial outbreak. They have enough vaccines to supply most of the world stockpiled in one of their warehouses located on-site at the complex."

"They have that much of the vaccine stored and haven't released it yet?" Cho questioned incredulously.

"Yeah, it's there," Ali reaffirmed.

"What were you able to find out about the lab in Belarus?" Duke asked.

"The pharmaceutical lab server there was much easier to gain access to, but the information on their hard drives were limited because they've recently been wiped. I don't know if I can retrieve the information remotely. I've done that sort of thing before, but only when I was actually in front of the computer. We can try if you want us to, but it'll be very challenging and time-consuming, and we can't promise you it will work," Ali informed Duke.

"No, let's not waste our time and energy on that right now," Duke replied. "Do you have anything else?"

"We did find out the facility is owned by a wealthy businessman named Grigori Shirokov, who also owns many other enterprises throughout Belarus and Russia. It seems that several years ago, Wu became affiliated with Shirokov and his medical company in Belarus. However, it doesn't appear that Wu is partnering with Shirokov in any other business. We're sending everything we've found to you right now."

"Thank you both!" Duke said before he hung up.

"If they have that many vaccines, it must have already been tested to make sure it worked. They wouldn't have produced that much otherwise," Steve said.

"And if it was manufactured before the outbreak…" Cho paused, deep in thought, and then continued, "They must have intentionally released COVID in order to profit off of its vaccine."

"But why haven't they released it yet?" Ami asked. "Wouldn't releasing it as soon as possible benefit everyone—including themselves?"

"Huh. That's a good question," Steve said.

"Whatever the reason, I don't think there's much else we can do here in Wuhan right now," Duke said, and the others nodded in agreement.

They decided to fly back to Hong Kong on the next available flight, scheduled for departure three hours from then. Steve and Cho returned to their room to pack.

As Duke and Ami were packing and getting ready to head down to the car, there was a knock at the door. Duke went to open it, naïvely thinking it must have been Steve and Cho. When he began to turn the knob, the door was violently slammed open, and four men barged into the room with their guns drawn. They pushed Duke and Ami against the wall, handcuffing them with zip ties. For a brief second, Duke thought about disarming the men, knowing that with Ami's help, they could have turned the tide on the assault. But he didn't want to risk escalating the matter further, which turned out to be a good thing because there were two more men standing in the hallway. None of them were in uniform; they all wore suits and didn't seem to be working for the police.

All six men surrounded them and herded them to the elevators down the hall, shoving them into one as soon as the doors chimed open. They pushed Duke and Ami out of the elevator and through the lobby, careful not to draw too much attention, and then out the front doors, where a van waited with the side door open. Once the door closed, the van sped off. Steve and Cho heard everything through their earpieces and rushed up the two levels to Duke and Ami's room, using Duke's spare key card to gain entrance. They searched for the keys to the rental car and found them sitting on the coffee table. Steve grabbed Duke and Ami's suitcases and one of their backpacks, Cho grabbed the other, and they rushed down to the parking lot.

Cho turned on the tracking app on her cell phone and found Duke and Ami's signals right away. She called out directions to Steve as they raced along, trying to catch up with the vehicle carrying their partners. All the members of the Syndicate had a tracking device implanted in one of their thighs, just under the skin. The device broadcasted a constant signal so they could be easily located, and their vitals were monitored to allow those tracking them to also know their physical condition. Ali and Valerie had designed an app that could monitor the tracking devices from about fifty miles away, depending on the weather and the terrain.

"They stopped!" Cho exclaimed, still watching her phone.

Steve and Cho were about two miles away from the tracking signal when the movement ceased.

"It looks like they're at a warehouse," Cho said.

"Let's go check it out, and we'll figure out what to do when we get there," Steve suggested.

"Okay," Cho replied, knowing that besides Duke, there was nobody else she would rather be in such a dangerous situation with than Steve. She was confident in his on-the-fly strategizing abilities.

Meanwhile, Duke and Ami were driven into a large industrial warehouse along the edge of the Yangtze River and placed in chairs. One of the men duct-taped Duke's legs and torso to the chair, leaving his wrists bound together behind his back. Then, the man did the same to Ami. A few seconds later, a Qiantu K50 electric sports car silently glided to a stop in front of them, and the warehouse doors slid closed. A hefty thirty-something Chinese man emerged from the vehicle and removed his sunglasses as he walked over to Duke.

"What are you doing here?" he asked in broken English.

"I don't know," Duke replied flippantly. "Ask those clowns. They're the ones who brought us here."

"What are you doing in Wuhan?" the man vehemently probed.

"We wanted to see the market and do some shopping," Duke quipped coolly.

"Liar!" the man yelled. "We have evidence that you're here as a spy. Who are you working for?"

"What gives you that impression?" Duke asked.

"We intercepted communications from you with someone in Hong Kong. We know you've been spying on the pharmaceutical lab," the man said.

Duke wondered how on earth they would've been able to figure that out. Had his team been followed when they drove by the lab? But how did the men know about his communication with Ali?

"I'm sorry," Duke said, "but you're mistaken. We aren't spies, and I don't have any idea what you're talking about."

"Yes, you do! Someone hacked into our mainframe and stole information. We have records of you making a phone call, and whoever you talked to called you back with information about Mr. Wu and his lab. Now, I want to know what you're doing here and who you're working for, or else you're going to watch your wife suffer," the man threatened, pointing at Ami.

"She's just my girlfriend," Duke replied nonchalantly, exchanging a telltale glance with Ami. "I don't care that much about her. I'm probably going to have to find another girlfriend after this ordeal anyway."

"Take her," the man told one of his associates. "We're going to see just how much this man really does care for his woman."

All eyes turned to Ami as one of the men whipped out a knife and began to cut the tape off her legs and torso, freeing her from the chair. He grabbed her by the arm and spun her around to cut the zip ties off her wrists, not at all worried about the tiny woman. Duke readied himself for what was about to happen, knowing that Steve and Cho had to be listening nearby. When the man cut Ami's zip ties, it was as if he'd unleashed the Tasmanian Devil. Ami swung around and kicked the man who had just freed her on the side of his knee. His leg buckled under him, causing him to fall to the ground and drop his knife as he pulled his knee up to his waist, groaning in pain. Ami grabbed the knife and tumbled around Duke's chair as she slipped the weapon behind him and into his hands.

The other five men began to close in around Ami, all of them leery given what they'd just witnessed but still underestimating the woman's abilities. The interrogator backed away to allow his men access to Ami and to get himself out of harm's way.

The warehouse was full of pallets of round plastic pellets about the size of baseballs that weighed about a pound a piece. It looked like they must've been stored in the warehouse for some plastic-manufacturing company. The pallets provided excellent cover for Steve and Cho, who had broken into a side door and were stealthily approaching, still undetected.

Steve quickly took stock of the situation and, without a moment's hesitation, took a couple of the pellets and threw one at the man opposite Ami, hitting him square in the back of the head and dropping him to the ground. The man next to him looked down at his writhing colleague on the floor beside him, giving Cho the opportunity to leap onto his back and grab his head. She twisted her body with all her might until she heard the man's neck pop. She let go and landed on her feet as he collapsed on the floor. The first man began to stagger back to his feet, holding the back of his head. Steve kicked him in the face while he was on his knees, and the man's lights went out.

The other men turned to see what was going on and began to draw their guns, but it was already too late. Duke had freed himself with the knife in about two seconds. He grabbed the gun from the man nearest himself and shot him and the other two who were still standing. Steve grabbed a gun from the guy he had knocked out and shot the man Ami had initially taken down, just as he reached for his gun to shoot Duke.

While all of that was happening, the interrogator had slipped away to his Qiantu. He slammed his car door shut when the warehouse doors opened and then sped away.

"Who was that man?" Steve asked.

"I don't know," replied Duke, "but whoever he is, he has some formidable resources."

"Should we chase him down?" Cho asked.

"No, let's just get to the airport and get out of here," Duke said.

* * *

They made it through security at Wuhan Tianhe International Airport and onto the plane with only seconds to spare. But the fact that they were able to board the plane without incident meant that whoever the kidnappers were, they weren't part of the government. Duke, Ami, Steve, and Cho all breathed a sigh of relief when they finally set foot back on the *Charaka* in Hong Kong, and Duke gave the order to get everyone back on board. They would leave as soon as Duke could get clearance from the General Administration of Customs.

The next morning, Duke took his document folder to the General Administration of Customs office to get his paperwork stamped and the ship cleared to depart. The *Charaka* always had proper documents wherever it went because Abe Lim could create any document, passport, driver's license, or whatever else the crew needed anywhere in the world. And between Ali and Valerie, they could ensure the information was put into the proper computer system for verification.

A little while later, three men from the General Administration of Customs returned to the boat with Duke, who had told the crew through his earpiece to assume their positions in the superstructure in anticipation of visitors.

The men boarded the boat, climbed the five flights of stairs to the bridge, and were greeted by Steve and Ali, who invited them to look around. The men glanced around and, still panting from their climb, asked if they could see the cargo bays.

Duke said, "Of course," and asked Ali to unlatch and open the bay doors.

"Where's the rest of your crew?" asked one of the inspectors.

"They're scattered throughout the superstructure—some in the engine room, one in the equipment room, a couple are sleeping, and the cook is probably getting something ready for lunch. I can take you around to each level and show you if you'd like," Duke said, knowing that the stairs were as much exploring as they'd want to do.

"Your cargo doors are hydraulically opened?" one of the inspectors questioned.

"Yes, sir," Duke responded. "They can be latched and opened from the bridge, reducing the manpower needed to operate the ship."

"High tech!" the inspector exclaimed.

"You have no idea." Duke smirked.

Duke and the three men went downstairs and walked out onto the deck to look down into the holds, only to see what looked like a full load of iron ore pellets. The three men nodded in satisfaction and didn't even look at half the holds before turning around and heading back to the pier. When they arrived at the gangway that bridged the ship to the dock, one of the men stopped and took the paperwork he'd been carrying. He laid it on the rail as he withdrew a stamp from his ink-stained pocket and proceeded to flip through the pages, stamping some of them. Then, he turned to Duke and handed him the folder, offering a "bon voyage." As the three men turned and exited the ship, Duke looked up to the bridge and motioned for the crew to retract the gangway. Valerie, watching everything on the monitors above her desk in the main control room, pressed the button that retracted the walkway. The few crew members in the superstructure headed for the elevator to join the rest below. Whenever an inspection took place, only the men took positions in the superstructure since it wasn't typical for women to crew a cargo ship and Duke didn't want to draw any unnecessary attention to his ship or his team.

The *Charaka* pulled out of port and headed north to Bohai Bay, a two-day cruise. From there, it would be a two-hour drive to Beijing, where they intended to interview Mr. Wu.

CHAPTER 6

Mingli had recruited his little brother when Minzhe was old enough to leave home and move out on his own. Minzhe had never been very good in school, and afterward, he was a laborer at one of the local factories, so he was happy to work for his successful older brother. Mingli slowly brought him up to speed on his companies and his business prowess. He felt certain he could count on his little brother's loyalty and would eventually entrust him to take care of certain unscrupulous business matters from time to time in order to keep Mingli's subordinates in their places. Minzhe was a natural in the position because he had developed a somewhat nasty disposition, perhaps because he had been raised by a stepfather who hadn't cared for him.

Mingli owned a commercial fishing fleet that operated hundreds of small fishing boats. The daily catches were given to larger processing vessels, and those canning ships would clean, cook, and package the product while still at sea. Then, the craft would take the seafood to the distribution center on shore once it met its quota. While at the dock, the ship would be resupplied with fuel, packaging supplies, and a fresh workforce. Mingli had made it a practice to visit all his businesses at least once a year, and on one occasion not too long after Minzhe had begun working for his brother, he joined Mingli on one of their processing ships. That day, they sailed with a seasoned captain who'd worked for the company for over thirty-five years. The captain told Mingli that his father had once fished with him on a vessel very similar to the one they were on.

While they were out at sea, the captain pointed out the fishing boats in Mingli's fleet that would soon transfer their catches for the day onto his ship. Then, he took Mingli and Minzhe belowdecks and showed them the sorting and processing facilities. The captain expounded on each step of the process and how, by the time the ship reached the dock, the cargo would be offloaded for transportation to the distribution center. At the end of the day, the fishermen on the smaller crafts could simply prepare their boats for the next day and return home without worrying about preparing the fish. That kept the men's spirits high and the profits even higher.

After the business lesson, the three men returned to the bridge, and the captain bellowed, "Darn it! There's an independent. Watch what I do to these guys."

The captain pushed the throttle forward, and his ship increased speed as he corrected his bearing and steered it directly toward the little fishing boat in the distance. The men in the boat were preoccupied with throwing their lines into the sea. The captain explained that his ship had a steel hull and large propellers ideal for smashing small wooden fishing boats, like the one getting closer to them, into pieces. Mingli and Minzhe watched out of the pilot-house window as the little boat drew closer and closer. A man inside of it jumped up and started waving his arms frantically.

"They all do that," the captain explained.

The man jumped back to the motor and began to move his boat out of harm's way, but the captain matched his direction, and soon, the men's screams were replaced with a deafening scraping sound under the ship that started at the bow, passed under Mingli and Minzhe, and concluded with a loud grinding noise at the stern as the remnants of the men and their boat were shredded and spit out into the sea behind them.

"I'll circle back and check for survivors," the captain said as he turned his ship around. "Well, look. There's somebody in the water. Looks like he needs help." The captain aimed the ship straight for the man. There was only a slight thud that time as the ship plowed over the helpless victim.

"More fish for us now," the captain said with a chuckle.

Minzhe was dumbfounded at first, while Mingli congratulated the captain for his fine work, then explained to his silent little brother, "You see, Minzhe, so many fishermen struggle because of overfishing—the largest number of fishing vessels in the world are concentrated here. Despite the fact that the waters are crowded with so many fishermen, Wu International's fishing branch still makes record profits, and little acts like this help more than you know."

Soon, Minzhe began to view those cavalier methods as the way successful men conducted business, his conscience becoming hardened to the point that he soon adopted similar approaches to promote his brother's prosperity.

* * *

One of Minzhe's earliest assignments was to eliminate one of Mingli's business competitors. Mingli had been looking to enter the shipping industry to expand Wu International's subsidiary portfolio when an opportunity arose to partner with Yoon Shipping. Mr. Yoon, a young man who owned a modest fleet of cargo vessels, wanted to expand his business venture but needed capital. Mingli exploited Mr. Yoon's naïve desperation to finance his company's expansion, and Mr. Yoon agreed to give Mingli a majority share of his business. Mingli was a savvy mogul and had a contract drawn up that not only made Wu International the majority stakeholder, but if Mr. Yoon passed away, Wu International would have the opportunity to purchase Mr. Yoon's shares for pennies on the dollar. Mr. Yoon had reasoned that it didn't matter; he was a young man that had decades of dividends to accrue before he sold his shares and retired.

Minzhe had never killed anyone before and was apprehensive about his task. But Mingli made it easy for him. All he had to do was take a vial of an odorless, tasteless liquid and administer three drops to Mr. Yoon's drink or food. Minzhe followed Mr. Yoon for several weeks to learn his routine and found that Mr. Yoon liked to frequent an upscale restaurant near his home. Minzhe ate at the restaurant a few times to get the feel for the atmosphere and decided to impersonate one of the waitstaff.

He was able to easily enter the kitchen through the back door without raising an eyebrow from anyone in the kitchen. As usual, Mr. Yoon was dining with a young lady. From a discreet area in the restaurant, Minzhe watched the waiter take Mr. Yoon's order and knew the server's routine—he would take the entrée request to the kitchen and circle around to the bar to place the drink order. Minzhe watched as the bartender made the drinks and surmised which cocktail was Mr. Yoon's and which one was his lady friend's. Minzhe sauntered over to the bar and nonchalantly dumped the entire contents of the vial into the glass he presumed was Mr. Yoon's and retreated to an area frequented by the waitstaff. The waiter collected the drinks from the bar and served them to Mr. Yoon's table. To Minzhe's despair, he had put the poison in the wrong drink! Within minutes, Mr. Yoon's date was grabbing her neck and struggling to breathe, bringing much attention to their table when she fell to the floor, dead.

While all the commotion was taking place, Minzhe retreated to his rental car and waited for the ambulance. Mr. Yoon followed the ambulance in his car, and Minzhe followed Mr. Yoon. Minzhe knew she was dead; all he'd needed was three drops, but he had used the entire vial. He followed Mr. Yoon into the parking garage and parked a few spaces down from where the man's car was. Then, he waited. He wasn't about to let his brother down, especially not on his first major assignment.

A few hours later, Mr. Yoon lackadaisically walked back to his car, intermittently sobbing, and didn't see Minzhe approaching him. Without a word, he grabbed Mr. Yoon from behind and lacerated his neck. Minzhe's lack of experience and pent-up anxiety caused him to not only cut Mr. Yoon's jugular vein but also almost cut his entire head off. He quickly returned to his car and headed to his hotel to clean up, barely able to drive because he was shaking uncontrollably.

After that first time, it became easier and easier until Minzhe was able to torture or kill someone without any remorse whatsoever. Minzhe evolved from having a somewhat nasty disposition to being a natural killer, solidifying his essential position in his brother's company.

Later, he helped his brother with the pharmaceutical side of the empire. He was to hire eight people—three women and five men—to test an experimental drug. He told them it could cause a runny nose and a slight cough for a while, but the symptoms should go away in a couple of weeks, similar to the flu. It wasn't difficult to find participants for the experiment because so many people in China were struggling, and six months' worth of wages was well worth the two weeks of suffering. There was only one requirement: they had to be five foot two or shorter. Each test subject received an injection, and then every day for two weeks, they were to go shopping at the Wuhan market with two thousand yuan to buy anything they desired. For those two weeks, each of them would be put up in a hotel with free meals, and a shuttle would take them to the market and pick them up at the end of each day. The eight subjects were happy to have such an opportunity while it lasted.

Two of the eight people died about a week after receiving their injection and were only able to visit the market a few times because they were too sick to leave the hotel. The others went a few more days than them, but they also became too sick to go to the market every day for the required two weeks. The scientists at Wu International determined that since the participants had been injected with the virus, their reactions were much more severe than what they could expect from the general population.

To avoid being noticed in the hotel, Minzhe had two men wait to dress in white hazmat suits, face masks, and respirators until they were outside of each deceased individual's room. After which, they collected the two bodies and placed them in five-foot, three-inch duffle bags. All eight rooms were grouped together on the same floor, making their task easier. Once the men had both bodies bagged, they discarded their personal protective equipment in plastic bags, sealed them, and disinfected their hands. They loaded the bags onto the luggage cart, pushed it to the elevator, and rolled it out to their van. As soon as the vehicle was loaded, they returned the luggage cart to the lobby and drove away without anybody giving them a second glance.

With the rest of the subjects too sick to go to the market, Minzhe had his two men return to the hotel and pick up the remaining six people, who presumed they were being brought home. They all crawled into the back of the van and took their seats, either too sick or too scared to say anything to the two men wearing white hazmat suits in the front seats. The men had driven a few miles to a warehouse and pulled in when one of the subjects finally got up the courage to ask what they were doing.

"Just get out. We need to change vehicles," one of the men said.

They all climbed out of the van as six shots rang out. The men loaded the bodies into duffle bags, piled them back into the van, and drove to another business Mingli owned—a funeral home with a cremation chamber.

* * *

It didn't take long after the virus was released at the market for it to rapidly spread throughout China, and soon after, the entire world became gripped by the pandemic. Mingli assigned Minzhe to erect a security fence and install guarded entries around his pharmaceutical complex because there were whispered allegations about their possible connection to the virus. Minzhe completed his task in just a few weeks, which impressed his brother. Mingli owned a technology company that made espionage equipment for the military and designed high-tech security software that prevented anyone from hacking the information systems protected by it. Mingli had thought it was totally impenetrable and the best in the world…until it was hacked by the Syndicate.

The security equipment installed in the lab complex had notified Minzhe about a firewall breach. Although it couldn't precisely locate the source of the intrusion, he was able to trace the break-in to the general area of Hong Kong. As soon as the alarm had sounded, supplementary espionage equipment scanned the surrounding cell towers and picked up on keywords that enabled them to triangulate the location of Duke's cell phone while he talked to Ali. Once the area of Duke's cell phone had been located, Minzhe dispatched his two best technicians in a sophisticated surveillance van equipped with eavesdropping gear that allowed them to listen to each and every cell phone conversation routed through a particular cell tower. Singling out keywords in English, they'd fine-tuned the direction of the signal until they'd determined a precise location in the hotel. The technology Mingli's company had developed was second to none, and within a short amount of time, Minzhe's security team had identified Duke's room and rolled up to the front doors, where six men had exited the van and headed up there.

Mingli wasn't happy that, in his opinion, his brother had failed him. Not only had he not discovered the mysterious man's identity, but he'd also gotten some of his men killed and let the suspects get away. Mingli knew his brother wasn't the best schemer and needed some direction at times, but tracking down the hacker should've been a no-brainer, the kind of thing his brother had done hundreds of times before. The perpetrators must've been admirable adversaries, Mingli reasoned, if they were able to kill all six of his men and escape his brother's interrogation without revealing a thing. By the time Mingli and Minzhe were able to deploy men to the airport in Hong Kong, the flight from Wuhan had already arrived, and the subjects were long gone. The two brothers had no idea where they could've gone, and after listening to the audio of the conversation, they didn't have a single name they could use to identify the culprits. But the one thing Mingli knew for certain was that someone was after him, and he needed to find out who they were and what they wanted from him. He had his own spies on alert in and around Hong Kong. But with the city's population of seven and a half million people, Mingli knew finding them would be harder than finding the proverbial "needle in a haystack," especially since the man and his crew seemed to be masters at playing cat-and-mouse.

Mingli was certain that whoever had escaped his brother intended to investigate his lab and, in turn, himself. He'd never expected suspicions would point to his lab when the virus had been developed all the way in Minsk. He'd made sure that the only thing manufactured in his Wuhan lab was the vaccine for the virus. But even that was top secret. Only seven researchers ever knew about it, and they'd been paid handsomely to keep it confidential. If money wasn't motive enough to keep them all quiet, Mingli had sent Minzhe to meet with the seven researchers just in case someone were to develop a good Samaritan complex. During the interrogation, he'd accused one of them of disclosing the classified information. Despite the researcher's adamant denial—and Minzhe's confidence in the man's innocence—Minzhe had reached into his coat and pulled a pistol from a holster under his arm. He'd shot the man in the forehead in front of the other six to make a point and ensure they kept silent.

But Mingli couldn't get one question out of his mind: *How did that man stumble upon him as the source of the virus?* He was perplexed, and it drove him crazy, but he knew he needed to get out of Beijing before the man tracked him down. Mingli called his pilot and told him to file plans to fly from Beijing to Minsk and then to Greece. There, Mingli would visit Grigori Shirokov to make sure things were in order in his lab before their stalker paid Grigori a visit as well. After that stop, he'd meet his father on his yacht in the Mediterranean.

Mingli's chauffeur took him to his private hangar at the airport and pulled up next to Mingli's Gulfstream V. The plane took off and was soon cruising at an altitude of forty thousand feet. Nine hours later and after a good sleep, Mingli touched down in Minsk and taxied to a Toyota 4Runner. He yawned as he exited the plane and climbed into the back seat next to Grigori Shirokov.

"It's good to see you, my friend," Grigori said to Mingli in broken English, their common language since he couldn't speak Mandarin and Mingli couldn't speak Russian.

"It's good to see you too, but we have a problem," Mingli told him.

"Hold on. Let's wait and talk at dinner. I have nice private table ready for us at excellent restaurant I own. You will love it," Grigori said.

After a short drive, they arrived at a small stone building. Inside, they were led to an elegantly decorated table in a small private room. The table had two settings of a small appetizer plate with a set of silverware framing it, a napkin folded in the shape of a turkey's tail feathers on top of the dish, a crystal goblet filled with water, a crystal shot glass next to the goblet, and a chilled $3,400 bottle of Stoli Elit Himalayan limited-edition vodka in the center of the table next to a bouquet of beautiful chamomile flowers.

The waiters slid the men's chairs up to the table, and Mingli said, "This is very nice. I hope dinner is just as impressive."

"Dinner will be excellent," Grigori said. "But first, let's enjoy some fine Russian vodka." He began filling the shot glasses. "Drink, relax, and we can resolve any issues that come up."

Mingli didn't waste a second before telling his colleague about their trouble. "Yesterday, a man and woman were snooping around the lab in Wuhan in search of the cause of the virus. I know this because my brother intercepted a phone call they made. They were inquiring about me and my lab, and we suspect they hacked into our server and stole information. Then, whoever they were getting their information from also linked me to our lab here and mentioned your name as my partner," Mingli told him.

"Most troubling," Grigori said, then took another shot. "Why do they suspect virus originated in Wuhan lab when we develop it here? Did you have any information about virus on your server?"

Mingli shook his head. "It's because of the media. To procure headlines and recognition, they invented the premise that the virus was developed and leaked out of my lab," he responded. "Thankfully, there wasn't anything about the virus on the server, but there was the formula for the vaccine on it."

"What should we do?" Grigori asked.

"We should clean up the lab here and make sure all evidence of the virus is gone."

"It's already done, my friend. I had them wipe server and get rid of all evidence as soon as we completed mission. Then, I disappeared scientists that were working on it."

"Good, good!" Mingli said with relief. "Then we don't have anything to worry about."

"No, we don't," Grigori said. "Now, let's appreciate rest of this bottle while we enjoy our excellent meal."

Mingli was relieved, but still, there was something about

his stalker that made him uneasy. It was just a feeling he had, but what could he do? He decided he'd try to relax and let things cool down before continuing with his agenda.

After dinner, Mingli said his goodbyes to his friend and business partner. He exited the SUV and boarded his plane for the two-and-a-half-hour flight to Athens.

* * *

They landed in the city well into the evening, and after a short taxi ride, Mingli was on a speedboat headed toward his father's yacht.

"Welcome, my son," Mr. Wu said with a smile. "It's so good to see you again. Choo will show you to your cabin, then come join me for a nightcap."

After stowing his belongings, Mingli went to the deck, where his father already had a glass of Maotai waiting for him. Mingli sat down in the recliner next to his father and began to sip his drink.

"You have been doing well with Wu International, my son—profits are soaring. But I believe it's time to start focusing on American commerce; that's where our future lies."

"Father, you know I have a large staff of researchers tracking businesses in the United States. I am just waiting for the right time to begin the takeovers."

"We don't want to wait too long. The global economy is going to explode over the next few years, and it could change the world's economic balance," Hui fang said.

"I intend to tip the scales in our favor, Father."

"I know you will, Son."

"It's been a long day, Father," Mingli said. "I think I'm going to finish my drink and turn in. We can talk more tomorrow."

"That'll be fine," his father replied. "I'll have the chef make your favorite breakfast, and we can dine in the salon."

"That sounds good." Mingli tipped his glass back to

swallow down his last bit of Maotai, told his father goodnight, then returned to his cabin.

* * *

While Mingli had been on his way to Athens, Grigori called his right-hand man, Yuri, and asked how the families of the scientists were faring. The five scientists had been given a top-secret assignment to manufacture a virus from a formula Grigori had given them. The virus had already been perfected; they'd just needed to create a vehicle or solution to contain the virus alive so it could be easily injected into a human while also preserving it in a state that would promote proliferation throughout a body and then readily spread to other bodies. They didn't have to create a great quantity; their objective had been to make just a few hundred doses. At completion, they'd delivered the vials to Grigori himself and dismantled the lab. The next day, the scientists had gone to work expecting a new assignment, but instead, they were called one by one into a soundproof office, where Yuri had waited for them with his gun.

The problem was that they'd all gone missing on the same day, and Grigori couldn't return the bodies to their families without them knowing how they'd died. He'd told the families there had been a terrible accident at the lab, exposing the scientists to a substance that had killed them instantly, and the dangerous nature of the contagion had rendered their bodies unable to be exposed to anyone else. The bodies had had to be burned immediately to prevent any further contamination. The families, however, weren't satisfied with the explanation and complained to anyone who would listen, even though the company gave each household a substantial sum of money as compensation for their loss.

It was up to Yuri to see to it that each of the surviving family members met an untimely death, just in case one of the scientists had mentioned their task to a wife or husband.

Yuri killed one of the scientists' spouses in an automobile accident by following her on a desolate highway one night and performing a pit maneuver on her car. He eased his vehicle up alongside her back-quarter panel like he was going to pass her, then suddenly turned his vehicle into hers, spinning it. As her car spun, he accelerated and pushed it just enough to let the momentum take over and roll her vehicle. He counted three rolls before the car came to rest on the driver's side. Then, after he stopped to check out the damage and saw that his job was done, he got back into his SUV and took off. The authorities assumed she had fallen asleep and lost control.

Another surviving family was made up of a widower and his two teenage children. One night, Yuri broke into their house and cut a natural gas line to the stove while everyone slept upstairs. He lit a candle in another room and left. About forty minutes later, an explosion rocked the neighborhood, and when the neighbors looked outside, they saw the house totally engulfed in flames. There were no survivors. The authorities ruled it an unfortunate accident.

The wife of another scientist had loved to swim in the pool at their house almost every day when the weather was warm. One day, Yuri climbed the fence in her backyard and hid behind a shorter enclosure screening the pool equipment from view. When the woman went outside to swim, Yuri waited until she was facing away from him and made his move. He jumped into the pool and held her head underwater until she quit struggling. He left her floating facedown in the water. It was ruled an accidental drowning.

Once the scientists and their closest family members were all dead and the lab was dismantled, nothing could've possibly linked the virus to Grigori or Mingli.

* * *

Grigori had handed off two boxes of vials on one of Mingli's earlier visits to Minsk, and Mingli had transported the virus back to Beijing on his personal jet. Two weeks after the illness was unleashed at the Wuhan market, Mingli had 192 other individuals injected. He'd sent them to forty-nine of the most populated cities throughout the world, covering six of the seven continents, excluding Antarctica. First-class seats on different airlines had proven to be a perfect mode for a rather prolific and speedy transmission of the virus. First-class passengers always boarded the plane first, forcing all subsequent passengers to walk by the infected subject on their way to their seats. If anyone somehow managed to elude the virus, the moist air conditioning system took the infected person's exhaled air and circulated it throughout the entire aircraft.

Mingli had ensured that none of his injected subjects had direct flights, making each one travel through connecting airports in order to expose more people in additional cities around the world. His plan had worked beautifully. The first exposures had occurred in Wuhan in late November of 2019. A month later, on December 31, 2019, Chinese health officials informed the World Health Organization about an outbreak of viral pneumonia cases of an unknown cause in Wuhan, Hubei, China. Within three months, the virus had spread throughout the world, and on March 11, 2020, the World Health Organization recognized the extent of COVID-19, labeling it a pandemic. Many governments had shut down businesses and limited social gatherings in efforts to slow the progression of the disease. However, despite those measures, the virus had continued to spread throughout the world until a vaccine was introduced by a Chinese pharmaceutical company named Wu International in August of 2020.

Within a few months, the vaccine had been administered to nearly everyone in the world, causing the virus to be nearly eradicated six months later. Wu International was touted throughout the entire world as the company that had saved the planet. Their pharmaceutical branch's revenue had topped that of Johnson & Johnson, the reigning world leader of pharmaceutical companies.

Despite the rumors, nobody ever knew for certain that Wu International was responsible for releasing the virus into the world or that Mingli's pharmaceutical lab in Wuhan had begun manufacturing the vaccine six months before the illness was unleashed on mankind. By the time the vaccine was introduced in August of 2020, Wu International had been manufacturing it for over a year. They'd stockpiled enough of the vaccine to adequately supply the overwhelming demand for it throughout the world, and they didn't need the assistance of any other pharmaceutical company to help produce it.

Nobody knew that the exploratory and preclinical stages of the vaccine's development had been accomplished over a year before the virus emerged on the world scene or that it had been thoroughly tested on unsuspecting individuals prior to its introduction. Mingli had covered all of his tracks, and to someone unsuspecting, it would appear as if Wu International had followed the proper protocols to the letter. Once word had gotten out that people in China were being cured by a vaccine approved by the National Medical Products Administration of China, other nations had followed suit, and the approval process was fast-tracked around the globe—regulatory reviews and approval procedures were completed in record times.

Many called the vaccine a miracle drug because it began eliminating symptoms within twenty-four hours and completely purged the virus from the body within seventy-two hours. The virus didn't even last as long as the common cold once the vaccine was administered. Wu International was publicized as the new world leader in pharmaceutical research and development, and humanity wondered what they'd accomplish next. Mingli's company had become the highest traded commodity on the stock exchanges, catapulting him to become the richest man in the world. But Mingli wanted more than money—he wanted to be the most powerful man alive, and he had just the plan to accomplish that.

CHAPTER 7

The *Charaka* had been approved to dock in the busy Port of Tianjin inside Bohai Bay to unload its cargo. The lines were tied, and the *Charaka* was secured to the wharf. Duke had Ali hack into the port's computer system and delay offloading procedures, so the crew members were free to operate unimpeded for at least three days—plenty of time to go to Beijing and pay a visit to Mr. Wu. They planned to send Cho Bai to Mr. Wu's office to see if she could get in to see him. Cho was the equivalent to men of what Steve was to women. They both had some mystical allure to the opposite sex that baffled Duke. Sure, they were both good looking, but the way people bent over backwards to cater to their every whim was inexplicable. Nonetheless, Duke hoped that if Mr. Wu saw Cho, he'd be enamored and willing to talk with her. If he wasn't at the office, then Abe and Ami would go to his house under the guise of offering home maintenance services. Abe Lim was of Chinese descent, so he and Ami would make an inconspicuous couple.

Abe Lim, although forty years old, had a boyish face that made him look much closer in age to Ami, who was ten years his junior. At five-foot-two, the black-haired, brown-eyed man was slightly taller than

Ami. His family had been in the US for three generations, and his parents couldn't speak a lick of Chinese, so neither could he.

Duke didn't want to take any chances with Abe's very limited Mandarin vocabulary. From Ali's research, they knew Mr. Wu was a traditional person and would expect Abe to lead the conversation. Mr. Wu was a very savvy man, and if Abe slipped up, Duke was afraid that Mr. Wu may finish with Abe and Ami what he'd started with Ami and Duke back in Wuhan. Duke was certain Mr. Wu was behind his kidnapping somehow because the interrogator had mentioned he knew they were spying on the pharmaceutical lab, and the lab was owned by Mr. Wu. It was crucial to get information from the businessman, so for two hours, Abe practiced saying "I will have my assistant tell you about our services" as well as a few other simple sentences that would hopefully direct the conversation back to Ami until it was time for them to leave.

The plan was to take the Syndicate's van and have Ali, Duke, Abe, Ami, and Tiny— Duke's number one during their Navy SEAL days—go with Cho to the offices of Wu International to see if Cho could get in to speak with Mr. Wu.

Valerie expertly guided the thirty-ton crane as it lifted the metal CONEX shipping container out of the hold and placed it on the dock. Tiny unlatched the doors, swung them open, and pulled out the ramps. Ali was much narrower than Tiny, so he climbed into the driver's seat and pulled the van out of the CONEX. Tiny latched the doors closed and gave the all-clear signal in the direction of the hidden camera Valerie was using from the control center below deck. Valerie tucked the shipping container back into the hold while Tiny, Duke, Abe, Ami, and Cho climbed into the van.

Edmond Wilson, aka Tiny, was a thirty-six-year-old man who intimidated many with his six-foot-six, three-hundred-pound muscular frame. But as daunting as his appearance was, his abilities far exceeded his rugged exterior. Tiny could run at lightning-fast speeds, outswim just about anybody, shoot the wings off a fly, and overwhelm the most able opponent with his proficiency in martial arts.

The van was loaded with surveillance equipment and could listen to a conversation up to five miles away or pick up on earpiece communicators from over three miles unless the signal was impeded by thick walls, which limited the range to about a mile. Strategically placed listening devices could be monitored for up to a ten-mile range, and drones could be controlled for over fifty miles on a clear day when aerial footage was needed. In addition to a stockpile of various weapons, there was enough equipment in the van to pull off any infiltration mission if the crew needed to access a highly secured facility. The van could handle just about any land mission and provided the means to deal with any surprises the Syndicate could encounter.

* * *

The team arrived at a twenty-six-story building in downtown Beijing—home to Wu International. The man at the information desk called Mr. Wu's office and explained that there was a woman in the lobby who wanted to speak to Mr. Wu about a confidential matter. He hung up the phone and told Cho she should take the second set of elevators just around the corner to the twenty-sixth floor. Then, he walked around the desk with a huge smile and said, "Let me show you." He offered his arm, and Cho embraced it and let him escort her to the elevator. Cho was used to unwanted attention; men catered to her everywhere she went.

Cho opened the large glass door when she heard the buzzer and walked straight into the offices of Wu International Headquarters, where an exceptionally beautiful woman sat at a large, exquisite receptionist desk.

"Hello. I'm Ju Li, and I'm here to see Mr. Wu," Cho said.

"Is Mr. Wu expecting you?" the woman asked.

"No, this is my first visit. I need to talk to him about a

confidential matter," Cho continued.

"I'm sorry, but Mr. Wu isn't in the office today, and I'm not sure when he'll be back."

"Just between you and me," Cho said, thinking on her feet, "I'm writing a book and wanted to interview Mr. Wu because it's about him and his rise from the son of a humble farmer to the most powerful businessman in China."

"You must be mistaken," the woman at the desk replied. "Mr. Wu was never a farmer. I heard that he was raised by a fisherman until his dad didn't return from the sea one day. He was raised by his biological father after that. Maybe Mr. Wu's father grew up on a farm, but not Mr. Wu."

"Oh my," Cho said. "I need to do some more research before I talk to Mr. Wu so our conversation will be more productive. Please let him know that I'd like to speak to him at his earliest convenience." Cho handed the woman a business card that simply had her fake name, Ju Li, with a phone number below it, then turned and walked out of the office. The man at the information desk jumped up when he saw Cho, smiled, and waved goodbye as he watched her walk out of the building.

Cho may not have gotten a meeting with Mr. Wu, but she'd learned some invaluable information. As the Syndicate was enacting plan B, on the way to Mr. Wu's house, Ali provided some background information.

"After hearing the fishing story," he said, "I did some further research and found that the receptionist was correct. Hui fang Wu is the founder of Wu International and is still listed as the owner of the corporation today. However, it seems as though he's no longer involved with the company. His son, Mingli Wu, is the CEO and runs the company's day-to-day operations. It seems that Mingli was the person the receptionist thought Cho was there to see. They have their business organized in a way that the closer you get to the top of their corporate ladder, the more blurred the organizational structure becomes. It's as if they're deliberately trying to make it difficult for anyone to know who's responsible for the company's leadership."

"I agree," Duke said. "A bunch of smoke and mirrors to make people like us go down the rabbit hole. Let's check for other houses, personal aircrafts, boats, and the like that could lead us to Mingli Wu. I doubt he's home or that he ever goes to the office. He has businesses all around the world and probably travels a great deal. He knows we're on his heels now; I imagine he's trying to dodge us."

With no other leads, they still had to check Mr. Wu's residence even if he wasn't home. They pulled up to Mr. Wu's house and rang the bell at the gate. To their surprise, the gate opened and allowed the van to pull into the long winding driveway. Abe and Ami got out, and when they stepped up to the front porch, the door opened, and an elderly man greeted them.

"Hello. I'm Wang Wei, and this is my associate, Li Jing," Abe said in almost perfect Mandarin. "We're here to offer our services, and she is going to explain them to you."

Ami started telling the man about their cleaning service, but he quickly cut her off.

"We already have all the services we need," he said as he began to close the door.

"Wait!" Ami blurted. "Can we speak to the owner of the house, please?"

"He isn't here."

"When do you expect him?"

"I don't know. He's rarely home and doesn't bother to tell me when he'll be back."

"How many workers do you have? Maybe you could use one or two more?" Ami pleaded.

"We have all the staff we need. I'm here full time, and we have two housekeepers who come in two or three times a week, depending on whether Mr. Wu is here or not. We have a groundskeeping company that comes once a week. As I said, the owner is rarely home, and the house requires minimal effort to take care of, so we have all the staff we need and aren't looking to make any changes. Now, if you'll excuse me, I need to get back to work," the man said and closed the door.

Abe and Ami returned to the van, drove to the gate, and waited for it to open. As Abe pulled onto the roadway, he asked, "Do you think we should break in and see if there's anything in the house that would help us?"

Duke said, "No, he won't have anything linking him to any malfeasance in there. If he does have evidence, it'll be on his laptop, and I'm sure he carries it with him wherever he goes."

"Then we're leaving with the same amount of information we came with," Tiny said with a tone of discouragement.

"That isn't necessarily true," Duke retorted. "We know he's rarely ever home, meaning he's also rarely ever at the office. If we ever need to get into the office, we know it's accessible from the roof, and if we need to get into his house, we now know it's most likely only occupied by an elderly servant. Both locations will be easy to infiltrate if we ever need to."

"Here's something interesting," Ali said, pointing to his computer screen. "The pharmaceutical lab in Minsk that Mr. Wu is partnering with had an accident not long before the virus outbreak, killing five of its scientists. All five were cremated without being returned to their families because they were exposed to an extremely deadly contagion. That sounds plausible, but here's the kicker: between the time of the accident until now, three of the five scientists' marriage mates died from various kinds of accidents. I find that to be rather unbelievable."

"I agree," Duke said. "Drop me off at the airport. You guys go back to the *Charaka,* and I'll contact you in a couple of days to let you know what we're going to do next."

"Where are you going?" Tiny asked.

"I'm going to go to Minsk. The last two surviving families are going to die next unless I can get to them before the assassin does."

"They're shoring up any loose ends," Cho said.

"That makes sense," Ali added. "They wiped their server, killed their scientists, and now they're disposing of their researchers' families."

"I would guess that's where the virus was developed," Duke stated. "But I bet any trace of it is long gone."

* * *

Duke landed in Minsk just as the sun was setting and decided to stay at the DoubleTree Hotel in a room overlooking the Svislach River. When he returned to his room after dinner, Duke checked his email to find a message from Ali with the addresses of the two surviving wives of the scientists killed in the lab. He looked them up on Google Maps and planned his route to pay them a visit in the morning.

Duke woke up to the boom of thunder and looked outside to see that a miserable rainy day awaited him. Thankfully, he had a rainproof jacket in the go bag he'd grabbed out of the van when the crew dropped him off at the airport. He showered, put on some clean clothes, repacked his bag, and went down the elevator to his rental car.

As he turned into the residential area where the widow of the first scientist on his list lived, he was stopped by a fire truck blocking his path. He parked his car and walked around the corner to see a house engulfed in flames, burning so hotly that even the steady rain couldn't put it out. He looked at the addresses on the houses around it and concluded that it was the residence he'd intended to visit.

He returned to his car and drove to the next location across town. It was a nice quiet neighborhood with very luxurious houses. Duke surmised that the scientists either made very good money or the widow had purchased the house with the cash Grigori's company had paid them off with. Either way, it didn't matter because she wasn't going to enjoy it much longer unless she heeded his advice. He knocked on the door, and a very attractive woman in her early forties opened it. She had long curly brown hair and a pretty but melancholy face.

"Hello, ma'am," Duke said in fluent Russian. Duke spoke Russian better than most native speakers. He continued, "My name is Duke, and I've come to talk to you about your late husband."

"Are you from the lab?" she inquired.

"No, ma'am. I'm here to find out what happened to your husband and to warn you about the danger you're in. May I come in?"

"I guess so. What kind of danger are you talking about?" she asked nervously, opening the door to let Duke enter her home.

He went on to tell her about the spouses of the other scientists who had died in the accident at the lab. He informed her that she was the only one left and that, if she wanted to, she could go with him, and he'd make sure she was protected. She remained silent, taking it all in and trying to decide whether or not she could believe the man sitting across from her.

"What did the company tell you about your husband's death? Did you ever see his body?" Duke asked.

"I never did get to see him. I didn't have any kind of closure." She looked at the floor. "How did he really die? I don't have any answers, and it's tearing me up inside not knowing. None of this makes sense to me. Ivan was so careful with everything he did, whether at work or at home. He'd come home and tell me some things about his work at the lab, but he couldn't tell me everything. I could see that he was working on something that bothered him very much, but he wouldn't tell me what it was."

"I might be able to find some answers for you. Did Ivan have a computer?" Duke inquired.

"Yes, but some men from the lab came right after the accident and took everything they claimed belonged to the company—his computer, one of his phones, his flash drives, and even his lab coats."

"You said 'one of his phones.' Did he have another?"

"Yes, but it was his personal phone, so I didn't tell them about it. They seemed like they wanted to take anything capable of storing electronic data."

"May I look at the phone?" Duke requested.

"Sure, why not?" she said as she got up and went into the other room. A minute later, she returned with an iPhone. The battery was dead, but she also brought a charger and plugged it in near where Duke was sitting. After it powered up, she unlocked it and handed it to him.

Duke looked through the phone, but nothing unusual jumped out at him except for a folder named WORK. He opened it and found an Excel app, but it didn't contain anything useful. He looked at the Word app next, but that didn't have anything either. Then, he looked at the Notes app and found a note with what looked like a chemical formula. He asked if he could email it to himself, and the woman agreed. He handed the phone back to her and asked again if she'd go with him.

She said, "Everything I have is here. I can't leave."

"If you don't come with me, whoever killed the other family members is going to kill you," Duke said. "You're the only one left. I'm not asking you to abandon everything you have. Once this matter is resolved and you're safe, you can always come back, but if you stay here, none of these things will matter because you won't be alive to enjoy them."

She looked at him for a long minute in silence, then said, "Okay, let me go pack a few bags, and I'll go with you."

"Grab your passport too," Duke said. "We're leaving the country. By the way, what's your first name?"

"I'm Larissa."

While Larissa was packing her bags, Duke emailed Ali and Valerie the data he had found on Ivan's phone. Larissa returned after a while, carrying two large suitcases.

Duke said, "Let me get those for you." He took the bags

and set them next to the front door while Larissa went back into the other room and reappeared with another large suitcase and a smaller one.

"I'm ready to go," she said.

The rain had turned to a heavy mist, and Duke took the luggage out to the car in two trips. When he went back to the front door, Larissa was locking it. He escorted her to the passenger door that he'd opened for her and closed it once she was inside, then walked around to get in the driver's seat. As they drove down the street, Duke noticed a tall, rather thin man sitting in an SUV a few houses away. Duke didn't say anything to Larissa but kept an eye on his rearview mirror just in case the stranger decided to follow them. Sure enough, the taillights lit up, the SUV made a sharp U-turn, and it started following at a distance.

Duke didn't try to lose the man; he just drove as he normally would and carried on a conversation with Larissa.

"Where are we going?"

"We are going to the airport to catch a flight to China. Have you ever been to China before?"

"No. What's there?"

"We're going to go on a cruise from there."

"That sounds exciting. Ivan and I went on a cruise once. For our honeymoon, we flew to Copenhagen and sailed to Berlin, Tallinn, St. Petersburg, Helsinki, Stockholm, and then back to Copenhagen. It was so much fun."

"I'm glad you like cruising," Duke said.

"I loved the casinos on the ship and all the stopovers."

"Well, this cruise will be a little different. We'll sail from Bohai Bay in Tianjin to Tokyo Bay in Japan. We won't see anything while we're in China. We'll be leaving as soon as we arrive to go to Japan."

Duke didn't want to burst her bubble, so he just let her talk and imagine going on another relaxing vacation.

"That still sounds like fun. I never had any desire to see China anyway," Larissa confessed.

"You can more than make up for any fun missed once

you get to Japan. I'll find a place for you to stay and give you cash to pay for anything you need. You won't be able to use a credit card during your stay there. The people who are after you could easily trace a credit card."

"Are you sure someone wants to kill me?"

"They have killed everyone's family associated with your husband's lab team except you. I'm certain you're supposed to be next."

"The thought of that really scares me!"

"I know it's scary, but I can make sure you're safe if you listen and follow my directions."

"Okay. But I just don't understand why someone would want to kill *me*."

"They think you may know something that could get them into trouble."

"I don't know anything."

"I realize that, but they aren't going to take any chances." Duke glanced into the rearview mirror, took a deep breath, and asked Larissa, "Is your seatbelt tight?"

"Uh, yes, I guess so."

With a tone of urgency, he said, "Tighten it up and hang on."

"What? Why?" she asked, beginning to turn in her seat.

"Don't turn around! There's an SUV behind us that has been following since we left your house."

"No! Are you sure?"

When they were still a few miles from the airport, Duke noticed the SUV start to pass him, and he was going to let it, but the car suddenly swerved into the back of Duke's sedan.

"Hold on!" Duke exclaimed.

Larissa shrieked in horror. Duke stepped on the gas and turned the wheel, causing the car to slide sideways instead of spinning. The sedan straightened back out swiftly, but then Duke saw the SUV rapidly approaching again in the left lane. He slammed on the brakes just before the SUV could cut over and smash into the back of his mid-sized car.

The heavier SUV couldn't stop as quickly and came to a screeching halt in front of Duke's rental.

Then, Duke went on the offensive and floored his car into the back passenger wheel well of the SUV, bending the rim and flattening the tire. Duke slammed his car in reverse and backed away from the crippled vehicle as it began trying to pursue them. But its larger wheel on the driver's side overpowered the flat tire, making the SUV turn in a way that gave Duke a clear line to the back wheel well on the driver's side. He didn't waste any time before ramming his shifter into drive and smoking his front tires as he quickly accelerated into the SUV's undamaged wheel well, flattening that tire too.

"Doing okay?" Duke calmly asked.

Larissa just looked straight ahead, breathing rapidly with both hands gripping the dashboard.

"Are you okay?"

"I-I-I think so," Larissa barely uttered.

Duke's rental was smoking from under the hood and making an awful noise as he drove around the SUV and headed to the airport. He only had a few miles to go and hoped he could make it. He grabbed his cell phone and called Ali on the *Charaka*.

"Ali, I need two first-class tickets—or whatever seats you can get us—on the next flight from Minsk to Tianjin. One for me and one for Larissa." Duke turned to Larissa, who was still flabbergasted, and asked, "What's your full name and date of birth?"

She stammered, "L-L-Larissa F-Furmanov. June twenty-fourth, nineteen seventy-eight."

"Did you catch that?" Duke spoke into the phone.

Ali said he had and started searching flights. "I found one leaving in fifty-five minutes. It's an eight-and-a-half-hour flight to Hohhot, China, where you'll have a thirty-minute layover before continuing for another hour and a half to Tianjin. Can you make it?"

"Perfect. If the car holds up, we can just make it," Duke

told Ali.

"What do you mean?" Ali asked.

"I'll tell you later," Duke said as he hung up the phone. "Don't worry, Larissa. I'll take care of you. I bet that was the man who was going to kill you tonight. He won't be driving anywhere for a while, so we should be able to make it to the airport before he catches up with us. As soon as we get there, we'll need to hustle; our plane takes off in fifty-five minutes."

"I-I-guess you must have been right," Larissa whispered.

"You're okay. I told you I wouldn't let anything happen to you, and I meant it."

Coming out of her semi-trance, she urged Duke, "Hurry!"

"We'll be at the airport in just a few minutes. You can relax now," Duke tried to reassure her.

All Larissa could do was nod her head, biting her bottom lip apprehensively. Duke figured she'd be okay in a little while. He parked the car in the return lot, grabbed the luggage and his go bag, and threw them onto a stray luggage cart. Pushing the cart, they ran into the airport. Duke threw the keys on the car rental return counter and said, "I'm glad I got the insurance."

The person at the counter hollered, "Do you want a receipt?"

"Email me!" he yelled back over his shoulder as they continued toward the terminal.

CHAPTER 8

When the plane touched down in Tianjin, Duke and Larissa walked through the airport with Duke pulling a cart of luggage behind him. They exited the terminal and found a black Cadillac SUV waiting for them. Duke opened the door to the back seat for Larissa, loaded the luggage, and then climbed into the front passenger seat.

"Tiny, this is Larissa," Duke said in English. Then, in Russian, he said, "Larissa, this is Edmond, but we call him Tiny."

"I heard you had a bit of trouble in Minsk," Tiny said in English, the only language he knew.

"Nothing too serious," Duke replied. "Is the *Charaka* ready to go?"

"Yes, sir," Tiny said. "Just waiting on you and a destination. What are we going to do with her?"

"She'll be staying in one of our guest cabins," Duke said. "I'll call ahead and make sure everything's prepared for her." Then, he called Ali and told him to have Ami prepare one of the guest cabins for Larissa.

Larissa had calmed down considerably after ten hours of flight time and a number of cocktails. "How far to the cruise ship? I'm tired," she said, slightly slurring her words.

"We'll be there in about fifteen minutes," Duke answered her.

When the SUV pulled up to the dock, Larissa was a bit astonished at the sight of the cargo ship. Duke noticed her stunned silence and said, "It's nicer than it looks, I promise."

"I'm still in shock, I guess. But at least I'm safe and out of harm's way. That's all that really matters."

When they walked across the gangway onto the deck, Duke introduced Larissa to his waiting crew members. "This is Ami and Rodney. They'll show you to your room while I go check on the bridge.

Before entering the superstructure, Larissa watched the ship's crane rotate to pick up the container housing the SUV they'd just arrived in. The huge crane swung it around and lowered it into the fifth bay, and the hydraulic door slammed closed as the lock sealed the door watertight. The gangway was retracted, the lines untied, and the *Charaka* was underway.

Duke had decided to take Larissa to Japan while the Syndicate continued their business regarding the coronavirus investigation. Japan wasn't very far from Tianjin and was an excellent tourist destination for their guest. The Syndicate would put Larissa up in a vacation rental and provide her with cash so she wouldn't have to use any credit cards that could be traced. Duke thought she'd be safe in Tokyo for however long was necessary.

They all entered the door leading into the main deck of the superstructure and headed up the stairs with Tiny and Rodney in tow carrying her luggage.

"Larissa, your room is this way," Ami said in the best Russian she could muster, which was spoken well enough that Larissa understood her. They proceeded down the short corridor while Duke continued up the next flight of stairs on his way to the bridge.

Ami opened the door to the guest cabin, and Larissa exclaimed, "Wow! This is nicer than the room Ivan and I stayed in when we went on our cruise."

Ami showed her how to work the remote for the big screen TV, how the coffee maker worked, and asked what kind of beverages she preferred. Then, she showed her how to operate the bidet and where extra linens were if she needed them.

Just as they were finishing up, Ethan walked in with a tasteful platter of crackers, cheeses, meats, fruits, vegetables, and dips. "Do you have any preferences for dinner?" Ethan asked, and Ami translated.

"I'm really tired. I think I'll just fill up on these delicious snacks and turn in for the night."

"Okay," Ami said. "When you wake up in the morning, just go down the flight of stairs to the next level, and you'll find the dining area."

"Okay. Thank you all so much for your warm welcome."

The group left her room and went to their assigned compartments on the same level. Despite the Syndicate's secret operations, the crew were accustomed to visitors. When crew members were assigned to be part of the fabricated staff, they had a second cabin of their own in the superstructure to keep up appearances during visits from anyone outside of the Syndicate. When a guest stayed overnight, the Syndicate crew members turned in for the night in their secondary staterooms in the bridge structure. If they so desired, they could sneak out of their rooms through a secret door in their closets and take an elevator below to their regular accommodations. The hidden doors in the back of the closets were the only thing different in the crew's pretend cabins. Since the hidden doors were electronically operated, they could be locked if there were ever an overflow of guests and additional berths were ever needed.

In the morning, Larissa looked out the window of her room to see only water. No land or another boat in sight. She went to the level below just as Ami had told her and found the dining area with Duke, Ami, and Tiny sitting at the table drinking their morning beverages and chatting.

"Good morning," Duke declared across the room.

"Good morning," Larissa responded.

"How did you sleep?" Ami asked.

"Incredibly well," Larissa said. "That's the most comfortable mattress I believe I have ever slept on."

Just as Larissa was sitting down, Rodney entered the room through the door leading to the galley with a tray of breakfast plates. He served them all around and took the last plate for himself, then sat down at the table with the others.

"This is delicious," Larissa said.

"I believe we have the best chef on the seven seas," Duke said in Russian, then again in English. The others all nodded in agreement.

"After breakfast, I'll show you around the ship," Ami said.

"That sounds great. I'm sure glad you saved me, Duke. In more ways than one. I was feeling pretty down about Ivan and everything. This is just what I needed—to get away."

"Enjoy your vacation. As soon as this passes, you can go back to your normal life," Duke promised.

"What do you guys do? How did you come to know my life was in danger?"

"We are just sailors taking iron ore around the world. We happened to stumble across some information and realized there were only two surviving family members from the lab left—maybe we have too much time on our hands between ports?" Duke said with a chuckle. "I wasn't in time to save the other widow, and I'm afraid a day later, you might not have been here either."

"I can never thank you enough," Larissa said with obvious gratitude.

"Just your being here is all the thanks I need. There is no greater feeling than knowing you saved someone's life. That's the greatest reward there is," Duke reservedly admitted. He then excused himself and went up to the bridge.

Ami took Larissa to all the public levels and showed her as much as she wanted to see. Larissa's favorite place, like most visitors, was the bridge with a great view over the horizon. Most people liked walking out onto the wings spanning over the sides of the ship, and Larissa wasn't any different. The breeze blew her hair back, and she could look straight down to the water below. The *Charaka* was set up so anyone in the bridge structure would think that area was the extent of the ship and everything else from the bridge structure to the bow was cargo storage. Nobody would ever suspect that below the deck was a state-of-the-art sailing vessel complete with an array of weapons, aircraft, watercraft, vehicles, and luxury accommodations that rivaled the most splendid yachts in the world.

The day passed fairly quickly for Larissa: a few good meals, a long walk on the deck, and an engaging conversation with Duke on the bridge. When she woke up in the morning and looked out her window, she could see land. Japan was on the horizon.

The *Charaka* provisioned fuel and food supplies while docked in Tokyo Bay, then headed back through the China Sea toward Malaysia, where they'd be centrally located to pursue their next lead. Sitting around the table in the conference room, Duke told his crew there was certainly something going on in Minsk. He told Ali and Valerie to look for a way into Grigori's server to see if they could find a way to remotely access the information that had been erased. If so, perhaps they could also find out exactly what was going on in his lab. They had already traced Mingli Wu's travels from Beijing to Minsk and then onto Athens because all flight plans had to be filed when crossing international borders. Mingli had made a mistake by registering his father's yacht under the Wu International corporate name, making it easy to trace and discover the yacht's unique AIS number. Satellite surveillance the United States' government had made available to the Syndicate showed an AIS signal emanating from a yacht in the Mediterranean Sea, and Duke presumed Mingli had boarded the company yacht after arriving in Athens.

Mingli, however, remained one step ahead of Duke. While the Syndicate sailed to Tokyo, Mingli had already boarded a private jet owned by Rasheen Attar, the uncle of Zikri Abdul Attar, the deceased Malaysia Airlines copilot. He left his own personal jet in Athens and then flew to Iran to meet him.

Rasheen Attar could be described as a Renaissance man; he excelled in many business ventures, but very few of them were legal. His most profitable business was trafficking arms. He didn't care who he traded with as long as they had money. In fact, he'd even sold weapons that were later used against his own people. As long as he made lots of money and *he* wasn't ever in harm's way, his callous decisions just made good business sense. He didn't have any problem sacrificing his sister's oldest son on Malaysia Airlines Flight 818 because Rasheen had made a deal to collect three million dollars in exchange for bringing his nephew into the scheme. Once again, extremely profitable business endeavors outweighed morality.

Rasheen also had a predisposition for hating the United States and anyone from there. It was believed that he had financially supported the Islamic terrorist group al-Qaeda's attacks against the US on September 11, 2001. But, despite the rumors and hearsay, there had never been conclusive evidence to convict Rasheen, and he'd remained at liberty. He was a financial supporter of various diabolical individuals, but he stayed behind the scenes and filtered his money through untraceable channels.

Mingli had called on his long-time friend and business partner Rasheen to fly him to Iran to discuss their objective. The venture would make the events of September 11 pale in comparison and would surely bring America to its knees. Mingli didn't need financing—he had more money than Rasheen could ever dream of. What Mingli needed was men who abhorred the United States and would be willing to do whatever it took to bring about the genocide of the American people. With the right planning, the death toll could exceed that of the Holocaust.

CHAPTER 9

Before the downing of Malaysia Airlines Flight 818, Mingli had constructed a secret pharmaceutical lab on North Sentinel Island, one of the Andaman Islands in the Bay of Bengal. Mingli had chosen the location because it was protected by the Andaman and Nicobar Islands Protection of Aboriginal Tribes Act of 1956, which prohibited travel to or within five nautical miles of the island in order to prevent the native islanders from contracting diseases to which they had no immunity. Mingli had thought it was the perfect place for a lab that would be located underground, making it undetectable from the air or by anyone on the island. The lab had been a challenge to construct because it had to be done in secret, forcing Mingli and his crew to evade the Indian Navy who patrolled the area to keep outsiders away—but that was the easy part. Mingli supplied his construction crew on the island by air drops after disabling the transponders on his aircraft and the AIS on his sailing vessels.

The most daunting obstacle of the construction process was the inhabitants of North Sentinel Island. The Sentinelese were famous for killing anyone who dared to venture onto their island. Two fishermen had been killed when their boat got too close to shore. Then, a decade later, a single missionary had thought he could introduce Christianity to the Sentinelese—but the tribe instead familiarized him with their own religious convictions, and he quickly learned his mistake as he too was subsequently slain.

Mingli had overcome that obstacle by sending amphibious armored vehicles ashore, each carrying a large box that proved to be impenetrable by the primitive weapons of the Sentinelese. The boxes were similar to shipping containers—almost as tall but shorter in length and nearly indestructible. The hauling process had been repeated over and over, linking the new box to the previously placed one until enough were linked together to make a continuous ring surrounding the chosen construction area. The area was dense with vegetation, which concealed the metal-box barrier.

The boxes were then electrified so anyone who touched them would receive an alternating current of two hundred and twenty volts at five milliamperes, a strong enough jolt that it would deter any human or animal from maintaining contact with the structure but not enough that it would kill them. After all, Mingli hadn't wanted to kill the Sentinelese people—he was counting on them to act as his watchmen.

While preparing for his lab's construction, Mingli had been able to bribe a low-ranking member of the Indian Navy to provide him with the patrol schedules. Then, he was able to airlift all the equipment needed to build his concealed lab during the times when the navy wasn't guarding that sector.

The Sentinelese were a high-spirited lot, and occasionally, they'd build up the courage to launch an attack while the construction was taking place. On such occasions, one inhabitant or sometimes even a small group had gathered outside to throw stones, spears, arrows, or other unsophisticated weapons over the enclosure. Although they rarely struck anyone, every once in a while, they'd made a lucky shot and hit an unsuspecting worker. If fatally injured, the person was then placed outside the perimeter, where the islanders were able to have their way with them. Mingli mused that it was his way of placating the locals.

Eventually, enough concrete had been placed over the excavation, and the remaining dirt was used to cover the roof, forming a large mound that quickly grew over with vegetation, completely hiding the lab. The exterior ring of boxes had been removed, and all traces of construction were gone. There was only one entrance into the underground lab, and that was well camouflaged to the unknowing eye. Mingli's lab was finally ready for his greatly anticipated wunderkind scientist, Quon Zhang.

* * *

Quon Zhang was born and raised in Beijing by middle-class parents, who realized when Quon was very young that he wasn't like their other children. When they enrolled him in school, it didn't take long before the faculty realized the same thing Quon's parents did. He quickly went through elementary and middle school and graduated high school by the time he was twelve years old. He was a mischievous boy who grew bored easily with the simple curriculum of each grade. The school's staff shopped Quon's resume around to the top universities in the world, and they all came running. Each college knew what a phenomenon like Quon would do for their reputation and future funding possibilities.

Stanford University in California was the top-rated engineering university in the world. They offered a full scholarship and a relocation package to move Quon and his family from Beijing to California. Stanford also offered them a house much nicer than where they had been living. Quon's parents wanted the best for their son, and all those things coupled with a monthly allowance that would cover their family's needs made the deal too good to pass up.

Quon eventually graduated from Stanford when he was

eighteen years old with doctorates in engineering physics and chemical engineering, making him one of the most sought-after individuals in both fields of study. Upon graduation, he was offered many jobs in California and throughout the US as well as the rest of the world. Any of the positions would've provided for his entire family's needs and more, but the Zhangs missed their homeland and their extended family, and they yearned to return to China. There were plenty of offers in China too, which were equally as impressive, so the Zhang family made the decision to move back to Beijing.

One job offer was particularly impressive—to work for Wu International—and Mingli Wu was furious that Quon had rejected his proposal. Quon Zhang had been on his radar since he'd heard about the engineering prodigy six years before, when Quon was just twelve years old. His attempts to recruit the boy had thus far failed. After Quon's graduation from Stanford, Mingli presented a proposal almost twice as generous as Quon's next-highest job offer. But Quon accepted a position with the China Space Administration instead of Wu International because space travel was his passion at the time. It offered less money but was more exciting. Mingli knew that eventually, Quon would tire of the space agency and accept his lucrative offer, but Mingli had a timeline to keep and didn't have the patience to wait for Quon's interest to dwindle. With the downing of Flight 818, he didn't have to.

* * *

When Quon Zhang awoke, he was lying on a bed in a strange room. Mingli sat in a chair across the room from him and stated triumphantly, "Welcome to your new home."

"Where…where am I?" Quon asked, still groggy from the anesthetic.

"You're on North Sentinel Island in the Bay of Bengal,

and you now belong to me," Mingli said with a grin.

"What are you talking about?" Quon questioned, his senses slowly coming back to him.

"I made all of this just for you. You'll live here and work for me, and in turn, you'll be provided with everything you need. A cook will be at your disposal as well as a housekeeper, and a scientist is available to work as your assistant. Anything you need, I will supply you with," Mingli promised.

"But I don't want to work here. I told you before that I didn't want to work for you. Take me home," Quon demanded.

"That's not possible," Mingli told him. "You're dead now. Your plane was lost at sea, and nobody will ever find it—or you. A smart man like you should know about North Sentinel Island."

"I've never heard of it," Quon said. "I just want to go home. I'm not going to work for you."

"I'm afraid you don't have a choice," Mingli told Quon. "You can't leave this place because if you go outside, the islanders will kill you."

"You're lying!" Quon shouted.

"Come with me, and I'll show you," Mingli told him. They walked out of the bedroom and down the hall into a control room with monitors mounted on the walls. "Here's the media room. You can watch television on these monitors or switch them over to show the area surrounding the lab. When I leave, you'll be able to watch me go and see for yourself that what I'm telling you is true."

Mingli went on to tell Quon the whole story of his kidnapping and the reason behind it. He told Quon that he could receive television broadcasting from satellites around the world, but the island didn't have internet, so his computer couldn't be connected to it either. Mingli showed the brooding Quon around the lab and introduced him to the staff, who were also being held prisoner. They had all initially accepted a lucrative job offer but then ended up being double-crossed by Mingli with no way out.

Before Mingli left Quon, he reiterated what was expected of his new employee and promised that if Quon generated the formulas he was required to create, then he would eventually be returned to his family. Quon didn't have any choice but to hope Mingli was telling the truth. After a few weeks of protest and a futile effort to open the exit door, he finally gave in and began doing research.

Provisions were supplied every two weeks or monthly. The tank containing the diesel fuel used to power the generator was so large that it only had to be refilled three times a year. Mingli had an employee who was responsible for making sure the lab was well supplied, making him the only regular visitor. But whenever Mingli or his employee did visit Quon, they always came with a troop of bodyguards to ensure that nothing happened to them. The prisoners had no opportunity to try to escape by overpowering either one of them. When Mingli, his employees, or supplies came to the lab, they arrived in an amphibious vehicle with a trap door at the bottom, which was shielded by a thick steel ring that could be lowered into place to surround the laboratory entrance and the vehicle's trap door. That allowed people to enter the lab without exposing them to the islanders.

Quon's research was a three-phase procedure. First, he was provided with viral cultures of SARS-CoV, a pathogen that caused a respiratory disease. Quon was instructed to manipulate the pathogens so they would replicate profusely. But there was one problem: Quon needed a host to develop the virus. He requested pangolins, which were mammals with large protective keratin scales covering their skin. Pangolins were in high demand in the Chinese and Vietnamese cultures because their scales were believed to have medicinal properties and their meat was considered a delicacy. The demand for pangolins resulted in overhunting, which made them the most trafficked animal in the world despite trading them being illegal.

Mingli, who had promised Quon anything he needed,

sent hundreds of caged pangolins to the lab, and Quon's work progressed at a swift pace until he finally developed an ideal virus.

But then the virus had to be tested on a human to make sure it worked as intended. It was designed to spread readily from one human to another, but it also had the ability to jump from animals to humans and vice versa. Quon made sure the virus was light enough to remain airborne for hours before it slowly sank to a surface, where it could continue to live for up to two weeks. It could be disturbed and become airborne again or transferred directly to another host through inhalation or absorption through the eyes, mouth, open wounds, or any other pathway into the body. Quon had developed the perfect virus for Mingli's purposes—it would be practically impossible to eradicate due to its long lifespan and the ease of infection. The only way to exterminate the pathogen would be to inoculate the population with a vaccine, and that was the second phase of Quon's work.

With the creation of the virus completed, it was time to begin his work on a vaccine, which ended up taking Quon much more time to develop. He tried many different compound configurations, formulas that worked on his computer models but still couldn't kill the virus.

One day, Mingli showed up at the lab with four scientists from Minsk and an interpreter to assist Quon with developing the vaccine.

Anatoli, the self-appointed leader of the new arrivals, asked Quon through the interpreter, "Why haven't you escaped from here?"

"We can't. The door is electronically locked and can only be opened remotely. But even if we could get it open, we would be killed as soon as we exited this facility," Quon replied.

"Surely we could make weapons and floatation devices from something in here and make our way to the ocean," Anatoli insisted.

"I thought like that when I first arrived too. But like I said, we can't open the door. One time when they brought supplies, I watched on the monitor and saw one of the men get out of his protected vehicle to urinate. There was no sign of natives when he got out, but they must have been hiding just beyond the tree line because just a few seconds after he unzipped his pants, a mob of men attacked him and killed him. He had a gun but was never able to fire a shot. The natives may be primitive, but they are smart and kept the vehicle between them and the armed man until the last second when they converged on him," Quon told them. "They hunt for their food here and are very proficient with their weapons. I don't think there is any way we could win a battle against them. Leaving this facility would be suicide."

"I guess we have no choice but to do our work and hope that they will keep their word and release us when we are done," Anatoli capitulated.

Over and over, they manipulated the formulas, but none were successful until a miscommunication between Quon and the scientists caused an accidental combination. When tested, it seemed to kill the virus. Quon duplicated the compound and tried it hundreds of times with the same result: it effectively killed the virus 100 percent of the time. Finally, after three years of tedious research, an effective vaccine had been perfected.

Quon hated developing the virus for Wu International, but he hated being held prisoner in the ten-thousand-square-foot compound even more. He decided his only chance at getting out was by cooperating with Mingli Wu. He knew the virus would be used to infect people, and he feared it would spread around the world quickly. If that happened before the vaccine was available to be administered, many people would die. So, Quon worked twice as hard on the vaccine as he had on the virus and withheld from Mingli that the pathogen had been completed until he also had the vaccine ready. Keeping information secret was no easy task for Quon because

Mingli constantly pressed him for results. In the end, it took Quon four years to develop both the virus and the vaccine, and Quon was confident the vaccine would offset the virus to a great degree. At the time, he'd envisioned Mingli using the virus to infect millions of people and then introducing the vaccine soon after in order to make billions of dollars, but he'd had no idea Mingli would wait to unveil the vaccine until the world had been dealing with the virus for nine long months.

Nonetheless, Quon had no choice but to hand over the formulas and cultures to Mingli after they were both completed. Mingli was so happy to see his vision finally coming to fruition.

"Now for the third phase of the plan. How long will it take you to develop the final formula?" Mingli asked.

"I still don't know if I can," Quon replied. "And even if I could, it might take years."

"That's unacceptable! I need that formula soon, within a year at most."

"I could try…"

Mingli could sense Quon's reluctance and said, "Fine. If it's an incentive you need, I'll give you one." Then, he stormed out of the room.

A week later, Quon saw on one of the monitors that an amphibious vehicle was approaching with many of the Sentinelese people in pursuit of it. Quon thought the islanders would have given up on trying to slay the vehicle, having seen it come and go hundreds of times, but every single time the vehicle landed on shore, it was pelted with spears and arrows. It stopped over the entrance, and Quon knew in a few minutes, Mingli would be there to hound him about the last formula. Instead, Quon heard his sister's voice say, "Quon!"

"Linh!" Quon shouted back as he ran to embrace his sister. But as he got within a few feet of her, two guards stepped in front of Linh and stopped him.

"Get out of my way!" he protested.

Mingli stepped in and said, "Quon, if you want to see your family again, you will produce the third formula. I'm going to keep your sister safe for a while, but if you take too long, I'm going to bring her back here so you can watch the islanders kill her."

Then, Mingli had two of the four guards take Linh away and returned to the vehicle while Quon sobbed. He was beside himself, but there was nothing else he could do except start working on the third formula.

Phase three of the viral trio was the most difficult for Quon to pursue, and he hadn't been able to motivate himself to start his work until he'd seen his sister after so many years in isolation only to have her torn away from him again. That was the most difficult day of Quon's life. He was determined to see her again—alive—and within three months, Quon had a formula that would do what Mingli wanted. He'd developed an odorless, colorless chemical compound that was benign by itself, but when ingested by someone who had been given the vaccine, it meant certain death within hours. Mingli had originally wanted the compound to spread just like a virus, but Quon explained to him that it was a poison, not a living entity, and couldn't be transferred from one host to another. It had to be ingested or injected to work.

Mingli didn't like the explanation, but it made sense to him, and he'd devise a way to use it. When Mingli returned to the lab to see Quon's progress on the coronacyde, the name he'd given his creation, Quon told him he was nearly finished with it, but until he had his sister there with him, he wouldn't do another day's worth of work. Mingli agreed to Quon's demands and told him he'd return in a few days with his sister.

Quon was watching the news one day when he saw that the coronavirus he'd developed had swept across the world over the past six months. He wanted to know when Mingli planned to introduce the vaccine. Mingli told him very soon, but first, he needed the coronacyde. Quon told Mingli he didn't need the coronacyde before distributing the vaccine because once the serum had been injected, for as long as it lasted in the body—which Quon estimated to be ten years or longer—the coronacyde would work the same as if it were introduced the day after the vaccine had been administered. The recipient would still die.

With that information, Mingli did just as he'd promised, and a few days later, he arrived with Linh. Quon and his sister embraced, cried, and celebrated their reunion. Quon was hopeful that Mingli might keep his other promise and let them go some day. All ten people living in the laboratory compound hoped to be freed as well. With Quon and his five scientists so close to completing the final phase of their objective, they knew they were either going to be returned to their homes or—what none of them could admit or dare vocalize—they'd be killed.

CHAPTER 10

Duke thought it intentional that the vaccine was introduced to the world at the same time Mingli Wu realized someone was seeking information about him and the source of the virus. So far, it seemed that Mingli was trying to revamp Wu International's global reputation and draw the focus on the origin of the virus away from his laboratory in Wuhan. After investigating, Duke was confident that Mingli had unleashed the virus so he could distribute the vaccine and augment his fortune. He just didn't know why Mingli had waited so long to release the vaccine or how he'd kept his employees from leaking information about it.

By that time, the Syndicate had gathered a great deal of information about Mingli Wu: he had eight residences in six different countries, sixty-two businesses in nine different countries, and a fleet of ships. Most of those were fishing vessels, but he also had construction ships, oil tankers, and cargo ships. The most expensive watercraft his company owned was a yacht, which his father resided on in the Mediterranean. Mingli also had three helicopters—one in China and one in the United States, but Ali and Valerie couldn't pinpoint the third's location. However, they knew Mingli's main source of transportation was his personal jet, which was currently sitting in Athens, Greece.

Duke decided he'd fly Ali and Tiny to China to plant a tracking device on the helicopter there, and Bubba and Kabir would fly to the US to do the same on the other one. Louis and Abe would fly to Athens and place a tracking device on Mingli's personal jet. Diego would fly all of them to Tan Son Nhat International Airport in Ho Chi Minh City, Vietnam, where they could take commercial flights to their respective destinations. After they completed their missions, they'd fly back to whichever international airport was closest to the *Charaka*. The tracking devices wouldn't be a problem getting through customs at the airports—they were very small, and unless someone was an expert in identifying surveillance equipment, nobody would have a clue what they were. Transporting the devices in continuous positive airway pressure (CPAP) machines discouraged any TSA from probing very much.

Duke planned on going to the Mediterranean to find the yacht so he could install a tracking device there too, but Valerie discovered the yacht was already traveling from the Mediterranean Sea to the Red Sea through the Suez Canal. It seemed that it was possibly headed toward them, so Duke had Steve alter their course and head for Singapore, where they could either travel back to China or pursue the yacht, depending on which course they decided to take.

* * *

Meanwhile, Mingli was concluding his negotiations with Rasheen in Iran. They had already finalized their plan and decided to have a nice dinner together before Mingli headed back to his jet in Athens in the morning. Mingli had developed a false sense of security after the vaccine was released, assuming the pressure to find him had been alleviated and nobody would be pursuing him any longer. He enjoyed his meal, said farewell to his friend, and returned to his hotel, where he slept like a baby. The next morning,

Rasheen had his driver pick Mingli up at the hotel and drive him to the airport, where he boarded Rasheen's private jet for the seven-hour flight back to Athens.

Abe and Louis had assumed Mingli was on the yacht, and they'd had no idea he'd taken a flight to Iran. They'd been on the ground in Athens for about a half hour by the time they deplaned and were able to get a rental car and drive to the general aviation terminal, where they anticipated the private aircraft would be located. When they finally found the plane, they were surprised to see it untied with the door open. They quickly boarded the private jet, and Louis knew exactly where he wanted to place the device so it wouldn't be found by anyone.

Louis Schmidt was a five-foot-eleven, fifty-year-old German with blonde hair and the bluest eyes Duke had ever seen. He was the Syndicate's second pilot. Along with Diego, they were both experts in the aviation field, and they knew how to operate anything that could fly as well as how to fix it if it couldn't. Louis had spent a number of years in the US military as an Apache attack helicopter pilot before Duke recruited him to be the primary pilot of the Syndicate's Boeing AH-64 Apache helicopter.

All of his experience made Louis sure that the panel on the Gulfstream V was the perfect location for the tracking device. However, right after Louis installed the device and was getting ready to replace the panel, two Chinese pilots boarded the plane and yelled at the intruders. Neither Louis nor Abe could speak Chinese, and they just looked at one another and then back to the two angry pilots, shrugging their shoulders. Louis answered in German that he was there to fix a problem someone had reported. Then, it was the pilots' turn to look at one another, then back at Abe and Louis, dumbfounded.

Just then, another Chinese man walked up the steps and entered the plane. He looked at Abe and Louis and then at the two pilots. He questioned the two Chinese pilots, but both of them just shrugged their shoulders. The Chinese man glared at Louis and Abe again and said in English,

"What the hell are you two doing on my aircraft?"

Louis spoke in German again and said they were there to fix the plane, then motioned that he was going to replace the panel.

Mingli stopped him and said something to the pilots, who quickly stepped up to the opening and looked around inside. They spoke to Mingli, telling him that they didn't see anything wrong. Mingli gestured for Louis to put the panel back on and then motioned for them to leave his plane. Two men in suits waited at the bottom of the stairs with suitcases in tow, and Mingli instructed them to take Abe and Louis away.

Abe and Louis were escorted to the terminal. The person working the service desk was multilingual, and one of the Chinese men asked him to find out who Abe and Louis were and what they were doing on Mingli Wu's plane. The man behind the desk held up a finger and picked up the phone. The two Syndicate members looked at one another, puzzled over what their next move would be. Although they had considerable fighting skills, they wouldn't be a match for the guns bulging from under the Chinese men's suit jackets. Because they flew commercially, Louis and Abe weren't able to bring any weapons, and they knew a physical altercation may or may not go in their favor—a chance they didn't want to take unless they had to.

When the service desk manager turned his attention back to Louis and Abe, Louis told him in German that he was there to fix the plane. The service desk manager understood German well and carried on a conversation with him. Louis pointed outside as he informed the man that someone had told him about an electrical problem with a plane and had wanted him to look at it. He explained that he must have misunderstood which plane needed to be repaired because he looked at it and couldn't find anything wrong. The service desk manager began talking quickly into the phone, then he handed it to one of the Chinese men, who listened while nodding his head before finally giving the phone back. The men motioned for Abe and Louis to follow them back out to the plane.

Mingli came to the opening in the jet, and the man who spoke on the phone told Mingli Louis's story. After he was done, Mingli stared at the strangers for a few seconds, then motioned for Louis and Abe to go. The two Chinese men picked up Mingli's suitcases and boarded the plane, then the door closed.

Abe and Louis began a fast walk toward their rental car. The jet engines started up behind them, and the plane taxied across the tarmac and headed for the runway. Abe and Louis looked at one another and breathed a sigh of relief.

"That was a close call," Abe said. "What did you tell them?"

"I just told them we were there to fix an electrical problem," Louis told him.

"We were fortunate. I was afraid we were going to have to try to disarm them and escape," Abe admitted.

"I'm sure glad it didn't come to that," Louis said.

"Me too. Let's check in and get out of here."

They called the *Charaka* and told Duke what had happened. With nothing more for them to do there and the tracking device working perfectly, Duke told them to buy two first-class tickets to Singapore and he'd have Diego pick them up from there.

Within three days, the two other teams had successfully installed the tracking devices on the helicopters without any complications or confrontations and were back on the *Charaka*. The Wu International yacht was rounding Sri Lanka and heading into the Bay of Bengal, and Mingli's jet had landed at Port Blair Airport on South Andaman Island. Mingli didn't have a residence or a business on South Andaman Island, so the members of the Syndicate were curious about his intentions there. They figured he'd be meeting up with his yacht soon, so they navigated the *Charaka* in the direction of the Bay of Bengal.

CHAPTER 11

The *Charaka* was about five hundred nautical miles away from Mingli's yacht when it entered the Andaman Sea and was closing the distance between them quickly. The ship in question was about fifty miles west of South Andaman Island, which puzzled Duke because he'd expected it to be anchored nearer Port Blair on the east side of the island, where Mingli could be picked up.

Ali called Duke from the control room and said, "I just picked up a bogie on the radar leaving the yacht and heading toward the island. From the speed, I'd say it has to be a helicopter. I think we just found the third one."

"Track it, and let me know where it lands," Duke said. Then, he called Louis. "Would you get the drone up and fly it over the yacht so we can see what we're looking at? It must have a helipad and who knows what else."

Duke walked into the control room, and Ali picked up their conversation where he'd left off. "There's another large ship in the vicinity of the yacht. It'd be a very odd coincidence for two vessels to be anchored in such close proximity so far out in the middle of nowhere."

"Well, we'll know soon enough. Louis is going to fly the long-range stealth drone over the yacht to get a better look,"

Duke said as Louis himself walked into the control room and took a seat at one of the desks that held the drone controls.

The drone was a collective creation of Mandy Graham, Ali, and Valerie that resembled a typical drone with four horizontal propellers. Unlike most drones, however, it was a little over four feet in diameter and could travel a total of twelve hundred miles under the right conditions. It also had a payload of thirty-six pounds, which meant it could carry a number of various items or extra fuel for longer missions. It was also undetectable on radar to anyone who might be keeping a close watch on the sky. The drone was controlled by powerful, futuristic electronics in the control room of the *Charaka* and had a camera that could fine-tune a square foot from an altitude of over ten thousand feet. It could travel at speeds of two hundred and twenty miles per hour, sometimes faster if the wind was in the right direction.

Louis had the video feed of the drone on the main screen, where everyone in the control room could see. It took the drone about an hour and a half to reach the yacht, and at ten thousand feet above, it was silent and completely undetectable to anyone below unless someone were to look up with binoculars. Louis switched screens so the horizontal camera used to steer the drone came into focus on one of the smaller monitors, and he broadcasted the rotating zoom lens image onto the main screen. Most of the Syndicate's crew were gathered in the control room—every eye mattered. The yacht came into focus, revealing a huge 310-foot luxury ship with an empty helipad, just as they'd concluded.

"Everyone still on the vessel must be inside," Louis said, "because I don't see anyone on any of the decks."

He panned the camera around, and the other ship came into view. It appeared to be some sort of cargo ship that resembled the type of military vessel capable of launching other watercraft into the sea, but like the yacht, it didn't appear to have anyone on deck. As he maneuvered the drone to see the transom, the name *WU INTERNATIONAL #9* came into focus.

Louis zoomed the camera back onto the aft section of the yacht to see the name of the boat. Duke read aloud, "*WU.*" In Chinese, Wu meant shaman or sorcerer, originally the practitioners of Chinese Shamanism or Wuism. The Syndicate thought it could've simply been their last name, but it could've also been their viewpoint of themselves. Maybe both.

As Louis panned over the *WU*, there was an abrupt commotion of people scurrying about the deck of the vessel. Louis backed the drone away from the yacht and gained altitude as he zoomed out with the camera, giving a much wider view of the surrounding areas. Then, a helicopter came into view.

Ali said, "How can that be? I never saw it on radar. It's as if it doesn't have its flight transponder turned on."

"All legitimate aircraft keep their transponders emitting at all times. Even if they don't need air traffic control, they would certainly want to be identified by other aircraft to avoid a collision," Louis added.

"They obviously don't want anyone to know where they're going," Duke said. "They're up to something they don't want anyone to know about."

"Let's just see what they are going to do," Louis said as he zoomed the camera in on the helipad.

As the helicopter landed, men began tying it down. Once Mingli Wu emerged from the aircraft, he was greeted by a gray-haired man who had emerged from within the yacht, and both went inside the vessel while the rest of the men on deck continued securing the helicopter.

Duke told Louis that he wanted a drone above the *WU* at all times and to have one of the backup drones on site when it was time to bring the first one back to the *Charaka*. Then, he told Steve to park the *Charaka* one hundred miles south of the two ships. Finally, he called for a team meeting to be held inside the ready room fifteen minutes later.

As the team assembled, they were able to watch the live drone footage on the giant theatre-like screen above the podium. Louis had positioned the drone at an altitude that allowed a visual of both ships, then placed the drone in stationary mode, which kicked on the drone's autopilot to maintain its coordinates without any intervention from him.

Duke updated everyone on what he had concluded so far, then Ali took his turn to offer some additional information. Within twenty minutes, everyone was up to speed. As they discussed their next plan of action, there was movement on both ships. The yacht opened a compartment on its aft end, and a power boat emerged and docked at the *WU*'s transom. Mingli boarded the power boat, and it took him to a military type of amphibious vessel that had been launched from the cargo ship. The amphibious vessel was camouflaged and completely enclosed in a metal structure. The Syndicate watched as Mingli transferred to the amphibious vessel and climbed aboard.

"That's strange. The vessel must be headed to South Andaman Island because North Sentinel Island is prohibited to visit," Valerie said as she stared up at the screen.

Ali piped up, "That's a long way off for such a small craft. It'll take them hours to reach the island at their speed."

"I think they're going to North Sentinel," Steve chimed in.

Ali went back to the control room, and the rest of the crew followed. "I'll track them and tell you exactly where they're going. It doesn't have a signal either," he announced. "I'm switching over to radar."

"Follow it," Duke told Louis. "We need to see what they're up to."

As the vessel neared North Sentinel, it became clear that South Andaman wasn't its terminus. The boat began slowing as it approached the beach, twenty-two miles short of South Andaman.

"What are they doing?" Valerie posed. "North Sentinel

is inhabited by extremely territorial islanders."

"Don't they kill anyone who invades their island?" Mandy asked.

"They certainly do," Cho responded.

"Are there any Indian Navy vessels in the vicinity?" Duke asked.

"None," Ali replied. "The closest one is over two hundred miles away."

All eyes were glued to the screen as they watched the amphibious vessel land on the beach and begin to travel inland. A dozen natives quickly emerged and started chasing the vehicle while chucking spears and shooting arrows at it. All the primitive weaponry just bounced off, and eventually the vehicle came to a stop in an area that was green with vegetation—a lighter, more immature vegetation. It was as if a large roundish area had been cut down and had recently regenerated. The Syndicate members waited for someone to exit the vehicle, but nobody emerged. It just sat there for an hour or so.

"Ali, get those exact coordinates saved," Duke said as he watched the monitor intently.

The natives were milling around the vehicle, looking under it and probing every inch. One of them got up on the hood and rammed his spear into the slits cut in the metal covering the windshield. Then, after about an hour and a half, the vehicle began to move again, turning around and heading back to the beach. It stopped briefly at the water's edge before continuing into the ocean. The amphibious boat returned to the ship it was deployed from, and Mingli returned to the *WU*.

Less than an hour later, men began untying the helicopter, and a few minutes after that, Mingli bid farewell to the elderly Chinese man and boarded the aircraft. It took off in the direction of South Andaman Island again.

"The copter has a signal now!" Ali exclaimed.

Duke thought he'd figured out what was going on. "There's something underground on North Sentinel

Island," he said. "The amphibious vehicle must've had a protected opening underneath it that would allow safe entry into the underground facility. I can only imagine what lies beneath, but I'd bet money that's where the virus was manufactured."

"The problem is that we don't have any amphibious vehicles like that one. If we want to get to the island, we have to come up with another plan," Steve said.

"Back to the ready room," Duke said. "We have to figure out a way onto that island."

CHAPTER 12

As they all took their seats in the theatre-like room, Steve said, "I think a few of us should drop onto the island at night while the natives are sleeping and work on the entrance. It must be electronically operated somehow since it was accessed from a hatch in the bottom of the amphibious vehicle."

"I agree," Duke said. "Doc, can you prepare tranquilizer darts that we can use if we need to?"

"I have just the thing. It's fast-acting. It takes effect in seconds and will keep someone down for five to seven minutes," Dr. Bai said.

"Excellent," Duke replied. "Steve, Ali, Mandy, Tiny, Kabir, and I will drop in around midnight while the natives should be sleeping. Ali and Mandy will work on getting the door open while the rest of us set up a perimeter and take out any natives that may stumble upon us. But we also need an escape plan in case we're discovered by Wu's men and need to make a quick exit."

"It looked like the clearing was big enough for me to drop the Osprey in without any problem. I could pick you up in a hurry," Diego said.

"That sounds like our best bet," Duke said, "but I'd like

to have the DSRV sitting just off the beach in case we're on the run and have to swim for it. On the way there, I'd like to have you swing by the *WU* and the other vessel and place a tracking device on each of them. We should be able to keep tabs on them until they clean their hulls."

"Ten-four," Louis said as the primary submarine pilot.

"Take Bubba with you, and then once the devices are in place, you two wait as close to the beach as you can get," Duke said. "Valerie, Abe, and Monica will be helping you in the control room, and Ami and Dr. Bai will go with Diego just in case we need to improvise on the fly."

"You got it, Duke," Monica stated, and the rest voiced their agreement.

Monica Thomas was Dr. Bai's nurse, but she also wore many other hats on the Charaka. *At five-foot-nine, the extremely attractive African American woman had long black kinky hair, brown eyes, and an athletic figure. Coupled with her martial arts abilities and the fact that she was an excellent markswoman and extremely intelligent made her a valuable asset on the* Charaka *no matter what role she played on a mission.*

Duke continued, "Diego, if you're out of earshot from the island, how long do you think it would take you to come get us in an emergency?"

"I think I could be there in three to four minutes," Diego said. "Any closer and the natives would be able to hear the engines."

"We don't want to wake them up, so stay far enough away that they can't hear you," Duke said. "I don't like the three-to four-minute waiting window, but I don't see any other way around it. Grab a couple hours of sleep if you want. We go at midnight."

Duke knew that nobody would want to sleep, but he liked giving them the option. Before a mission, nerves and adrenaline made it impossible to sleep for most of the crew, and he knew they'd start preparing right away.

Louis and Bubba went to the sub pool and began the checklist for departure. One of the submarines on the

Charaka was a deep-submergence rescue vehicle modified by the Syndicate to carry out a variety of missions. It was sixty-three feet long and twenty-three feet wide with a capacity for one pilot and six passengers to sit comfortably, but it could hold up to twenty-two additional people standing or a substantial cargo and remain submerged for fifteen days. Once the exterior checklist was completed, Bubba lowered the submarine into the pool of water and removed the straps that secured it to the ship when it wasn't in use. Louis climbed into the DSRV and went to the pilot's seat as Bubba climbed in after him and closed the hatch. Louis activated the clamshell doors in the hull of the ship and began to descend into the depths of the sea.

At twenty-two knots, it wouldn't take them long to reach the *WU,* so Bubba began donning his scuba gear. Once under Mingli's ship, he opened the bottom hatch and swam to the yacht, where he checked to make sure it was anchored and not relying on its bow and stern thrusters to maintain its position. Once he saw that the anchor was holding the *WU* in place, he swam over to the bow thruster and placed a good amount of underwater epoxy onto the tracking device before sticking it into the bow thruster tube as far as his arm could reach—far enough in that even if the hull was cleaned, it would still be difficult to detect. He held pressure on the device for a couple of minutes until he was sure the epoxy had cured, then swam back to the DSRV and knocked on the hull. Louis knew that was the signal for him to steer the submarine over to the other ship, so he slowly maneuvered the DSRV while Bubba held on to a handhold on the side of the watercraft.

Once under the ship, Louis stopped the engines so Bubba wouldn't have to fight the current from the propellers. The second ship had a metal hull, so Bubba had its tracking device equipped with a heavy-duty magnet. Once he'd placed it, he wouldn't be able to relocate it because the magnet's force would be too strong, so he would have to make sure to secure it correctly on his first attempt.

He swam to the bow of the ship and was almost sucked into the thruster as he neared it. In that moment, all he could do was swim frantically—he wasn't even able to scream or curse. The silence, somehow, made everything more frightening. He kicked against the current as hard as he could, his muscles burning, his breath panting, the air pressure in his tank dropping rapidly. Finally, he was able to inch his way out of the bow thruster's stream maintaining the ship in its location. Extremely relieved that he was still alive, he breathed a heavy sigh into his regulator as he regained his composure.

Bubba swam to the centerline of the bottom of the hull so the thruster jets wouldn't affect him again and continued to look for a place to put the device. There wasn't a place inconspicuous enough, so he swam to the stern of the ship and found an opening just big enough to slip the device into. He placed it in and pulled the plastic layer that limited the magnet's strength out from between the ship's metal and the device. Without the plastic, the magnet stuck to the ship with a clank that Bubba could only hope nobody heard. He swam back to the DSRV and climbed inside, shutting the hatch behind him.

"All done!" he exclaimed to Louis without a hint of anxiety from his near-death experience. "Tell Valerie we're ready to test them out."

Louis steered the DSRV toward the beach and radioed the *Charaka* to tell them the sub would be in place in twenty minutes. Valerie told Louis she had a strong signal from the tracking devices and two fresh drones in the air—one over the ships and one over the island.

Diego held the Osprey at twenty-one thousand feet just a few miles west of North Sentinel Island and lowered the rear door. A minute later, he flipped the green jump-light-indicator switch, and the six crew members leapt from the plane, Duke, Steve, Kabir, and Tiny each carrying tranquilizer pistols that only had an effective range of about one hundred feet. They also had rifles that could shoot up to three hundred feet if the conditions were right, but with the dense jungle on the island, a long shot wasn't likely. Duke hoped they'd be well camouflaged and able to hit a target before they were seen, otherwise the natives' bows and arrows would rival the tranquilizer guns. Mandy and Ali each had a bag of tools and electronics to use to hopefully penetrate the mechanism securing the door.

They saw a couple of fires burning about a mile away from their landing site as they glided down into the clearing and quietly touched down. Ali had his GPS turned on before they landed and headed directly for the door as soon as he shed his parachute, grabbing it up and taking it with him. Mandy was right behind him, dragging her parachute with her as the duo made their way to the area where they suspected the entrance to be. They began scanning their surroundings for an electronic keypad while Duke, Steve, Kabir, and Tiny spread out to cover four points around them just outside the clearing at the edge of the jungle. The nighttime jungle air was thick and heavy, and there wasn't a sound, only complete silence.

Mandy and Ali couldn't find any kind of a keypad anywhere and guessed that the door must operate remotely, similar to the way a garage-door opener worked. But Mandy was prepared for such a situation and had brought a device she'd designed that automatically sent industrial, scientific, and medical (ISM) radio frequency bands throughout the entire radio spectrum within seconds. If the door was remotely controlled, her device could send a signal that would open it. Within thirty seconds of sending random codes, Mandy's device stopped at seven digits, and two doors camouflaged with rocks and stones slowly opened, grinding softly, revealing a long staircase down into a sterile-looking white interior.

"We're in," Mandy whispered over her communication device, and the four other men came running from their hiding places in the jungle, carrying their parachutes with them.

"Can you shut the door once we're all inside?" Duke asked Mandy.

"Of course," she replied. "I know the code now and can open the door immediately. It won't take thirty seconds again."

They all went down the stairs with Duke and Steve in the lead, Kabir and Tiny just behind them, and Ali and Mandy trailing the group. There was a corridor with numerous doors lining each side, like a hotel hallway with one door directly across from another. Duke quietly turned the knob on the first door, and it opened. Inside, someone was sleeping in a bed. Duke gently nudged the sleeping body, and a Caucasian man opened his eyes in fear as he saw the pistol aimed at his forehead.

"Who are you?" the man asked nervously in Russian.

"Keep your voice down. My name's Duke. Who are you?"

"I'm Anatoli. Where's Mr. Wu?"

"Mr. Wu isn't here. He doesn't know we're here either, and I'd like to keep it that way."

"Are you here to save us?" Anatoli asked hopefully.

"Yes, we are," Duke said as Anatoli ripped the covers off himself and leapt out of bed to embrace his savior. Duke let the man hug him. He put his arms around Anatoli and patted his back. "There, there, big fella. Tell me what you're doing here and how many others there are. How many armed men does Mr. Wu have here?"

"There aren't any armed men here. The only ones here are me and five other scientists, a cook, a housekeeper, one scientist's sister, and an interpreter," Anatoli said.

Duke turned to Kabir and said, "Go wake the rest of them. There shouldn't be any resistance." Then, he turned back to Anatoli and asked, "Why are you all being held here?"

"We created a vaccine for the coronavirus, and once we'd completed that, we had to create a poison that would kill anyone who'd been injected with the vaccine," Anatoli said. "I can't believe you're here. I thought I'd die and never get out of this place. They promised to release us as soon as we finished the poison, but the last time Mr. Wu was here, he said we weren't going anywhere just yet. He said he may need us to develop something else."

"When was that?" Duke asked.

"Today or yesterday. What time is it?" Anatoli asked.

"It's almost one a.m."

By that time, the other prisoners were all up and excitedly chattering in the hallway. Duke and Anatoli walked out to see everyone smiling, embracing, and carrying on in anticipation of being rescued.

"Before we go," Duke said, "we need to have a quick tour of the complex here to see exactly what's been going on."

A man named Quon took the lead and began showing Duke around the laboratory and all of the rooms in the complex while explaining his entire story about being abducted by Mingli. He described being forced to develop the virus, the vaccine, and then the poison, which Mingli had picked up the day before.

Duke tried to contact the *Charaka* from the underground structure, but he couldn't get a signal through the layer of lead in the walls. He wouldn't be able to make any contact until he returned to the surface. As Quon was showing him the laboratory, there was suddenly a rumble.

"Oh no!" Quon exclaimed as he ran to the media room. "They're here. Look!" He pointed at one of the monitors.

Duke looked at the screen and saw the amphibious vehicle approaching. "Tiny, go grab the parachutes and drag them into one of the rooms. Everyone, get in this room, and stay put," Duke said in Mandarin and then repeated in Russian. "Kabir, you and Steve hide in one of the bedrooms. I'll stay down at this end of the corridor. After they get past Tiny, he can shoot them in the back while we shoot them in the front. Remember, though, the darts will only last five to seven minutes. Once they're down, we need to get them tied up quickly."

Seconds later, the door opened, and four men walked down the stairs. They started knocking on the bedroom doors while hollering for everyone to get up—they were finally going to get to leave. There was a short rumbling sound right after the entrance doors closed, which could only mean the amphibious vehicle had moved from covering the door. Duke reckoned it was so the prisoners could be forced out onto the island to fend for themselves against the natives. Actually being allowed to go home was a naïve thought. It wasn't a real release; the scientists knew secrets Wu would want suppressed forever.

Just then, the bedroom door closest to the entrance opened. Tiny stepped out and shot one of the men in the back with his rifle and another in the back with his pistol as Steve and Kabir each popped out of bedrooms in front of the men and shot the other two. The men instinctively began pulling the darts out of their bodies, but it was too late. The plungers pushed the sedative into their systems upon impact, and within ten seconds, all four men dropped to the ground. The amphibious vehicle must have awakened the natives because the monitors showed a number of them milling around it, spears in hand.

"We only have five minutes before these guys wake up," Steve said. "Let's get them zip-tied. We'll bind them to chairs and lock them in one of the rooms."

"Good idea," Duke said. "Strip them down to their underwear to make sure they don't have anything hidden up their sleeves, and then secure them in the room with the pangolins. We can't contact anyone to come get us, and the amphibious vehicle isn't over the entrance anymore. We're in a tight spot."

Ali said, "Don't forget about the drone. Valerie can see what's going on at the entrance."

"We only have one shot with each gun before we have to reload, so if we were to all shoot a native, we could only take down eight of them, and there are at least twice as many out there. We'd never be able to reload and get the rest before they got us," Steve said.

"We could open the doors and let them come down a few at a time, then close the doors back up," Tiny said.

"That might work," Duke replied, "but I don't want to take a chance on one of them getting stuck in the doors, which would crush them and prevent the entrance from closing. Maybe whoever is in the amphibious vehicle will get curious and come down to see what's going on. Let's wait for a half hour and see what happens."

Everybody agreed, and they all nervously stood around watching the monitors. It didn't take ten minutes before they saw the amphibious vehicle returning.

"Everyone, stay here," Duke instructed. "Steve and I will go to the first bedrooms and lay in wait. Tiny, you and Kabir stay at this end of the corridor in case more than two come down."

The doors opened, and one Chinese man walked down the stairs and opened the first door to the bedroom where Duke was. As he peered inside, Steve opened the door across the hallway and shot him in the back. With the structure's entrance still opened, Duke and Steve cautiously entered the vehicle and found it empty. They returned to the underground complex and saw that the last man had been zip-tied and bound to a chair with the others, who were all awake.

"Mandy, how far away will your door opener work?" Duke asked.

"One hundred yards, maybe a little more," Mandy replied. "But just in case, you keep it." She handed the device to Duke, knowing he'd be the last one out because it was his style to make sure everyone else was safe before taking care of himself. Then, Mandy continued, "It's already been programmed and saved, so all you have to do is push this button, and the doors will open or close."

"Mandy, you're the greatest! Tiny, go get into the driver's

seat of the amphibious vehicle, and then Mandy, Steve, Ali, and Kabir will ride in the back with you. You'll draw the attention of the islanders to the beach. When the Osprey arrives, I'll open the doors, and the rest of us will get in so Diego can fly us out of here. Once we're in the air, Tiny will drive out to the DSRV, and you guys can go back to the *Charaka* in the sub. Just before you abandon the amphibious vehicle, put it in gear and send it out to sea," Duke instructed.

The five Syndicate members took off in the amphibious vehicle, and the islanders followed just as Duke had anticipated. Once outside, Steve was able to contact Diego to tell him they were ready to be extracted. Tiny drove to the beach and turned away from the laboratory, drawing the natives as far away from it as he could. A few minutes later, the whir of the Osprey caught the islander's attention, and they watched it fly past them to the clearing. The rotor wash of the aircraft shook the entire underground complex, alerting Duke and the others of its arrival.

Diego knew the coordinates of the entrance and sat the Osprey down with the ramp open just a few feet from it. Duke checked the monitors and saw that no islanders were around, so he opened the doors and stood just outside, ready to shoot anyone who approached. Quon and his sister were the first to exit, with the rest of Mingli's prisoners right behind them. Everyone was inside the aircraft in less than a minute, and Duke closed the lab doors as it began to lift off, the ramp closing with everyone safely inside. Within seconds, the Osprey was headed back to the *Charaka*.

As Valerie watched the events unfold via the drone, she saw some of the islanders run out to the Osprey as it was lifting off. But they soon stopped their pursuit, as the extreme prop wash and heat of the giant propellers drove them back. Tiny turned the amphibious vehicle around and headed back down the beach, where the best entry into the sea was located between outcroppings of coral. As he motored out into the water, he could see the islanders getting into their canoes, ready to pursue the vehicle. Steve radioed Louis and told him to remain submerged at thirty feet and that the five of them would swim down and enter through the bottom hatch. He received the coordinates from Louis and told everyone when to jump out of the vehicle. Tiny was the last one to jump after he'd tied the steering wheel to the door so the vehicle would maintain a steady course. With the amphibious vehicle heading back out to sea and the passengers diving into the water never to resurface, the islanders eventually tired of the pursuit and returned to their island.

CHAPTER 13

Duke and those on the Osprey arrived back at the *Charaka* first. Duke had called ahead and asked Rodney and Ami to begin readying the guest rooms in the superstructure for their visitors.

Back on the ship, Duke said, "Ami, lead our guests across the deck to their accommodations, and show each one of them the rooms they'll be staying in."

She first took the group to a room they called the Store, which was a room the size of four cabins lined with racks of clothes in many sizes and styles. Every person the Syndicate had ever rescued had always wanted a hot shower, a clean set of clothes, and a good meal—the perfect combination to help with the recovery process after being traumatized. To feel clean, comfortable, and safe went a long way in compensating for whatever suffering a person had experienced, and the people from the lab were no different.

It was the same way for the crew. After a mission, they all liked a hot shower, a clean set of clothes, and a great meal. The routine helped them unwind after a harrowing experience. Most of the crew involved in the rescue cleaned up and stayed in the superstructure with the guests because they had already been introduced to the people from the lab.

After the rescue mission on the island, the superstructure would host the highest number of guests it had ever had, but the scientists deserved comfortable accommodations where they could feel safe. More importantly, though, they were free for the first time in years.

Before Duke began his after-mission routine, he went to the control room and asked Valerie, "How are things going?"

"There hasn't been any movement from either ship," she said, "but I think that is about to change. See the amphibious vehicle? They should be able to see it from the *WU* and the *#9* as it passes by them."

"Contact the Indian Navy and report the secret lab. Hopefully they'll arrive before Mingli has his men rescued or blows it up," Duke told Valerie.

By the time Duke finished eating with their visitors, he invited them all up to the conference room in the superstructure, where he offered everyone a nightcap—or rather a morning-cap since the sun had just risen. Everyone had been up for hours, and a drink seemed appropriate. As the drinks arrived and the small talk ended, the rest of the crew that had returned on the DSRV had finished their after-mission routines and joined everyone else in the conference room. They too placed their drink order with Rodney. Two long rectangular tables had been placed end to end, and there was more than enough room for all nineteen people to sit and debrief. Duke had every newcomer tell their story, starting with Quon.

"I was flying back to Beijing aboard the missing Flight 818 after enjoying a week in Malaysia before starting my new job with the space agency. I noticed everyone else was falling asleep just before I lost consciousness. The next thing I knew, I woke up in strange surroundings, my bedroom in the lab complex. Mingli was sitting across from me with a smug grin on his face and basically told me that I was his prisoner. He had previously tried to recruit me to work for him, but there was something about the man that

I never felt comfortable with—he was creepy. He told me that my only hope to be released was to develop three formulas for him," Quon related, and everyone at the table was fixated on his every word.

He continued, "The first formula he wanted was a super virus, one that would spread from person to person easily and live for a long time. He gave me a sample of SARS to work from. It took a little while to perfect it, but eventually I developed it into a virus that could live for up to two weeks outside a body, and once it was ingested, it would spread from host to host very easily and then turn the creature's cells into virus-making factories. I used pangolins as the hosts because they are resilient creatures that the virus wouldn't kill.

"The second formula was the vaccine. But I couldn't develop a vaccine that worked well enough. Mingli's patience with me waned, and he brought in four other scientists to help. I was happy to have the help, but between all of us, we still couldn't develop an acceptable vaccine until we accidentally combined the wrong…well, right elements. When we discovered that the formula worked, we just had to retrace our steps to reproduce it. Soon, all the pangolins were completely healthy again," Quon divulged.

"I convinced myself that the virus wouldn't kill that many people—surely the vaccine would be administered before many people died. It was just a money-making scheme. But after I gave him the virus and vaccine, I saw on the news day after day how the virus was sweeping across the world month after month without any mention of the vaccine. It was then that I realized just how evil Mingli really was. Over a million people died before he introduced the vaccine. How could anyone do that? I just regret I had any part of it and don't know how I will ever be able to forgive myself," he confessed.

"The third formula was the hardest for me to work on," Quon went on. "I really had an emotional battle within myself. Mingli wanted me to create a poison that would kill anyone who had been vaccinated. I honestly thought about letting Mingli kill me instead of developing the poison. It only has one use—to kill people. I refused to do anything and had decided death was the better option until Mingli brought my sister, Linh, to the lab as leverage to get me to complete the deadly formula, which I named coronacyde. At that point, I didn't have a choice. Coronacyde is inert by itself. Only when it is ingested by someone who has been vaccinated will it react and kill that person. I had just finished the coronacyde formula when Mingli came yesterday to take possession of it. That's when he recanted his promise to release us. We weren't surprised and figured our days were numbered—until you guys showed up and saved us."

"If it has to be ingested, then someone would have to have it injected, eat it, or drink it," Cho said.

"If he just picked up the formula, then it hasn't been mass-produced yet. We still have time to figure out what the target is and stop it," Steve said.

"We are chasing Mingli right now, and I hope to stop him before he even gets started making the coronacyde," Duke said. "How did you end up at the lab, Anatoli?"

"We worked at a lab in Minsk for Grigori Shirokov. He came to me in January and offered me a promotion and a relocation to a lab on a tropical island. Do you know how cold it is in Minsk in January? Of course, I was interested. He told me he was going to double my salary and pay for my relocation. And the best part: I was going to get to help stop the pandemic because I would be working with a team to create an effective vaccine. He had me at 'tropical island.' Little did I know I was going to be held captive in a concrete bunker on that tropical island."

The other scientists from Minsk all confirmed that the same deal was struck with them.

Quon's assistant told them, "After I'd graduated college, Mingli promised me a salary three times as much as my father had ever made. It was more money than I'd ever dreamed of, so I readily accepted the offer. I didn't even realize I was actually a prisoner until I arrived at the lab. And even then, it really wasn't so bad. I had comfortable accommodations and good food. I just couldn't ever leave. It was a nice enough place, but after about six months, it really began to weigh on me, and I began feeling claustrophobic and needed to get out of there, at least for a little while. However, when I watched the island's natives savagely kill one of Mingli's men, I realized I couldn't ever try to escape."

The cook and the housekeeper were the first to move into the lab, and they told similar stories about how they had been promised lucrative jobs and ended up prisoners. The interpreter told the same story as well. She'd been promised a rewarding salary for a temporary, six-month position as a Russian-to-Chinese translator.

Then, Quon's sister related her story. "My family was devastated when we heard that Quon's flight had disappeared. We waited months for the investigators to find some evidence of a wreck or something, but they never found the plane and eventually gave up on the search, declaring everyone dead. Our grandfather was sitting at the kitchen table when my mother went in to tell him about Quon's flight. He put his head down and rested it on his hands and was never the same after that. We don't know if he had a mild stroke or what happened, but he died less than a year later. For years we never gave up hope and yearned for a miracle, but eventually we concluded we'd never see Quon again.

"Then, one day after work," she continued, "I went to get in my car when someone grabbed me from behind and put a chemical-smelling rag over my face. I tried to scream and kick, but after a few seconds, I was out cold and didn't wake up until I was on a plane with Mingli. He told me not to worry, that he'd found my brother and was taking me to him. I knew that couldn't be true. Why would somebody have grabbed me like that, and why would I wake up in a plane? None of it made sense, but I'd longed to be reunited with my brother for so long that it overwhelmed my logic. I didn't put up any resistance, even when we got into an armored boat that turned into a truck when we reached the beach. When I saw it was true, my heart jumped with joy, until I went to hug my brother and they wouldn't let me. Then it all made sense; they were using me to torment Quon in order to get something from him, and that's why they'd kidnapped me. Quon told them that if they didn't bring me back to the lab, he wouldn't finish his last formula, so eventually they took me back, and I've been there ever since."

Duke thoroughly questioned them again about the poison they called coronacyde and how it was going to be used, but none of them knew how Mingli intended to produce it, utilize it, or any other details. All they could tell Duke was how it worked. The coronacyde was actually a relatively simple compound that had to be ingested or injected. It was a colorless, odorless, inert compound that wouldn't do anything to a human who hadn't been vaccinated for the virus, but if someone *had* been vaccinated, the coronacyde would kill them within hours.

* * *

After the meeting, everyone went to their cabins to get some much-needed sleep. The crew said goodnight as they went into their fake rooms and then slipped down to their normal cabins through the secret doors. Duke and Steve talked in the elevator on the way down.

"We need to catch up to Mingli before he starts to produce the coronacyde," Steve stated.

"Agreed. That's what I plan to do next. We'll track his plane and pick him up at his next destination."

"He seems to always be one step ahead of us," Steve surmised.

"He'll eventually stumble, and when he does, we'll catch

up."

"Linh said Mingli's father resides on the *WU*. I think he knows about Mingli's objectives. We should question him too," Steve said.

"Agreed. Let's get a good sleep and then reconvene to make a plan of action to question the Wus."

Before going to bed, Duke stopped by the control room for an update from Valerie, who told him that the Indian Navy had sent a ship to North Sentinel Island.

"It's stationed just offshore, waiting to receive permission from their leadership for further action," she said. "The two ships are still sitting in the same place, but when the amphibious vehicle went cruising by, they sent a speedboat to intercept it and returned it to the *#9*. Mingli's men haven't been able to go to the island because one of the navy cruisers showed up right after that."

"They must know something's up," Duke said. "Keep an eye on them and wake me if they start to leave."

"Okay," Valerie replied.

A few hours later, Valerie called Duke's cabin.

"Sorry to wake you, but I thought you'd want to know that a second Indian Navy ship showed up, and they've requested any information we can contribute to help them gain access to the lab. I sent them the entrance access code and told them the ISM radio frequency band to use. I believe they're going to try to breach the lab. The *WU* and the *#9* have both set sail and are heading toward Singapore."

"Thanks," Duke said, rubbing his eyes. "I'll be right there." He crawled out of bed, relieved himself, brushed his teeth, and dressed. He was in the control room about ten minutes after his call with Valerie. "Let's set a course to follow the *WU*," he said, getting right to business. "Where's the Gulfstream?"

"Mingli flew directly to Minsk from South Andaman Island and has been there since," Valerie said.

"Keep following the *WU* at a safe distance, matching

their speed, and we'll see where they end up. Aren't you about ready for a break? Have you been here all night?" Duke asked.

"I'll switch off with Ali as soon as he wakes up, and I'll be ready to go again after a few hours of sleep," Valerie replied.

"Why don't you go ahead and get some sleep now. I'll watch things until Ali wakes up," Duke stated, and Valerie knew better than to argue.

"Sure, boss. I appreciate it."

CHAPTER 14

Mingli touched down in Minsk and was picked up at the airport by Grigori's driver, who took him to a hotel where Mingli then spent the night. Grigori had promised Mingli that the laboratory in Minsk had been dismantled and the personnel working on it had been taken care of. He'd assured Mingli that the scientists who knew about the top-secret project were killed, as were their families—except Larissa. Other than her, there was nobody left who could talk. The only four scientists still alive, who had worked in the same department but not directly on the project, were transferred to Mingli's lab on North Sentinel Island. Grigori had his servers completely wiped of any evidence that could trace the virus's origin to them.

"There are absolutely no loose ends in Minsk," Grigori had promised.

But Mingli viewed Grigori himself as a loose end and didn't like the fact that one of the scientists' family members had survived after eluding Grigori's assassin. Whoever had helped her knew what was going on, and that worried him. Coupled with the laboratory on North Sentinel Island possibly being compromised, Mingli's peace of mind was diminishing. He knew he had to find out who was after him and what they knew.

Mingli told Grigori that he had to take care of a business matter elsewhere and would be leaving Minsk for a day or two but would return to discuss their future endeavors. He had to check on another lab to alleviate his worries. There couldn't be a single piece of evidence linking him to the virus—Mingli would make sure of it.

* * *

Mingli booked a commercial flight to Sardar-e-Jangal International Airport in northern Iran, where he was picked up by Rasheen Attar. They drove to an old, isolated concrete-block warehouse in southeastern Armenia. Inside was a makeshift laboratory with a large storage area full of fifty-five-gallon drums.

"How do you like it?" Rasheen asked.

"It's pretty gloomy in here, but it'll do," Mingli responded. "Do you have enough people to prepare the coronacyde?"

"We only need eight people. I have one scientist who will make sure the chemicals are mixed in the correct quantities in this large vat over here," Rasheen said, leading Mingli to a large, nine-hundred-gallon metal tub shaped like an enormous mixing bowl. The vat was supported by a large frame, suspending it about six feet off the ground. It had a makeshift catwalk around it that allowed people to walk around the top.

"See the I-beam mounted to the ceiling?" Rasheen asked. "We have a hoist that travels on it. We pick up a full barrel and pour the contents into the vat, and then we place the empty barrel on a pallet on the floor and repeat the process until we have four barrels on the pallet. Then, we slide the pallet under the tank with the pallet jack and fill the barrels through this hose."

The two men walked into a small office with big windows to continue their conversation behind the privacy of closed blinds.

Rasheen continued, "We can fill sixteen barrels with each vat of the coronacyde. If we work fourteen-hour days, we can produce one hundred barrels a day. At that rate, we'll have the eight hundred barrels ready in a week and should be able to have them on the ship within ten days."

But Mingli wanted to know for sure. "You're absolutely positive you can have the shipping containers to the loading dock in Wilhelmsen in ten days?"

"Yes, ten days for sure," Rasheen reassured him.

"Then I'll have one of my cargo ships ready to receive the containers at the Wilhelmsen port in Batumi ten days from tomorrow," Mingli told him. "It'll take thirty-six days to transport them to Quebec. Will we have our vehicles by then?"

"I was told that all of our vehicles are scheduled to be delivered thirty-two days from today," Rasheen told him. "It takes a while to fill an order like that. But most of the men are already in the United States, a few are in Canada, and the rest will be travelling to Canada over the next month. I'm confident that everything will be in place and ready to go by the time the coronacyde arrives in Quebec."

"Very nice work, Rasheen! I've always been able to count on you to get the most difficult things accomplished that I can't entrust to anyone else," Mingli told him. "What will become of the people working here in the lab?"

"The seven laborers will return home; I can always use them again for other confidential matters. They're uneducated people living in one of the poorest countries in the world. They don't have a clue what they're doing in the lab. Since the coronacyde isn't harmful to them, nobody has to wear any protective equipment, and no one suspects a thing," Rasheen told Mingli. Then, he continued, "The scientist, however, will have to be…transferred, as we like to call it. He's the only one who knows the formula's ingredients, but he doesn't know what it's used for. I told him it's simply a chemical compound that's going to be used for manufacturing. But just to be on the safe side, I'm going to have him disposed of when we're finished and remove the hard drive from his computer."

"I want that hard drive. Either I'll come personally to collect it, or I'll have my brother, Minzhe, come to get it," Mingli said.

"Of course. I'll keep it safe for you until then," Rasheen assured Mingli.

"I also need to take a vial with me. Would you get one for me?" Mingli asked.

"Yes, of course," Rasheen promised. "I'll get one right now, and then we can head back to the hotel."

They returned to Rasht, Iran, where they had a meal and spent the night before Rasheen dropped Mingli off at the airport for his return to Minsk.

* * *

Back in Minsk, Minzhe was waiting for Mingli at the airport in a rented SUV. Minzhe had arrived earlier on a commercial flight upon Mingli's request. He'd been heavily involved in his older brother's technology company that created espionage equipment and high-tech security software and had become somewhat of an expert in digital data management.

"I want you to go with me to the lab tomorrow and personally see to it that the hard drives have been wiped clean," Mingli told Minzhe. "I don't want anything remaining that could verify that the virus was produced there."

"There is no way to completely erase a hard drive. With the proper equipment, erased data could still be retrieved," Mingli told his brother. "It would be best to remove the existing hard drives from the server and replace them with new ones. That's the only way to ensure that all the data is gone. We can incinerate the hard drives when we get back home."

Mingli plucked his phone out of his coat pocket and dialed. "Grigori, it's Mingli. I would like for my brother to swap out your hard drives and reset your system. That way we can be certain nobody can retrieve any information regarding the virus."

"Okay, no problem. You are security expert after all," Grigori replied.

"I may own the company, but my brother's the expert."

"I think good idea. How about we go to lab, then to my restaurant for elegant dinner?"

"We are on our way to pick you up now."

"Okay. I'm ready."

Minzhe drove the SUV and Mingli sat in the back seat as they drove to Grigori's villa to pick him up. Grigori came out of his beautiful mansion at the end of a tree-shaded driveway overlooking the city. He got in the back seat beside Mingli and gave directions to Minzhe as they drove to the laboratory. On the way, Mingli brought Grigori up to speed on the events that had transpired over the last week.

"I'm still worried someone is after me. While I was in Athens, I found two men in my jet at the airport. They said they were there to fix an electrical problem and must have mistakenly entered the wrong plane. They had a panel off of an electrical compartment and said they couldn't find any problem. I'm going to have my mechanic go over the plane thoroughly when we get back to Beijing."

"That's odd. But maybe just coincidence?"

"Maybe, but then someone gained access to my lab on North Sentinel Island and rescued Quon and the other scientists."

"Oh no. That's big trouble! They must be stopped before they talk."

"I agree. But I don't know who is doing this. Right now, all I can do is make sure they can't prove anything. That's why we need to replace the hard drives at our lab here," Mingli told him.

"With your security company, you can't identify them?"

Grigori asked.

"My brother has exhausted all the resources at his disposal and found nothing. Whoever is following me isn't leaving a trace. They paid for their hotel and plane tickets using an offshore account in the name of a shell company, and there is no way to trace it back to anyone. None of my many contacts can identify the men or the company they work for; it is as if they are ghosts. I'm sure they'll show up here eventually."

"Sure, sure. The scientists from here don't know about virus. They were working on something else," Grigori worried out loud. "Everything here is taken care of, but you are more than welcome to see for yourselves that there aren't any loose ends here."

When they arrived at the lab, Grigori ushered them in and showed Minzhe to the server room. Minzhe had brought hard drives to replace the ones he took so that, while there wouldn't be any data remaining, the system would still have complete functionality. While Minzhe was taking care of the hard drives and restoring the operating system, Mingli and Grigori toured the rest of the laboratory, which was only manufacturing two drugs at the time. Mingli was satisfied that the lab was clean and their connection to the virus would be untraceable, especially after his brother finished with the server room.

With their minds at ease, they all left together for Grigori's restaurant, where Grigori promised a meal that would surpass the last one Mingli had eaten while in Minsk.

Grigori had his favorite vodka waiting and poured three full shot glasses, one for each of the three men.

"To best business partner who makes us rich, and to even better future," Grigori said in broken English as he held up his shot glass, waiting for Mingli and Minzhe to return the gesture.

"Za vashe zdorov'ye," Mingli replied. He then translated, "To your health," for his brother's sake as the three men raised their glasses and gulped down the vodka.

"Please excuse me, my friends," Grigori said as he stood up and placed his napkin back onto his plate. "I must use bathroom. I'll be right back."

While Grigori was gone, Mingli pulled the vial Rasheen had given him out of the inside breast pocket of his suit coat and opened it. He poured a few drops into Grigori's glass and refilled all three shot glasses with more vodka. Grigori returned just a few minutes later, and Mingli said, "My dear friend, I hope you don't mind, but I poured another drink for us to toast our trusted friendship."

"Excellent!" Grigori exclaimed.

"Za nashu druzhby. To our friendship," Mingli said and raised his glass to Grigori.

"Thank you, my friend," Grigori replied as he raised the potion to his lips and swallowed it down. "Let's eat!"

Minutes later, the waiters brought in course after course until the bottle of vodka was empty and they were too full to eat another bite. Mingli and Minzhe agreed that it was truly an exquisite meal. Grigori told them to go on without him—he'd have his driver take him home. So, Mingli and Minzhe returned to their SUV and drove to the hotel, where they spent the night waiting for news about Grigori's untimely demise.

* * *

The next morning, Mingli called Grigori's cell phone, but there was no answer. Mingli had to know for sure the state of his business partner, so he had Minzhe get the rental and drive him to Grigori's house. Upon arriving, they found many cars parked outside and people scattered all over the grounds. Minzhe parked, and Mingli walked up to the house to ask what had happened, but nobody there spoke Mandarin or English.

Just then, another vehicle pulled into the driveway—a van with Russian writing on it. Two men got out, opened the back doors, and pulled out a gurney with a folded black bag on it. Mingli stayed and watched. About half an hour later, the two men reappeared with a body inside of the black bag on top of the gurney. The elixir had worked.

With all of the loose ends resolved in Minsk, Mingli and Minzhe flew back to Beijing on Mingli's private jet. Mingli decided the first thing he'd do was have his aircraft mechanic check behind the panel the men in Athens had been messing with. He had a feeling there was a correlation between those men and the people pursuing him. He couldn't help but wonder, though, that if they'd been that close to him on his plane and had later discovered the lab on North Sentinel Island, why hadn't the authorities detained him already?

CHAPTER 15

The Indian authorities were reluctant to investigate the report of the lab on North Sentinel Island because it didn't seem plausible that anyone could've built such a structure without the navy or the government knowing. The decision was pushed from one government branch to another until it ended up in a to-do folder on someone's desk, or in other words, a dead end. Without direction, the navy returned to its normal patrolling schedule, which left North Sentinel Island unprotected for days at a time.

Duke would've liked to return Quon and the other guests back to their homes and families, but someone was killing anyone even remotely linked to the virus, and Duke had no doubt that the families of the *Charaka*'s current guests were in grave danger. Duke had Ali purchase first-class tickets for all of the laboratory prisoner's families to be flown to Singapore, where they'd be picked up and brought to the *Charaka* for their protection. Talking them into coming and staying with strangers on a ship hadn't been easy until they'd heard the voices of their loved ones on the phone. Each family member only had hours to pack a suitcase and get to the airport. That minimized the chance of them telling anyone where they were going, even though they were warned not to mention anything to anyone. Duke was worried that Mingli's assassins could already be following the family members and might choose to kill them on their way to the airport. Once the family members landed in Singapore, the Syndicate would pick them up and transport them to the ship. Aboard the *Charaka*, Duke was confident they'd be out of harm's way.

In the meantime, the *Charaka* followed the *WU* from a distance on its course to Singapore to pick up the new passengers while the *WU* continued to motor past Singapore toward Hong Kong. Duke was frustrated that the Indian authorities weren't doing anything about the lab, especially because *#9* accompanying the *WU* had turned around and seemed to be heading back toward North Sentinel Island. Duke decided to have Louis and Kabir follow the ship in the combat submarine and torpedo any amphibious vehicles that tried to approach the island. Hopefully the ship didn't contain more than four amphibious vehicles because the combat submarine only had four torpedoes.

Although the combat submarine was half the size of the DSRV and could only carry two passengers, it could still travel at twenty knots, almost as fast as the DSRV, while submerged. Duke wasn't worried about the *WU* getting away—Valerie was monitoring the boat on radar, and the *Charaka* could catch them very quickly because it could travel at about five times the speed of the luxury yacht.

Duke needed a plan, and he needed it ASAP. Mingli was going to use the coronacyde somewhere in the world, and the Syndicate needed to stop him before it was too late. After only a few months, most of the world's population had been vaccinated and would be susceptible to the poison. After Louis and Abe had gotten caught on Mingli's jet, Duke figured it was only a matter of time before Mingli's people found the tracking device, and when they found it, Valerie wouldn't be able to trace Mingli's travels anymore. Duke decided it was time to capture Mingli and force him to reveal his intentions. They knew he was in Beijing, and their best bet was to go there to get him immediately.

Steve and Tiny went with Duke from Singapore to Beijing—he needed his two best men for such an unpredictable mission with no weapons. They planned to go to Mingli's office first, and if he wasn't there, they'd wait for him at his house. One way or another, they needed to apprehend Mingli and find out what his plan was. Duke was certain that the team he had with him would either apprehend Mingli or devise another plan if things didn't pan out at either location. Duke didn't like missions that were arbitrary—so many things could go wrong. But they were desperate. Unfortunately, desperation could easily cause mistakes.

* * *

All of the new passengers showed up while Duke, Steve, and Tiny were in the air, headed to Beijing. Fortunately, they all made it to the *Charaka* alive and well without anyone following them, as far as they could tell. A celebration beyond description ensued as one by one, family members were reunited with loved ones they'd assumed were dead. They spent hours embracing and crying in their private rooms as each family caught up on years missed together until they finally all gathered in the dining room.

When Rodney walked in to see if they were ready to eat, they engulfed him with hugs and handshakes. They were so thankful that he'd saved their loved ones' lives. Rodney told them he wasn't one of the crew members who had rescued them, but despite his protests, they were determined to show him their gratitude because he was the only one around to receive their appreciation. To the families, Rodney was a megastar who deserved their best commendations.

One by one, as the rest of the *Charaka*'s crew entered the room, each received the same greeting. All of them told the same story, explaining that they had done very little, and it was the other team members who weren't there who'd really been the heroes. There were no glory hogs in the Syndicate.

When everyone was ready to eat, Ethan made sure they dined like royalty by preparing the best of his specialties for them to sample, although he was a little afraid to show himself in person for fear of the reception he'd receive. He wasn't an overly friendly sort of man, and the attention would've been too much for him to bear, so he had Rodney run the food from the kitchen to the dining room. None of the *Charaka*'s guests had ever had a meal like they did that evening, and never had any of them been so content and joyful.

* * *

When Duke and the other two men landed, Valerie informed Duke that Mingli's helicopter had just left the coordinates of his office building in Beijing and was headed to Pyongyang in North Korea.

Darn it, Duke thought. He always seemed to be one step behind Mingli. He decided it was time to place bugs in Mingli's office and home to catch him should he return. The only problem was that the portable devices didn't have the power or range they had when in closer proximity to the *Charaka*. All the same, they could still monitor the two locations so long as the team was within a few miles of the devices.

After setting up shop in the hotel across the street from Wu International headquarters, they decided to tackle Mingli's office first. They knew getting in would be difficult because they had to go through a security person at the lobby desk, and this time, they didn't have Cho with them to persuade the desk attendant. All three men stuck out like sore thumbs in Beijing: Duke was the palest man on earth with his freckles and cropped auburn hair; surfer Steve, with his blonde hair and Australian accent, attracted attention everywhere; and Tiny was a giant Black man who could've been mistaken for the larger brother of John Coffey from the movie *The Green Mile*. But because Duke was the most fluent in Mandarin and got to call the shots, he decided he would go and take Steve with him, mainly because Steve also spoke Mandarin and Tiny only spoke English. Duke was sure he could at least get them up to the office, then Steve could sweep the receptionist off her feet—since he had some mystical effect on women. Tiny would keep in contact and come to save the day with brute force if necessary. Duke figured he had his bases covered as best as he could.

When he got to the front desk, Duke reasoned with the security guard, explaining he had business with Mingli. He certainly looked the part of a professional colleague with his briefcase and three-piece suit, and Steve had even slicked his own hair back for the occasion to better look like a well-polished businessman. The man at the desk called up to Mingli's office and told the receptionist that Mingli had two men there to see him about a business matter. He hung up the phone and motioned for them to go around the corner to the elevator.

Both Duke and Steve smirked but remained silent on their ride to the twenty-sixth floor. They approached the glass doors, and the buzzer sounded, allowing them in. The receptionist was immediately smitten with Steve. As Duke watched the receptionist respond to Steve's coquetry, he couldn't understand why women always seemed to be so enamored by him. But he reasoned that even though he may never comprehend Steve's magnetism, he sure as heck would use it to their advantage.

Steve applied his charm, and the receptionist was, as expected, infatuated. He was setting up for a diversion when the light on her desk phone flashed, and she picked it up, said a few words, and set it back down again. Both men's hearts dropped when the receptionist said, "Mr. Wu will see you now. Please follow me."

Duke and Steve looked at one another and followed the

receptionist down the hallway. Neither of them had expected that. They had been prepared to distract the receptionist and sneak a couple of bugs into Mingli's office, but they'd never suspected he would be there. The question that immediately popped into Duke's mind was if Mingli Wu was in Beijing, who was on his helicopter to Pyongyang?

Never one to be intimidated, and without missing a beat, Duke began in Mandarin. "Hello," he said and stuck his hand out to shake Mingli's. "I'm David Duncan, and this is my associate, Steven Wilson. We represent Matson Incorporated from the United States. We're here to discuss a partnership between our two companies for full-truckload shipping between China and North America. We believe that partnering with Wu International's shipping division would be a profitable endeavor for both companies."

"Nice to meet you," Mingli said as he shook Duke's hand. "Won't you have a seat?" Mingli gestured to two chairs across from his desk, then said, "What are your intentions?"

Duke's initial bluffing faltered ever so slightly, but Steve chimed in with his fairly well-spoken Mandarin dialect and said, "As you know, we're the largest container shipping company in the United States, and we're looking to take on additional cargo ships to increase our supply chain from China to the US. We don't want to partner with a larger company because, frankly, we think we can get a lower price from your firm here, and we're certain you'd be open to the growth this would create for your multinational venture as well."

"That's a most interesting proposition, and I might've considered it if I hadn't already spoken to another man from Matson late last year before the coronavirus broke out. I initiated the conversation, but we couldn't reach an equitable agreement," Mingli said.

"Well, that's why we're here," Duke bluffed. "To see if we can renegotiate and reach some kind of mutually beneficial arrangement."

Just then, there was a knock at the door.

"Come in," Mingli said. He gestured at Duke and Steve, and the four men who entered stood and faced them. Mingli said, "I recognize you from the video surveillance at the Westin Hotel some weeks ago. I've been expecting you."

* * *

While Mingli introduced his thugs to Duke and Steve, four more men were knocking on Tiny's door back at the hotel. They tried to enter the room with guns drawn, but Tiny grabbed the first man and took his gun as he flung him back into the three others who were preparing to rush in, knocking them off balance and making them pause for a fateful second. Tiny shot all four men and dragged them into his room.

After taking their weapons, he grabbed his backpack and surveillance gadgets bag and headed down the hallway to Duke's room. As was the standard practice, each of the men had a keycard to the others' rooms just in case such a situation arose. Tiny let himself into Duke's room with the spare keycard and, over the hidden communication device buried in his ear canal, told Duke and Steve what had just happened. So, while Duke and Steve were being introduced to the four henchmen in Mingli's office, they knew Tiny was aware of their situation and would be heading across the street momentarily.

* * *

"Well then, let's just go ahead and disperse with the formalities so you can tell me what your designs are with the coronacyde," Duke quipped as he stretched his neck muscles, preparing for the inevitable.

Mingli was taken aback by Duke's terminology since only a few of his most trusted people knew the name of the secret compound. "How do you know about that?" Mingli asked with narrowed eyes.

"I know way more than you think," Duke said, sneering.

"I'm not too worried about what you think you know," Mingli said. "Your ship left Singapore just a little bit ago, and as soon as it makes it to the middle of the South China Sea, I'm going to send it to the bottom with Quon, his family, and everyone else on board."

Steve whispered to Duke, "I guess they did follow the families to the ship after all."

"I know more than you, but I need to know one thing. Tell me, why are you pursuing me?" Mingli asked. "Who sent you?"

"Why don't you tell us what your intentions are with the coronacyde, and then maybe we'll tell you who sent us," Duke said.

"I'm the one with the power here, not you. I'll make the demands, and you'll obey me," Mingli threatened.

In their earpieces, Duke and Steve heard Tiny say he was out of the hotel and positioned downstairs in one of the shops in the lobby.

"I have four 9mm Glocks, but one of them is short four bullets," Tiny informed them.

"Okay," Duke said to Mingli. "We were sent here by your president, Bo Xiong, to investigate your corruption so that when he has the military execute you, he can legitimize to the people and the rest of the business world why he had you killed. He's very upset that you brought reproach upon China with the coronavirus."

Mingli was furious. "Liar!" he exclaimed, startling the four henchmen for a split second.

That was all the time Duke and Steve needed. They each grabbed a man by the wrist before they could draw their guns and then jerked them around so that their backs were to them like human shields. The other two men drew their guns but hesitated to shoot out of fear they'd hit their associates. With their free hands, Duke and Steve each drew their human shields' guns and shot the other two men. They released the men they were holding and motioned for them to stand by Mingli. The entire sequence of events took place in a span of less than three seconds. Steve demanded all of their ammunition, and each man reached into his suit pocket and tossed a clip that Duke and Steve caught. Duke held them at gunpoint while Steve retrieved the guns and ammunition from the two dead henchmen.

"You won't get away with this," Mingli said menacingly. "I have your friend across the street at my hotel, and I can have him killed with just one word."

"You do that," Duke said as he heard Tiny warn them that there was a small army coming up the elevator. "I think we'll bid farewell until another time, Mingli."

Duke and Steve exited the office and headed down the hallway to the stairwell, then started down while Mingli shouted behind them, "Go after them!"

At the first landing, Duke stopped and waited for the door to open. Taking aim, he waited until he could see the pursuing men and shot them both in the knee, then turned and tried to catch up to Steve.

"They all went to the twenty-sixth floor. You should be free to come down the elevator if the stairs aren't safe," Tiny said over his communication piece.

Steve said, "We got a head start on them. Let's stick with the stairs." They both jumped down a half flight of stairs with every stride.

"I've got a cab ready. Hurry up!" Tiny exclaimed.

"Right behind you," Duke said. "Open the doors."

Tiny opened the front and rear passenger doors, showed the driver his gun, and motioned for him to get out. The driver didn't hesitate—he climbed out of the car as fast as he could. Seconds later, the stairway door burst open, and Duke and Steve ran out of the building with the security guard in pursuit. They leapt into the cab's opened doors, and Steve hollered, "Step on it, Tiny!"

They drove two miles and abandoned the taxi, hotwired another car, and drove three more miles. They repeated the car thefts at progressively longer intervals until they arrived at Mingli's house. Steve jumped over the gate and ran to the front door. He knocked, and to his surprise, an older gentleman opened the door.

"Open the gate," Steve told him. "Is anyone else here?"

"Excuse me?" the man inquired.

Steve pulled his gun out, pointed it at the man's head, and said, "The gate. Now!" He pushed the elderly man into the house, and the man led Steve to a control panel with a monitor showing the front gate, then pushed a button that opened it.

"Where's the button to the garage door?"

The man motioned to a button on the wall, and Steve opened the garage door and shut the gate.

"Anyone else here?" Steve asked again.

"The housekeepers," the man said and motioned upstairs just as a young woman was descending the steps. She smiled brightly at Steve until she saw his gun, then a frightened look spread across her face. A minute later, an older woman descended the stairs, and Steve motioned them all over to the sofa.

Tiny and Duke entered the room, and Duke said, "We're in a pickle now. Anyone got a suggestion?"

CHAPTER 16

Duke called the *Charaka* and told Valerie that Mingli knew the people from the laboratory and their families were aboard the ship. He'd had the families followed to Singapore and had allowed them to board the ship in hopes of sinking it in the South China Sea along with anyone who could testify against him.

Valerie informed Duke that the Wu International helicopter had left Pyongyang and was already back in Beijing. She also updated him that Grigori Shirokov was found dead in his house. She and Ali were currently searching for ships, trucks, planes, and trains that could be transporting coronacyde, and they came up with a list of over one thousand potential vessels. But Mingli could've also filled a CONEX shipping container and had the coronacyde shipped through a competitor's shipping company. The possibilities were endless.

Before Duke could tell Valerie about the predicament that they were in at Mingli's house, a phone chimed, and the butler said, "The gate."

Duke and Steve peered out the window to see the gate partially opening, and they heard the garage door activate. Steve bolted for the control panel and pushed the button to close the garage door. A car pulled into the driveway, and the door activated again, but Steve closed it before it could open more than a few inches. Duke told the butler to shut the gate, and he did, enclosing the automobile in the driveway. Steve continued to counter each attempt to open the garage door until a very angry Chinese man got out of the car and headed for the front door. Duke recognized the man on the surveillance video screen as the interrogator from his mission a few weeks before. He opened the front door before Minzhe had a chance to ring the bell.

Minzhe immediately recognized the man pointing the Glock at his forehead.

"Come on in," Duke said. "Looks like the tables have turned since our last meeting."

Duke slammed Minzhe up against the wall and relieved him of his own Glock. Duke used the zip ties he always carried with him and hog-tied him on the floor. With his hands and feet bound behind his back, Minzhe was completely helpless and had to strain to look at anything higher than knee-level.

"Where's the coronacyde going?" Duke started.

"I don't know," Minzhe replied.

"You're going to tell me, and you're going to tell me right now or else you won't like the consequences," Duke retorted.

"I really don't know," Minzhe insisted.

Looking at the butler, Duke asked, "Do you have any branch clippers?"

"No," the butler replied. "The grounds crew does all the yard work. But I do have a pair of kitchen shears."

"That'll do," Duke said. "Go get them, and don't try anything heroic."

"Yes, sir," the butler replied and went into the other room, returning a minute later. "Here you go."

Duke took the pair of heavy-duty scissors and grabbed Minzhe's little finger. "Okay, one last chance to do this the easy way," Duke said.

"I told you. I don't know anything about coronacyde," Minzhe uttered just before Duke took the tip of his little finger off at the first joint. Minzhe cried out in pain, but Duke ignored him and said, "I have two more cuts to make on this finger, then I'm going to move to the next one. Want to talk, or should I continue?"

"I'm not lying," Minzhe pleaded. "Please stop." Another loud snip as Duke made the second cut, and Minzhe cried out again and began to sob. "Okay, okay. I'll tell you what I know."

"That's better," Duke said. "Where's the coronacyde going?"

"I really don't know," Minzhe said as Duke grabbed the last stub left on Minzhe's little finger. "Wait, wait. The man my brother's dealing with is in Iran. He's the one who's organizing everything. But I really don't know what the plan is."

Nobody had bothered to look out back to see there was a helipad in Mingli's vast backyard until they heard the roar of a helicopter's engine as it descended onto the pad.

"Tiny, don't let that helicopter leave," Duke ordered. "Steve, you get whoever gets off of it."

Steve and Tiny raced for the back door of the house and waited for the passenger door to open on the Sikorsky S-76C++, a lavish executive's helicopter. The copilot got out and opened the rear passenger door, then Steve and Tiny made their move. They bolted out toward the helipad, guns drawn. Tiny focused on the pilot, keeping his pistol trained on him, while Steve held Mingli and a bodyguard at gunpoint and motioned for them to get out of the helicopter.

"Shut it down!" Steve yelled at the top of his lungs in Mandarin, and the copilot echoed his demand into his communication gear. The engine began to wind down as Mingli's bodyguard pulled out his Glock and tried to surprise Steve, but it was the last mistake he'd ever make— Steve, with his gun already drawn, just flipped his wrist and put a bullet through the man's head. Then, he escorted Mingli and the copilot into the house, and Tiny and the pilot followed once the aircraft had been completely shut down a few minutes later.

"Look what we found," Steve announced, throwing Mingli to the floor. "How about we continue our conversation? Looks like we're the ones with the power now, not you. We'll make the demands, and you'll be the one to obey."

Mingli noticed his brother lying on the floor with his mutilated hand and blood-stained suit. It was difficult to tell whether Mingli was mad or terrified, but the look on his face made it clear he was distressed. In fact, Mingli had never had to be submissive to anyone in his entire adult life, and now he found himself in a position where he was certain his life depended on it.

"Where is the coronacyde going?" Duke asked.

"I'll never tell you!" Mingli bellowed.

"That's basically what your brother told us…at first," Duke mused. "Go ahead and hog-tie him, Tiny."

"Don't you dare!" Mingli demanded.

Tiny grabbed Mingli by the back of the neck and picked him up like a rag doll. He kicked his leg up enough to catch Mingli's feet and keep them from stepping forward as he slammed Mingli face-first onto the floor, knocking him unconscious.

"What'd you do that for?" Steve asked.

"I didn't think he'd hit his head that hard," Tiny said in defense.

"Is he okay?" Duke asked.

Tiny felt for a pulse but couldn't find one and shook his head. Duke jumped down to Mingli's head and felt for a pulse too, but he didn't find one either. He rolled Mingli onto his back and started cardiopulmonary resuscitation on him but to no avail. After ten minutes of futile efforts, Duke determined that Mingli was gone.

"Darn it!" Duke shouted.

"I'm sorry! I'm sorry!" Tiny repeated.

"He must've had other issues, Tiny. I know you didn't mean for this to happen. There isn't anything we can do about it now, so let's just figure out what we need to do next," Duke said. He turned to the pilot and asked, "What's the range of your helicopter?"

"A little over three hundred nautical miles."

"We'll have to refuel a few times, but because we'll be travelling over Chinese airspace, we shouldn't have any trouble with authorization," Steve said.

"Let's do it," Duke said. "Load up, and we'll make our way to the *Charaka*." Then, he turned to the two women and said, "Do either of you two ladies need to call someone to let them know you won't be home tonight?"

The older housekeeper said," My husband will be expecting me home this evening."

The younger woman said, "My parents will be waiting for me to get home so that we can all eat dinner together."

"Call your families and tell them Mr. Wu has requested you to help with the needs of some special business guests tonight. Because it'll be very late when you're done, you are going to spend the night and return home tomorrow after Mr. Wu's guests leave and you're finished cleaning up. No funny business," Duke warned.

After the phone calls, everything was all set—they just needed enough time to get back to the *Charaka* before anyone discovered their exploits.

All nine of them proceeded to the helicopter, with the pilot and Tiny sitting up front. The copilot, Duke, Steve, Minzhe, the two housekeepers, and the butler all climbed into the back. The Sikorsky S-76C++ had two rows of five luxury leather reclining seats that faced each other, so the seven of them fit comfortably with additional seats to spare.

The pilot flew to Qingdao and refueled, then made four more stops before a final refueling in Hong Kong that got them close enough to rendezvous with the *Charaka* in the South China Sea.

CHAPTER 17

While Duke, Steve, and Tiny were pursuing Mingli and then trying to get back to the *Charaka*, the crew on the ship were dealing with their own problems. After leaving Singapore and heading north on the South China Sea, they encountered three large fish-processing vessels and one military patrol boat. The first fish-processing ship tried to ram them, but upon seeing the course the smaller ship was heading in, Ali and Valerie were able to maneuver the much faster *Charaka* to avoid a collision.

The kamikaze ship turned and began to make a futile second attempt. Ali spun up the GLPG and fired a round into the bow at the waterline of the vessel. The large hole the shell created swallowed up the sea, filling its bulkhead with water and rendering the ship dead in the water. By the time the visitors were able to look out at the deck to see what had caused the blast, Ali had already lowered the weapon back into its bay so that the source of the deafening boom would remain a mystery. One of the *Charaka*'s crew members told them it must've just been cargo shifting, which seemed to appease their guests' curiosities.

On the second encounter, two ships identical to the previous one tried to approach the *Charaka*, but Valerie and

Ali were able to easily outpace them and slowly pull ahead until they were out of sight and, hopefully, out of mind. By that point, they'd caught up to the *WU* and were in plain view. The yacht slowed to a stop as the *Charaka* sailed past, and Valerie and Ali soon realized why the *WU* had stopped. Suddenly, its helicopter took off, and the transponder was deactivated, rendering it invisible to the *Charaka* once it was out of range because they had never been able to install a tracking device on it.

Soon afterward, the *Charaka*'s radar picked up a patrol boat that appeared to be a Chinese military craft or one belonging to another nearby country. But then, its AIS signal was identified as belonging to Wu International. Immediately, the boat gained Ali and Valerie's top attention, and they watched as it approached on a southerly course while the *Charaka* steadily headed north. At six thousand yards, the vessel altered its course to a direct heading to intercept the *Charaka*. Ali spun up the GLPG again and let the computer calculate the coordinates, hitting the boat in the center of its helm station and creating a spectacular explosion that resulted in a fireball. The disintegrated vessel began to sink instantly.

"Incoming!" Valerie alerted. "We have two torpedoes coming in at five thousand yards. They must've launched them just before we nailed their boat."

"I'm preparing countermeasures," Ali called out.

"Three thousand…two thousand…" Valerie counted down, trying not to panic.

"Firing one…and two—two anti-torpedoes away!" Ali said.

All they could do was wait, but they didn't have to wait long to see if they were successful or if the *Charaka* would take a hit. The next-generation countermeasures were fully programmable three-inch-diameter mini torpedoes fired from underwater tubes at the bow or stern of the *Charaka*. The small, shrouded propellers hidden in the tail of the mini torpedoes were driven by a pressure-controlled motor that received energy from a thermal battery. The torpedoes hovered vertically at a computer-selected depth and emitted an amplified acoustic signal, which acted as a tractor beam to the approaching torpedo to draw it to the decoy until they collided and destroyed each other.

"Stopping hard!" Valerie shouted as the adrenaline flowed through her. She increased power to 90 percent and reversed the magnetohydrodynamic drive, virtually stopping the *Charaka* in her tracks, which tossed everyone and everything on the ship forward. But the maneuver put the maximum possible distance between the *Charaka* and the impending explosions. Seconds later, one explosion followed by another, and they knew the threat was over.

Other than a few bumps and bruises, the guests were fine, just confused about what had taken place. Ami told them they had hit an unknown object under the surface of the water, but that there hadn't been any damage to the ship's thick hull. They were still safe and secure.

But the crew members on the *Charaka* weren't the only ones having an exciting day. Louis and Kabir spotted two amphibious vehicles deployed from #9 off of North Sentinel Island and fired two torpedoes to sink each of them. The first vehicle exploded with little fanfare compared to the second amphibious vehicle, which exploded with a blast that shook the submarine violently and created a mushroom fireball that resembled a miniature atomic bomb. Louis began to frantically search the control panel, quieting one alarm after the other. "Make sure we aren't taking on water," he shouted to Kabir.

Kabir jumped out of the copilot's seat and headed for the rear of the submarine, checking every square inch as he went to make sure water wasn't trickling in. "I believe we just destroyed their explosives," he said with a grin.

"Their explosives almost destroyed our submarine," Louis noted. "If we were any closer, we might be swimming now."

The #9 turned into a busy ant mound with men

scurrying everywhere. Loud alarms blasted over the emergency sound system on the ship, and three more power boats launched into the water to investigate. They searched for the source of the attack, but Louis and Kabir's submarine was well hidden in the depths of the bay and undetectable unless the ship had sophisticated sonar equipment. But even then, the sub could always rest on the sandy bottom and wait them out. The sub had ten days of air and had only used up two of them. Before the oxygen was depleted, the *Charaka* would be back to save them if necessary.

Between Xiamen and Hong Kong, Duke received an update on the happenings with the *Charaka*, the *WU*, the helicopter, and the combat submarine. He ordered the combat submarine to put its last two torpedoes into the ship and head back toward Singapore. That would effectively disable the ship if it didn't sink her, and they would pick the sub back up in a few days.

* * *

The pilot of the Sikorsky didn't like flying over the sea, especially when the fuel gauge showed that they were too far out to return to land. Steve reassured him that there was a place to land on a ship, but that wasn't very comforting to the pilot either because he'd never landed on a ship before. About an hour later, Steve pointed to a vessel in the middle of the sea and said, "That's our landing spot."

The pilot was as happy as he was nervous because the fuel supply wouldn't have lasted another half hour. He settled the helicopter down with a thud as the *Charaka* rose to meet it while riding the waves. They all disembarked from the aircraft, and Minzhe was taken to one of three special rooms below, in the main part of the ship, that were specially designed to hold prisoners. The others were shown to their cabins and were treated just like the rest of the guests, which eased their fears and made them gain a little trust in the three men who had essentially abducted them. Even though Duke had explained to the butler and the two housekeepers the circumstances, it was difficult for them to put much faith in him, especially given the fact that Duke had sliced off pieces of another man's finger in front of them and Tiny had body-slammed their boss so hard it had killed him instantly.

Duke went down to interrogate Minzhe with Doc Bai while Steve organized a boarding party for the *WU*. They were going to seize it and question Mingli's father, if he was still aboard, but they assumed he'd departed on the helicopter that had left earlier.

Duke sat across the table from Minzhe, whose wrists and ankles were bound to the arms and legs of the chair with leather belts. His torso was bound to the back of the chair, completely immobilizing him.

"Tell me everything you know about the coronacyde," Duke began the interrogation.

Minzhe didn't put up any resistance and began spilling all the gory details while Doc Bai stitched up his finger and bandaged it. He started with his trip to Minsk to pick up his brother and their trip to the laboratory to swap out the hard drives. He went on to tell Duke that his brother had used the coronacyde on Grigori Shirokov at dinner, and then the two of them had gone to his house the next day to verify that he was dead.

Minzhe told Duke about his brother's trip to Iran to talk to Rasheen Attar, but because he hadn't gone with his brother and had never been to Iran or met Rasheen, he didn't know what they'd talked about. Mingli had never confided in him about his plans for the coronacyde or anything else until he'd needed Minzhe to carry out a task for him. But even then, it had been on a need-to-know basis. Minzhe confessed that his brother had treated him in a subservient manner, but he eventually became used to it and was appreciative that he'd been treated much better than most who worked for his brother. Minzhe had accepted his role of being kept out of the loop. All he knew for sure about the coronacyde was that Rasheen was manufacturing it somewhere, then shipping it to another location. He didn't know either location, but he knew Rasheen and his brother were planning something big.

Duke was very good at reading people and believed Minzhe's story. After all, Minzhe didn't have any reason to lie, but he had every reason to try to preserve his life. Just then, Duke received a message through his earpiece that Steve, Tiny, Abe, Bubba, and Rodney were ready to board the *WU*.

"Excuse me," Duke told Minzhe, standing up. "We're about to seize the *WU*, and I'd like to go see it unfold. I'll be back later, and we can continue our conversation then, hopefully with Mingli's father." He turned and headed for the door, but Minzhe kept talking.

"Mr. Wu isn't there," Minzhe said, "but I'd be happy to tell you where he's going if you'd like to negotiate."

"You're in no position to negotiate, but we'll discuss it further when I get back," Duke stated.

He went to the control room to watch the monitors that showed the body-cam footage as his men boarded the *WU*. The yacht had remained in place ever since it had launched the helicopter. The invading crew members had boarded two RIBs that were stationed in their cradles on a large platform and then lowered into the water until they began to float. The men piloted the RIBs until they flanked the *WU*, one on the port side and the other on the starboard side. The men boarded and began to search every level but only found a handful of crew members and no resistance. The yacht was truly a pleasure boat and wasn't equipped with any weapons, only a few bodyguards on board. There was also a chef, a butler, a couple of engineers, several stewardesses, some deckhands, and what appeared to be a couple of prostitutes.

Because the *Charaka* was already overflowing with guests, they decided not to take the *WU*'s crew with them back to the ship. Instead, Steve and Bubba would remain on the yacht with them while the others returned on the RIBs with the three bodyguards, who would reside in one of the holding cells. Steve was an experienced captain and could navigate any boat, and Bubba, the *Charaka*'s mechanic and engineer, could fix anything on the *WU* or at least figure out how everything worked. With the yacht's crew remaining behind, Steve could always ask one of the crew members in Mandarin if he needed help with anything.

After the mission aboard the *WU*, Duke headed back down to Minzhe to find out the location of Mingli's father. But Minzhe held his ground and demanded for Duke to let him go. He asked Duke to look the other way when the chaos was over if, in turn, he'd disclosed Mr. Wu's location.

Why not? Duke thought. He knew Minzhe wasn't going anywhere for a while, and a lot could happen in the meantime. Plus, getting along with his prisoner wasn't a bad idea, as he might need Minzhe's cooperation again later.

"Okay," Duke told Minzhe, "when this is all over, I'll drop you off in Tangshan or fly you to Beijing, and you can live with your demons. But this deal rests on you providing accurate information that allows us to find Mr. Wu."

"I'll tell you the truth. But how can I trust you?" Minzhe asked.

"I'm a man of my word, and I'll keep my promise to you. You're just going to have to trust me on that," Duke responded.

Minzhe went on to tell Duke that Mr. Wu flew to Ho Chi Minh City and then took a flight to India to talk with a friend of his to keep the lab on North Sentinel Island from being searched. Mr. Wu had connections there in the government, and he was sure he could get the investigation dropped with enough incentive. Mingli had been worried that if the government inspected the lab, it would lead them right back to Wu International—there was too much corrupting evidence there. That was why they'd sent the other ship back to the island to go in and destroy all the evidence they could find and then take the hard drives from any device that could identify and possibly incriminate the people there.

"Is Mr. Wu returning to the *WU*?" Duke asked.

"I think so. That's his home now. But I don't know what he'll do when he finds out you killed his son," Minzhe said.

"What airport?" Duke asked.

"All I know is that he was going to Ho Chi Minh City."

Duke spoke into his earpiece, "Valerie, tell Steve to maintain his position at the coordinates where the *WU* is anchored and wait for the helicopter to return. Can you find out which airport the helicopter landed at around Ho Chi Minh City?"

"I'll try to," Valerie said.

"How are you talking to someone else? Are others listening to our conversation?" Minzhe asked.

"We all wear communication devices hidden in our ear canals," Duke replied, gesturing to his ear.

"Maybe I should start working for you when this is all over," Minzhe mused.

"Sorry, Minzhe. We have a ten-finger requirement to work here," Duke said with a smirk.

But Minzhe didn't appreciate the remark and winced a little, undoubtedly still in pain.

Duke heard Valerie say, "Tan Son Nhat International Airport."

"Have Diego fly Abe and Ami there and place a tracking device on Wu's helicopter," Duke said. "Then we can track him if he decides to take it somewhere."

A few seconds later, Diego's voice came over the earpiece. "Can we take the Sikorsky?"

"Sure. If you like it, we can keep it," Duke said. "We can trade it out with our old Bell helicopter."

A twelve-million-dollar helicopter would make a nice addition to the Charaka*'s toy collection*, Duke thought to himself.

"Now, let's talk about Mr. Attar," Duke said out loud. "Where can we find this guy?"

"That's going to be tough," Minzhe said. "I know my brother visited him in a different location every time he went to Iran. He seems to live in every town in that country, or at least he travels a lot."

"Hmm," Duke said, moaning. "One last question, for now. What were you doing in North Korea?"

"I went there to talk to a government official about supplying military training to our bodyguards. Wu International doesn't get along very well with the Chinese government, and we were hoping the North Koreans would help us if we offered the right price."

"What'd they say?"

"The man I spoke with said he'd have to talk it over with President Jong-un and get back to me, but he thought it sounded like a good proposition," Minzhe said.

"What did you offer them?"

"One billion dollars and the formula for coronacyde," Minzhe told him.

"Well, that deal isn't ever going to happen. How many people have the formula?" Duke asked.

"Mr. Attar, Mr. Wu, and I are the only people alive who know it. Oh, and Quon, but you already knew that," Minzhe said. "But I don't have the formula memorized or anything. I don't even understand it. I have it on my computer, which is in my car at my brother's house."

"I appreciate your candor, and now I'm going to unbind you and show you to your quarters. But if there's any funny business, you'll end up like your brother," Duke threatened.

"As long as you return me home, you'll have my full cooperation," Minzhe promised.

CHAPTER 18

Meanwhile, Rasheen was busy with his part of the plan, unaware of the fate of his business partner. He had completed manufacturing eight hundred barrels of coronacyde and had them trucked to the Wilhelmsen dock in Batumi, Georgia, where five forty-foot containers were loaded onto one of Wu International's cargo ships headed for the Port of Quebec in Canada. Rasheen wasn't concerned that he hadn't heard from Mingli and knew he might not until they'd completed their operation. It was a beautiful plan.

Rasheen had purchased eighty-two Ford Transit cargo vans that had the storage capacity of ten barrels each. The vans were purchased from a Ford dealership in Montreal under the pretense of starting a home delivery company to supplement vendors who'd been inundated with a surge of online purchases due to the pandemic. Even after most of the people in North America had received the vaccine, the trend for non-contact purchasing hadn't waned, either due to people's uncertainty of the vaccine's effectiveness or simply because of the convenience of having things delivered directly to their front doors.

Rasheen was able to do all of this over the phone and

online, never appearing in person. He'd provided a list of drivers who would come into the dealership and pick up the vehicles. A week after the vans had arrived at the dealership, the drivers took them to Quebec, where they checked into a hotel and waited for the shipment to arrive.

Amassing one hundred and seventy qualified men was the most daunting task Rasheen had ever undertaken. Most of the men had already resided in the US for several years, having arrived when immigration rules and regulations were much more lenient. Once someone arrived in the US, false documents were obtained that showed the person to be a US citizen, complete with a social security number. They could obtain a driver's license and employment and fit right into society without ever standing out.

The men waited for Rasheen's instructions. He was anxious to exact revenge on the country he believed was responsible for oppressing his people for generations, and he needed like-minded people to carry out the plan he and Mingli had devised.

Crossing the border from the United States to Canada would be relatively easy for Rasheen's men because US or Canadian citizens crossing from one country to another didn't raise much suspicion. Some men flew to Mexico from the Middle East with false documents and then flew to Canada, bypassing the more stringent US Customs and Border Protection screenings. Rasheen had been arranging travel plans for years and had devised a foolproof system that had enabled him to fill all 160 driver positions he needed for his massive mission.

Once the shipment arrived in Quebec, the containers would be loaded onto five trucks pulling container trailers. The trucks would drive to a rented warehouse where they'd be unloaded, and then the barrels would be loaded into the vans, each vehicle carrying ten of them. The vans would then head to the town closest to the border crossing, where they'd enter the United States.

The second part of the operation—and the most

difficult—was the logistics. The vans would be split into two groups. Forty vans would be loaded first and start their thirty-two-hour drive to Coronach, Canada. Each van would have two men, and each man would take turns driving while the other man slept on a mattress on top of the barrels in the back. The forty-first van would have the five men who were to breach the border along with an electromagnetic pulse device. Once they arrived in Coronach, they'd wait for the specified time to cross the border at the Land Port of Entry in Scobey, Montana. The other forty-one vans would drive a much shorter distance of three and a half hours to Sutton, Canada, and wait for the specified time to cross the border at the Land Port of Entry in East Richford, Vermont.

The first van to cross the border would have five men instead of barrels. The men were specially trained in stealth combat tactics and would wait until 1900 hours to approach the border station after it'd been closed for the day, giving the officers plenty of time to leave. The van would stop short of the Canadian Border Services Agency, and four men would leave the van and secure the house on site by executing anyone inside. Once the all-clear signal was given, the driver would stop just short of a visual line of sight to the border facility and detonate an electromagnetic pulse from a device in the back of the van, rendering the electronics within three hundred yards of the facility inoperable. The four men on foot would then breach the border station, cut the power, disengage the backup generators, and open the gates. Then, they'd proceed to the US side of the border and repeat the process.

With both border crossings open and all cameras and alarms unpowered, they'd signal to the lead van carrying the barrels that the coast was clear, and the caravan would cross the border. In time, the authorities would become aware of the breach, but by then, all the vans would be safely in the United States and heading to their assigned destinations. They wouldn't leave a trace of who'd attacked the Land Port of Entries because there wouldn't be any visual record of what had transpired.

All of the vans would have the dealer's temporary tags on them until they crossed the border, then they'd be switched with temporary tags generated online for the US. They would then proceed to their predetermined locations to await the day and time of the next phase of the operation. The farthest destinations were in California, Florida, and Texas, which would each take twenty-six hours of travel. The plan was to arrive at their final destinations, get a hotel room, and then wait until the night-shift personnel change occurred at the first public water system on their list.

There were over one hundred and forty-eight thousand public water systems throughout the US, so Mingli and Rasheen had known they couldn't possibly target all of them. They had chosen the eight hundred systems with the most customers in each of the states they were targeting. Most public water system facilities were maintained by minimal personnel and had minimal security measures in place. Rasheen's hitmen would be able to breach the facility without causing any noticeable damage, eliminate any employees they encountered without causing a commotion, and proceed with their mission.

Often, one or two employees were able to monitor the water plant's operation from a control room and only needed to replace barrels of chemicals when they ran out. The barrels Rasheen's men brought would replace those of the chemicals used to treat the water, and they'd place a sticker on it to disguise it as the proper chemical. If they had to eliminate an employee, they'd put the bodies in their van and abandon the vehicle after they'd completed the mission. More than likely, the authorities wouldn't be notified of any missing persons until the next day or later, and even then, nobody would suspect that the barrels had been switched until it was too late.

CHAPTER 19

After all the Syndicate had been through, Duke thought it was time to update Johnathan Rosenthal. So, from a private line in his cabin, Duke called him. As usual, he answered after the second ring.

"Rosenthal. What've you got for me?" Johnathan asked.

"We've discovered the source of the virus, the vaccine, and the plot to poison an unknown target. This was all devised and orchestrated by the late Mingli Wu, the CEO of Wu International," Duke started.

"Excellent work," Rosenthal said.

"We also discovered that Mingli was behind the disappearance of Flight 818," Duke continued. Then, he went into detail about how the flight's disappearance was connected to Mingli's plan with the virus. He concluded his narration by telling everything he knew about Rasheen Attar, and then he asked if Rosenthal could help give him any information regarding the man.

Johnathan went on to tell Duke that he did know of Rasheen and that he'd been on their radar for some time. They suspected the man of many crimes, including funding the attacks on September 11, but they could never get any substantial evidence to convict him. However, Rasheen was slated to meet his demise as soon as they could pinpoint his location.

"If you find him, let us get him," Duke urged. "We need to find out his plan before he initiates it."

"I'll let you know as soon as we have eyes on him. For now, I'll send you all the photos we have so you can identify him when the time comes," Rosenthal agreed.

Johnathan Rosenthal liked using the Syndicate in those situations because unlike the Federal Bureau of Investigation, Central Intelligence Agency, or Department of Homeland Security, the Syndicate wasn't bound by criminal's rights. They did whatever was necessary to extract vital information from bad guys, even if it meant being insensitive to the terrorists' feelings or harming them. No matter how tough an individual was, Duke and his team believed proper persuasion could always get the information needed to avert disaster and save lives.

* * *

While Ali and Valerie were busy trying to find as much information about Rasheen Attar as they could, Diego, Abe, and Ami were returning from Ho Chi Minh City after successfully planting the tracking device on Wu International's third helicopter, which had eluded them before. Duke decided to pick up Louis and Kabir, so he guided the *Charaka* around Singapore and into the Andaman Sea, where he met up with the submarine. With most of the crew and a record number of guests onboard, they turned and headed back into the South China Sea to stay closer to the *WU* and hope for Mr. Wu's return.

What nobody knew, however, was that Mr. Wu had learned of his son's death and had decided to fly to Iran to meet with Rasheen instead of returning directly to Ho Chi Minh City. Hui fang Wu had ingrained in his son his own desires and values from the moment he came to live with him so many years ago. He always knew what was going on with his company and had put the notion in Mingli's head about kidnapping Quon and eventually bringing down the biggest businesses in the United States. By targeting the largest cities, they were actually targeting the largest manufacturers and businesses in the US. After amassing billions of dollars through the pandemic and subsequent worldwide sales of the vaccine, Wu International would be in a position to take over any company they desired. By killing off masses of company owners, presidents, CEOs, and board members of the most powerful companies in the world, it would open the door for Wu International to take over those companies and become the most powerful global business leader as well as the most influential family in the world. With that kind of clout, world leaders would cater to their wants and needs in exchange for financial stability in the new alignment of the world's wealth and power.

Rasheen's father used to do business with Hui fang Wu frequently until he passed away and Rasheen took over the family business. Mr. Wu had introduced Mingli to Rasheen early in Mingli's introduction to the business matters of Wu International, so Rasheen knew the Wu family well.

Mr. Wu landed in Tehran the evening after leaving his friend in India and was met at the airport by Rasheen's driver, who took him to one of the most luxurious houses Rasheen owned. He welcomed Mr. Wu at the door and embraced him.

"It's been a long time, my friend. How are you?" Rasheen inquired.

"Not so well, not so well," Mr. Wu said dejectedly. "They've killed Mingli."

"What? Who killed Mingli?" Rasheen said, flabbergasted.

"Somebody has been investigating his connection to the coronavirus and killed him when he went home. They took his staff, his helicopter, and the pilots. I had the helicopter tracked, and it disappeared somewhere over the South China Sea."

"I can't believe it!"

"I need to know that everything's still in place. We need to do this in Mingli's memory."

"Absolutely, my friend. It's already done. Everything's in place. The containers arrived two days ago, and the men are already mobilizing as we speak. The mission will be carried out within days. By this time next week, America will be on its knees," Rasheen said proudly.

"Good. Now let's talk about the people who killed my son. I believe they've raided my secret laboratory on North Sentinel Island and have taken the scientists who worked there. If I'm correct, they also know everything about the virus, the vaccine, and the coronacyde, but they don't know about the operation itself—the only three people who know about it are you, Mingli, and me, and I'm certain my son didn't give up any information. That must be why they killed him. I need your help to get rid of these vermin. I know the ship they're on. We need to sink her, but I don't have anything capable of destroying such a large ship. I had a torpedo boat try, but we lost contact with it just before I left for Ho Chi Minh City," Mr. Wu told him.

"Can't you get the Chinese Navy to sink her?" Rasheen asked.

"No, the president doesn't care for me. We go way back, but let's just say we're not friends," Mr. Wu said, shaking his head and looking at the floor. "If I could lure them close to North Korean waters, I could possibly get their government to take action, but not the Chinese government."

"I don't know anybody with enough fire power in that part of the world," Rasheen said. "I did sell some arms to a group of pirates in Malaysia, which could possibly help, but I don't know how far into the South China Sea they'd be willing to go. Hold on, I'll find out." Rasheen grabbed his phone and made a call.

"Wani? It's Rasheen. Good, good. Listen, I have a proposition for you. I need a cargo ship by the name *Charaka* sunk. You need to kill everyone on board and can sell the goods and the ship if you'd like. Name your price. Eight million?" Rasheen looked at Mr. Wu, who was nodding his approval. "Okay, eight million. But the crew and everyone on board has to die. Yes, the *Charaka*, somewhere in the South China Sea. You'll have to find them. Yes, I'll wire you four million now and the rest when the job's done. Okay. Bye."

"Do you think they'll be able to do it?" Mr. Wu asked.

"Yes, they need weapons, and they won't want to double-cross me," Rasheen said. "Why don't you stay here with me until they've been disposed of so you won't have to worry about them getting to you?"

"Yes, that's an excellent idea. I think I will. I'm sure that won't take more than a week or two."

* * *

Wani was known as one of the most dangerous and successful pirates operating out of Malaysia in the South China Sea. His modus operandi was to ply nefarious activities on cargo ships and other vessels that could earn him a handsome ransom. He was often responsible for killing entire crews when owners or authorities refused to cooperate—and sometimes even when they did. A number of governmental agencies were looking for him, but he was able to move to a new ship often enough that he hadn't been caught. He had a masterful method when taking a ship: always at night when most of the crew were asleep. He used black RIBs with electric motors, so his approach was silent, then his men would cast rubber-coated grappling hooks over the rails so they could silently climb up the hull and onto the ship. Overwhelming the crew and taking them by surprise, twenty to thirty specially trained men dressed in black would enter the superstructure and go straight to the bridge to take control. Then, they'd begin a systematic search from level to level, rounding up the rest of the crew and holding them hostage in one of the cabins. His system had proven very successful in the past and had purloined him millions of dollars.

Rasheen's deal was a win-win situation for Wani. Taking the cargo ship would be a piece of cake. Once he had possession of it, he could decide if the cargo was worth anything, and if it was, he could sell it along with the ship. If it wasn't worth the effort, he could just as easily sink it. Either way, he'd make eight million dollars at the minimum. Money didn't come much easier than that, and he didn't even have to play the negotiation game in an attempt to get a ransom. Wani liked catchy phrases and sayings and couldn't help but think that good things happened to good people.

"That is why life always smiles on me," he often told his crew after a successful heist.

And why not think like that? Nobody knew who he was—he could stroll down any city street, and nobody knew he was a notorious pirate who had made millions before he was thirty years old. *Yes, life was good for Wani!*

Wani gathered his crew, and they loaded the luxury yacht he'd commandeered from some rich guy who was traveling with his family from the Mediterranean to Singapore on his way to the Philippines. The yacht's captain and engineer had been shot and thrown overboard just to make sure the rich man knew the pirates were serious about the ransom. The man wired three million dollars into Wani's account to gain his and his family's freedom, and Wani kept his word. He gave the man and his son-in-law their liberty when he pushed them overboard as the yacht continued on. He reasoned that he'd given them a sporting chance; they could swim the few hundred miles to shore if they really wanted to. Besides, they wouldn't have wanted to stick around to see what he and his crew were going to do to the man's wife and daughter. By the time they'd finished with the women, the two ladies ended up in the water along with the cook, whom they kept as long as possible. No other pirate was smart enough to procure a new luxury yacht, good food, and female entertainment for his crew as easily as Wani could. *Yes, Wani was smart!*

The twenty-six men who made up Wani's crew had all worked for him before. They didn't even need instructions anymore—they worked well together and knew just what to do and when to do it. Together, they had taken many other cargo ships and split sizable bounties between them. Paying the crew well certainly kept Wani's men happy, but it also had its downfalls. Some of the men only wanted to work until they made enough money to settle down with a family and lead a normal life. Wani didn't understand that way of thinking and was thankful he'd held his group of men together as long as he had.

As they cruised north in the South China Sea, Wani couldn't believe his luck. Just sitting there was the *Charaka*, not even moving. She was just maintaining her position in the middle of the sea. As Wani and his crew passed by, they wondered what was wrong with the ship. Had it broken down? It didn't seem to be moving anywhere, and if it had broken down, surely it would be drifting. Were they waiting for a load? Usually, a ship did that at port. Wani was puzzled, but he wasn't going to dwell on it. After all, he had four million more dollars coming as soon as he boarded the ship. They passed on by because it was still daylight, and they figured they'd circle back and hit them later that night. His crew had never boarded a ship that wasn't moving before, so he imagined it would be the easiest job they'd ever pulled off.

As Wani's yacht continued on, they spotted another yacht just sitting in one spot: the *WU*. It was completely still like the *Charaka*. After he took the first ship, he'd have a few of his men take it to Singapore and sell the cargo and then the vessel. He'd then take the rest of the crew to the *WU* and use it for a while as his new base of operations while a couple of men sold his current yacht in Singapore. Wani couldn't believe his luck. *Yes, Wani was a lucky man!*

Wani circled around and approached the *Charaka* from

behind. He unloaded the RIBs when he was still about eight miles behind the ship. It'd be a long ride, but the RIBs wouldn't show up on radar because they were too small, and the yacht was so far away that nobody would think anything of it. He knew from experience—it had always worked in the past. As soon as his men took the ship, he'd drive his yacht up beside the *Charaka* and take charge. The men knew their directives and would have everything in order by the time he arrived.

On the *Charaka*, though, Valerie was on watch and called Duke and Ali when she noticed something unusual on her radar. "Hey, something is up with a small yacht eight miles to our aft," she said. "It just expelled four objects, and they're headed right for us."

"Keep an eye on them. We'll be right there," Duke said as he headed to the control room.

By the time Duke assumed his position in the Picard chair, the RIBs were still six miles out. Ali came in soon thereafter and took his seat next to Valerie.

"I bet they're RIBs," Ali said. "Probably pirates. Should we let them board?"

"No," Duke said. "We have too many civilians on board, and we can't take any chances on something happening to them. We'll let the pirates commit to boarding us and then electrify them."

The *Charaka* had the ability to divert some of the power generated by the MHD accelerator to the insulated metal hull, thereby electrifying the hull's exterior with three-phase power at ten milliamperes for three-second bursts. It could effectively knock anyone unconscious if it didn't kill them, and even then, they'd likely drown before regaining consciousness. Anyone who did make it on deck would be an easy target once the floodlights came on, or they could be taken out by the M134 Minigun using the *Charaka*'s infrared motion-detection system that could pinpoint even the smallest of mice running across the deck. Either way, getting on the deck of the *Charaka* was a sure way to commit suicide.

What Wani didn't realize was that the *Charaka*'s radar could pick up electric motors from fifty miles away, as well as any other metal object for that matter. His RIBs were being tracked from the moment they'd left his yacht.

Once his men reached the *Charaka* and threw their grappling hooks over the rails, they began to climb the ropes that would lead them to a big payday—or so they thought. The men started scurrying up the four ropes, hand over hand, while their feet walked up the hull. Then, there was a loud hum, and the men started dropping back into the water one after another. A new group of men would then start to climb and only make it a few feet before falling. The first RIB to arrive had all of its men electrified before the pirates realized what was happening. The remaining men in the other three RIBs decided to abort the mission and headed back to where they'd come from, leaving their associates to drown in the water.

As the pirates headed away from the *Charaka* as fast as they could, Duke told Ali to splash them. Ali opened one of the bay doors, brought the M61 Vulcan up, set the laser on the last RIB, and fired. A two-second burst and two hundred rounds disintegrated the RIB along with its driver. Ali set the laser on the next RIB with the same result and then again with the third one, completing the trifecta.

The M61 Vulcan was a Gatling-style hydraulically driven six-barrel rotating machine gun that fired twenty-millimeter bullets at six thousand rounds per minute. It could obliterate objects up to a thousand yards away, making it an excellent short-range weapon.

After Ali finished off the pirates, Duke gave the order to spin up the GLGP and take out the yacht. Wani had begun to approach the *Charaka*, figuring his men should've been in control by then. From about seven miles out, he couldn't see much, just the glow of light on the horizon from the Vulcan's spray of fire. Then, he heard the hum of the repercussions about seven seconds later and the same thing three seconds after that and again three seconds later.

"I wonder what that was," Wani said to himself. When his yacht had driven by the cargo ship, there hadn't seemed to be any guns on it.

Then, he saw a huge flash of fire in the distance, and during his last three seconds of life, Wani thought to himself—*Smarts only get you so far, and luck eventually runs out.*

CHAPTER 20

Mr. Wu's trip to India turned out to be futile. With a substantial sum of money, his contact had agreed to subvert the investigation. But when the *#9* cargo ship was discovered partially sunk just off the coast of North Sentinel Island, the Indian Navy initiated rescue efforts for the survivors and opened an investigation of what had caused the sinking. The crew on the navy's patrol boat quickly realized they couldn't accommodate every survivor and summoned a larger navy frigate to take them aboard. An officer on the frigate began interrogating the survivors about why they'd been in forbidden waters and how the massive damage to their ship had occurred. The holes in the hull, just below the water line, looked to be caused by explosions powerful enough to cause the three-quarter-inch metal to shred and the jagged edges to protrude into the hull.

Each crew member was taken privately into an interrogation room on the Indian Navy frigate and offered immunity if they were honest with the interrogator. In exchange for their freedom, several of the men told the officer that they'd been instructed to go to the island to retrieve important equipment from an underground lab and set explosives to destroy the entrance. They explained how they had planned to carry out their mission using armored amphibious vehicles to protect them from the natives. But the multipurpose crafts they'd sent were destroyed and they couldn't reach the lab. Then their ship had been torpedoed, and that was how they came to be found.

Once the interrogator passed his findings to the officers in charge, the leaders in turn reported the matter to higher government authorities, who gave orders to carry out another investigation to find out if there was indeed an underground lab and, if there was, what it contained. The navy carried out the investigation and proceeded to reach the island just as the crew members had outlined. They modified their own amphibious assault vehicle and rolled to the coordinates they'd learned from their interrogations, where they found the entrance and entered the lab, only to be met with the horrific smell of decaying bodies. The men who had been tied up had died of thirst sometime before they were discovered. The Syndicate had thought the men they'd tied up would've been discovered before they died— they'd never suspected the Indian authorities would resist investigating the lab once they'd reported it.

The bodies were removed and given a proper burial. The computers and hard drives the Syndicate had left intentionally for evidence were taken from the lab, and the door was closed one last time. Authorities finally determined the lab would be left as it was. The vegetation would continue to reclaim the area, and the natives would never be able to access it, so it posed no threat to their way of life. Nobody ever learned of Mr. Wu's dealings with his contact within the Indian government. Eventually, the government uncovered the data on the hard drives, deemed them top secret and classified, and delivered them to the World Health Organization. The WHO placed the files in a vault for future reference but hoped they'd never have to deal with them again.

* * *

Duke received a call from Johnathan Rosenthal, who notified him that they'd verified Rasheen Attar's location at one of Rasheen's residences just outside of Tehran. With the address in hand, Duke had Diego fly Kabir, Ali, and him to Ho Chi Minh City, where the three men took the first available flight to Tehran. Their first stop in Tehran after they'd gotten a rental car from the airport was the local hardware store. They didn't have any weapons and needed something to defend themselves with until they could acquire the needed armaments.

After a short shopping excursion, Kabir began making guns. He took a half-inch schedule 80-piece PVC pipe and cut it down to make three four-foot tubes. He took a cap, glued it to the end of each cylinder, and drilled a quarter-inch hole in the side of the first pipe an inch away from the cap. He grabbed a half-inch ball bearing and stuffed it about three feet down the pipe. The ball bearing was nearly the same size as the inside diameter of the pipe, so it fit very snuggly and wouldn't move. Then, he handed the makeshift weapon and a can of starter fluid to Ali.

Kabir duplicated the process two more times until all three men were equipped with a single-shot weapon. He explained that after spraying the starting fluid into the quarter-inch hole for about twenty seconds, they would then light the hole with a lighter. When the starter fluid ignited, there wouldn't be any place for the explosion to go except out of the quarter-inch hole until enough pressure built up and expelled the ball bearing out the end of the pipe.

"That's how it's supposed to work," Kabir said, concluding his explanation, "but there are many things that could go wrong with it. For instance, the cap could blow off the pipe if it isn't glued on well, or the pipe could have a weak point itself and blow apart."

"And if there isn't enough starter fluid in the pipe, it

might just flame out the quarter-inch hole and not push the ball bearing out, or the bearing might be too tightly pressed in, and the pipe could explode," Ali said, contributing to the group's worries.

"You might not have time to spray enough starter fluid, and you could get shot while filling the pipe. And, of course, the lighter just might not light," Duke said, silencing the other two. "These things are all possible, but there's a chance it could work and project the ball bearing with enough force to do some damage to someone, at least long enough to relieve the criminals of their weapons."

Ali and Kabir nodded, and Kabir said, "A primitive weapon is better than no weapon at all." Then, they headed to their destination.

Rasheen's house was located north of Tehran on a mountain overlooking the Caspian Sea. His property was surrounded by a nine-foot stone wall with palm trees and tropical plants adorning the landscape. The house itself didn't cover a huge footprint, but it was three stories tall, probably to give better views of the sea. Access to the property wouldn't be easy—surveillance cameras could be seen strategically placed around the perimeter of the house. Duke thought Ali would look the most like a local and have the best chance at gaining entrance, so he sent him and Kabir to the gate to see what would happen. There wasn't any answer.

They regrouped and watched the house for a few hours but didn't see any activity. They finally decided that Kabir and Ali would help Duke over the wall, then they'd position themselves for a clear shot of the front door. Duke would knock on the door, if he could get that far, and hope for the best.

Duke landed quietly and waited for Ali and Kabir to get into place. Then, he sprinted to the front door, but nothing happened. He knocked—still nothing. He pounded on the front door, but there still was no sign of life inside. Kabir kept the entryway in his sights, and Duke stood beside it while Ali scaled the gate. Ali took a position where he could cover the front door while Kabir climbed over the gate. Still nothing. With all the surveillance equipment around the house, it didn't make sense that they weren't greeted. Duke peered into a nearby window and didn't see any motion, so he knocked a hole into the glass and prepared for the worst. Nothing happened. Duke cautiously finished knocking out the window and climbed into the house, but no one came running to stop him. He went over and opened the front door to let Ali and Kabir in, then they searched the house and found Rasheen slumped over the kitchen table, not breathing. They continued to search the house and found four more men dead.

"What do you think happened?" Ali asked. "I don't see any signs of trauma or a struggle."

"It looks like there could have been someone else sitting here with Rasheen," Duke said.

"The other four men look like bodyguards who were having relaxed conversation when they died," Ali stated.

"I think the killer was someone they knew and trusted," Duke said.

"Look here," Kabir announced. "There are six glasses in the sink."

"Five dead men and six glasses," Duke thought out loud.

"I don't see fingerprints on any of the glasses. The sixth person must have poisoned the others, washed up, and left," Ali deduced.

"None of them have any identification or phones on them," Kabir stated. "The killer must have taken them."

"Maybe there's a computer someplace?" Duke wondered. But after a thorough search, they couldn't find one.

"I found the surveillance camera data storage location, but the computer is missing," Ali said.

"Whoever did this was meticulous and knew how to cover their tracks," Duke concluded.

"They would have needed a suitcase to pack all the

electronics," Ali declared.

"A man like Rasheen has many enemies, and there's a long list of people who would've liked to have done this to him," Duke alleged.

"Looks like we hit another dead end," Kabir pronounced.

"Before we leave, I have to know if Kabir's homemade rifles work," Duke said.

The grown men felt like young boys as each of them took turns filling up their pipes with the starter fluid, starting with Kabir. He aimed the pipe at the wall and lit the lighter. As he moved the flame close to the hole, the gun erupted, and the ball bearing exploded out of the pipe with a flash of fire. It crashed through the wall, and they heard the sound of glass breaking. The three men went to the doorway leading to the adjacent room and saw that the window on the outside wall had been broken by the projectile.

"Wow!" Duke exclaimed. "It worked! I believe that would've gone right through somebody."

"Here, let me try mine," Ali said. He lit his pipe with the same result.

"My turn," Duke said before shooting his gun.

"That went through two interior walls before exiting the house through the exterior wall," Ali reported after a quick investigation.

"Wow, Kabir! You actually made guns from simple hardware store items—who would've thought?" Duke applauded.

All of them were satisfied with their accomplishment, but no one felt as much gratification as Kabir.

* * *

Mr. Wu was on his way back to Beijing when Duke, Ali, and Kabir arrived in Tehran. He'd brought an untraceable poison concoction that his lab had experimented with years before the coronavirus outbreak. He had used it a number of times to finalize business deals, and he'd needed it in Tehran to cover his tracks connecting him to Rasheen. He didn't need the man anymore with the attack on the United States already underway. As Rasheen had said, it was already done.

Mr. Wu called the hotel where his pilot was staying at in Ho Chi Minh City and told him to take the helicopter back to the *WU* and have the captain take the yacht to Bohai Bay. He was headed back to Beijing and would contact his men later. Mr. Wu planned to bury his son and take control of Wu International once again. He needed to call his lawyers and financial executives to start preparing to buy the American companies that were about to be ripe for a takeover.

Meanwhile, Duke called Rosenthal to tell him the bad news. They hadn't discovered Mr. Wu's plan yet, but on the bright side, he no longer had to worry about Rasheen Attar. Duke told him he was hopeful that Quon would discover an antidote to the coronacyde. If or when something happened, they could respond quickly to prevent too many people from dying.

Johnathan assured him that Homeland Security, the Department of Defense, the FBI, and the CIA were all monitoring the US carefully for any outbreaks of sudden deaths across the country. So far, there hadn't been any. He'd contacted the heads of state of other countries around the world, and they were also on the lookout. US President Robinson had called Chinese President Xiong and told him that Wu International had developed the virus and the vaccine before the virus had broken out. His country as well as the rest of the world needed to be on high alert for the coronacyde, which was developed to kill anyone who had been vaccinated for the coronavirus.

President Bo Xiong had demanded proof, and President Robinson told him he was in the process of compiling evidence to bring those responsible to justice. However, it was still early in the investigation and things were still coming together, as more information was being discovered by the hour. But he'd promised to keep President Xiong updated when he learned more.

President Xiong had been furious, and although he'd demanded proof, he knew it sounded exactly like the kind of thing Hui fang Wu would do. Bo Xiong had grown up in a privileged family that could afford to send him to the most prestigious college in China: Peking University. At the start of his first year, he had been assigned to room with a less fortunate student—a young man who'd grown up on a farm and who would've never been able to attend a college like Peking University if it weren't for his exceptional grades and the perfect score on his college entrance exam.

Amid their quest for worldwide dominance, China had realized that the most dominant country in the world needed to have the most advanced technological resources as well as a powerful military. They'd started educating the most promising individuals in the country to help China emerge as the new world superpower. In order to facilitate their goal, China had initiated a program that provided financial scholarships to individuals who couldn't afford to go to college but had academic skills exceeding the ninetieth percentile. That was how Mr. Wu had been able to attend college.

Bo hadn't had any reservations about his roommate and thought the program that had enabled him to attend college was going to be the best thing for his country. However, soon after the two young men had begun living together, Bo realized that what Hui fang excelled the most at was cheating. He had tried to persuade Bo to cheat too by teaching him his clever tricks.

Bo soon lost all respect for Hui fang and had insisted on diligent study habits and personal perseverance to accomplish the level of scholastic achievement he'd desired. Over the next few years, he'd parted ways with Hui fang, and the two young men from different walks of life rarely crossed paths after that. Bo couldn't help but despise Hui fang. It had been Bo's integrity and hard work that had catapulted him to the top of his class, graduating with honors. He'd continued to strive to be the best he could be until he'd reached what he'd considered to be the pinnacle—the highest office in China. Because of him, his country was one of the three most powerful countries in the world and was poised to outpace the other two to become the most dominant.

Throughout their adult lives, Bo and Hui fang had never found themselves in the same social circles, but they'd heard of each other's accomplishments. Hui fang had watched Bo succeed in life and garner the love and admiration of the people of China. Hui fang, on the other hand, had achieved business success, but most often, it had been coupled with rumors of corruption and unfair business dealings. He'd used others as stepping-stones as he climbed his way to the top of the business world. President Xiong didn't like Hui fang Wu, and he wouldn't take responsibility for the dishonor the man brought to his country. It wouldn't be long before the entire world knew that someone in China had developed the virus to profit off of the vaccine and intended to use the coronacyde to terrorize the world. As soon as the news broke, he'd show the rest of the world he didn't tolerate terrorism, and justice would be served to Mr. Wu.

CHAPTER 21

The tracking device on Mr. Wu's helicopter alerted Valerie that it was on the move, traveling out of Ho Chi Minh City and heading over the South China Sea toward the *WU*. She called Steve and Bubba and warned them to expect company in the next couple of hours. Steve and Bubba planned to let the helicopter land, then as soon as it cut its engines and began to wind down, they'd rush it. They'd demand Mr. Wu and his pilot get out, and then they'd tie them up inside the *WU* and contact the *Charaka* for further instructions.

Almost simultaneously with Valerie's call to Steve and Bubba, Duke called to tell Valerie they'd hit a dead end and to ask how Quon's research to find an antidote was coming along.

"Quon, Cho, and the other five scientists have set up a makeshift lab in the conference room of the superstructure," Valerie told Duke. "They're working on a way to neutralize the coronacyde but haven't found the right formula so far."

"We're boarding a plane and would like Diego to be standing by to take us back to the *Charaka* in about eight hours."

"I'll let him know," Valerie responded. "As we speak, I'm tracking Hui fang's helicopter from Ho Chi Minh. It looks like he's heading back to the *WU*. Steve and Bubba are standing by to take custody of him as soon as he lands."

"Tell Steve to use whatever means he deems necessary to get the truth out of him and to do so ASAP."

"Will do. I hope you have a good flight. I'll see you in about ten hours." As always, Valerie waited for Duke to hang up before she disconnected.

Steve was ready, as it wouldn't be his first time trying to get someone to talk. He'd never had anyone resist his methods before. Although, there had been a few times where a stubborn individual who tolerated pain well would hold out for a while. But in the end, whether it was the pain or the drugs, they'd all eventually given in.

In the meantime, Quon and his five assistants were busy poring over notes and formulas. The five-by-twelve-foot whiteboard they were using was completely covered with formulas, mathematical equations, and notes. They were still scribbling on it between brief conversations, which took twice as long since the interpreter was translating as fast as she could.

Doc Bai studied the whiteboard for a long time, then blurted out, "Let's boil it!"

"What?" Quon asked.

"What if we boil it?"

Quon stared at the formula for a minute in stunned silence and finally exclaimed, "That will work! The polarity of the hydrogen bonds will be weakened by the kinetic energy supplied by the heat, and the attraction of the bonds will release a hydrogen molecule, making the coronacyde ineffective when combined with the vaccine! That's so simple; we were trying to complicate things by altering the formula with another chemical reaction. You're brilliant!"

Quon hugged Cho and kissed her, pretending to let the excitement allow him to do what he'd been fantasizing about since the first time he'd seen her.

"Valerie, where's Duke? I have great news!" Cho chimed through her earpiece as the others in the room looked at her like she was off her rocker. "Sorry, I was just excited and was talking to myself," she told them when she recognized their dubious stares.

Valerie told Cho through her earpiece that Duke was in the air on his way back to Ho Chi Minh City but that she'd tell him as soon as she could. Then, Valerie made a joke about a crazy lady talking to someone who wasn't there and chuckled. Cho smiled meekly, unable to reply.

Steve and Bubba were getting frequent updates from Valerie until they could hear the beating of the helicopter's rotor blades. They ducked out of sight and waited for the engine to shut off. As the rotor slowed, the pilot's door began to open. Steve ran to the bewildered pilot, and Bubba flung open that back passenger door only to find the helicopter empty.

"Where is he?" Steve asked forcefully.

"It's just me," the pilot replied. "Who are you guys?"

"Where's Mr. Wu?" Steve questioned.

"He's going to Beijing. He told me to bring the helicopter back here. Who are you guys, and where's everyone else?" the pilot asked again.

"Valerie, we have a problem. Wu isn't on the copter. The pilot says he flew to Beijing," Steve said over his earpiece. Then, to the pilot, he said, "Tell us everything you know, mister. Your life depends on it."

"All I know is that Mr. Wu told me to bring the helicopter back here. He's going to Beijing. He told me to tell the captain to take the ship to Bohai Bay and that he'd contact me later. That's all I know—I swear!" the frightened pilot stammered.

"Okay, then that's what we'll do," Steve said. "Valerie, we're taking the *WU* to Bohai Bay per orders of Wu. That's what the pilot told us, and I believe him."

"We'll sail toward Ho Chi Minh City and cut down on Duke's travel time, then follow you up there, I imagine,"

Valerie said.

When Duke, Ali, and Kabir landed, they were happy to have a short flight back to the *Charaka* and were elated to hear the news about boiling the coronacyde.

The members of the Syndicate all gathered around the conference room table in the belly of the ship to relate the events they had all experienced and brainstorm what the target could possibly be.

"The coronacyde has to be ingested," Cho stated.

"What is the best method to get minute quantities into humans?" Kabir asked.

"The water system," Ali blurted. "If they could contaminate a city's water system, they could kill thousands of people."

"I believe you're right. But what country? What city?" Duke asked.

"That's the million-dollar question," Mandy said. "Would it be his own country? Does he hate any other country?"

"The targets could be endless," Ali responded.

"We have to warn everyone," Duke said. "I'll call Rosenthal and see how he wants to handle this. But I think we have to conclude that a water system—or water systems—are the targets, even though we can't validate which ones. Everyone rest; we need to be ready to spring into action at a moment's notice."

Duke dismissed the meeting and went to his cabin. He immediately called Johnathan Rosenthal, and as always, he answered on the second ring.

"Tell me you got something, Duke."

"I can't prove this, but I believe the target is a water system or multiple systems. I can't tell you what country, but the US definitely needs to be on guard."

"Why do you think it's the water system?"

"Coronacyde has only been developed to kill people—people who have been vaccinated. It has to be ingested, and the only way to reach thousands of people at one time is to pollute the water or air. Since this is an odorless and tasteless liquid, it makes sense that it is going to be deployed in the water. Everyone drinks water or uses it for ice, or washing dishes, brushing teeth, bathing, and so on. I'm convinced that the intention is to unleash it through a water system. I just don't know where yet."

"Why would Wu want to do that?"

"I don't know. Maybe he hates someone or some country, maybe he is just diabolically insane, or maybe he wants to hold a country or the world for ransom. I don't know the guy, but what I've learned about him is that he's simply a businessman. Granted, he doesn't have any respect for human life; he just loves money and power as far as I can tell."

"I'm going to put our nation's water systems on alert and put out a warning to all of our national security agencies. Then I'm going to warn the rest of the world's governmental agencies to be vigilant to such an attack on their infrastructure."

* * *

Not everyone took the warning seriously, though, and many police departments were short-handed due to a lack of funding and the escalating social unrest throughout the US. While Duke and his team were scrambling to prevent a tragedy unlike anything the world had seen before, Mr. Wu was approaching Beijing. He called his driver as soon as he had cell service and landed shortly thereafter.

Mr. Wu only had a carry-on bag and was quick to deplane from his first-class seat. As he exited the jetway, he was greeted by four uniformed officers who were comparing a photo on their phones to each of the passengers deplaning. When they saw Mr. Wu, they motioned for him to stop and asked for his identification. He showed them, and one of the men told him to follow as two men flanked him on both sides and the fourth man followed close behind. They walked Mr. Wu to a room with concrete block walls and no windows. The steel door had a narrow-wired security window in it and was the only way in or out. The room only had a small metal table in the center with two steel chairs facing each other on either side of it. One of the men told Mr. Wu to have a seat and wait as two of the men left and the other two stood on either side of the door with their backs to the wall.

After what seemed like an eternity to Mr. Wu, a man in a three-piece suit walked into the room as the two officers continued their posts beside the door. The man pulled out the chair across from Mr. Wu, sat down, and introduced himself as Mr. Li, the chief executive director of President Xiong's security council.

"Mr. Wu, first let me say that I'm sorry about your son. My condolences," Mr. Li said. "But despite my sympathy and knowing this is a most difficult time for you, we still must have a conversation. It has come to President Xiong's attention that your company, Wu International, developed and introduced the coronavirus to your own country but not until you'd developed a vaccine to combat the virus. Is this true?"

Mr. Wu said nothing and just looked at the man.

Mr. Li continued, "We understand that despite having the vaccine prior to introducing the virus, you allowed the disease to spread for more than six months, creating a worldwide pandemic and causing the deaths of almost one million people before introducing the vaccine. Is this also true?"

Mr. Wu said nothing and continued to stare at the man.

"Now, we also understand that you've developed something called 'coronacyde' and that you hope to kill millions of more people with it. Is this true?"

Mr. Wu still said nothing and glared at Mr. Li.

"I need to know your plan for the coronacyde, Mr. Wu. Are you going to cooperate with us?"

Mr. Wu refused to say anything, but finally, he looked

away.

"I suggest that you cooperate with us right now because if you don't, I'm going to have you moved to a more private location, where I'll turn the questioning over to an information extraction specialist. Trust me, Mr. Wu, you don't want that. Now, tell me your plans for the coronacyde. Are you going to inflict more mayhem on the world?"

"I'd like to consult with my attorney," Mr. Wu finally said.

"I don't believe you understand what I'm saying. Until we have answers, you aren't going to talk to anyone but the people the president has authorized you to speak with, which are just me and my specialist friend. For the last time, do you want to cooperate?" Mr. Li demanded angrily, but Mr. Wu said nothing. "Very well. Secure the prisoner, and escort him to the van," Mr. Li said as he stood and replaced the chair, then turned and walked out of the room.

One of the officers opened the door and motioned for the other two to surround Mr. Wu. They handcuffed him, removed all of his personal articles, and placed them in a plastic bag. They employed the same formation they'd used to escort Mr. Wu to the interrogation room, with the officer trailing holding Mr. Wu's carry-on bag while the leader carried the plastic bag with Mr. Wu's personal effects. They led him through a *No Entry* door and out to a van that was waiting for them with a driver and another man. After they all climbed in, the man closed the side door and got into the front passenger seat, and they took off.

CHAPTER 22

As was often the case, screwups occur in every group, especially in one as large as 170 men. Rasheen's men were all in position and ready to go at the designated time the following day. The plan was to hit one public water system after another until they'd unloaded a barrel at each of the ten treatment plants on their lists. However, two men assigned to Montana were the first to arrive at their hotel just a few hours after crossing the border and had to wait two days for the other drivers to reach their destinations, particularly the ones driving to California, Texas, and Florida.

The two men in Montana became confused about when they were to start their task and began their route twenty-four hours early. The public water systems on their route were small in comparison to many of the other treatment plants around the US, and some of them weren't manned continuously, leaving them with little to no security beyond a locked door. As the two terrorists pulled up to their first target in Havre, they noticed a locked chain-link gate on a secluded street. A pair of bolt cutters and sixty seconds later, they were inside and had the gate shut so a passerby wouldn't notice anything out of the ordinary. They found an unlocked door, rolled their barrel in on a dolly, and had it hooked up in a matter of minutes. They were at the facility for less than ten minutes.

The next city on their list was Great Falls, which was slightly less than two hours away. Serving a city of almost sixty thousand people, the water treatment plant drew its water from the Missouri River and was much more sophisticated than the one in Havre. Once again, the bolt cutters allowed them entry to the premises, and they knew exactly which building to go to. They knocked on the door, but there wasn't any response. Habir used his lock-pick set, and they were in the building less than a minute later. They walked into the treatment area with their dolly in tow and quickly exchanged the nearly empty chlorine barrel for their barrel of coronacyde, then left undetected.

They continued their route an hour and a half south to Helena, where they came to a mid-sized water treatment facility. There, too, they knocked on the door. A man opened it a minute later and asked what they wanted as he peered around them. While the water department employee was looking at the barrel on the dolly, Habir shot him in the head with a silenced pistol. Habir began cleaning up the mess as his partner, Rabbel, wheeled the barrel into the treatment area and exchanged it with the chlorine. Both men were back in the van within fifteen minutes and tossed the water department employee in the back under a tarp.

Their next destination on the list was Missoula, the second largest city in Montana with a population of about one hundred and twenty thousand people, an hour and forty-five minutes away. The water treatment plant, although large, was easily infiltrated by the two men utilizing the lock pick when nobody answered the door. The two men pulled the dolly along until they came to the water treatment area and began craning the nearly full barrel of chlorine down so they could replace it with their barrel of coronacyde. Just as the barrel landed on the concrete floor, a man entered the room.

"Hey, what are you doing in here?" he yelled.

Habir pulled his gun out and shot at the employee, but the worker ducked around the corner when he saw the gun and headed back to his office to call 911. Habir and Rabbel pursued the man with weapons drawn. As the employee reached the office door and began to turn the knob, he felt a burning sensation in his side and grabbed at it with his other hand while he continued with the door. But before he could get it opened, he heard a second muffled shot, and then everything went black.

Habir closed in on the man and shot him in the side of the head with his third shot, killing him instantly while his blood oozed out onto the concrete floor. Habir began to wipe up the evidence and wrapped the man in some plastic bags to keep the blood contained while Rabbel went back to crane the barrel of coronacyde into place. Habir had just finished taping the two open ends of the large plastic bags together around the employee's midsection when he looked up to see another man staring and pointing at him. The man tried to yell but couldn't. Habir pulled his gun back out and shot him as he turned to run. Now, with another mess to clean, he wondered how many more people he'd encounter before they got out of the building.

Rabbel came back to see what was taking Habir so long and saw him pulling a plastic bag over the second man's head. He helped tape the two bags together as Habir had done before and then propped one of the men on the dolly and dragged the other man out. They placed them both in the back of the van, covered all three victims with the tarp, and left.

After that nerve-racking experience, the two men were looking forward to the hour and a half drive to Anaconda, their next target. Upon arriving, their nerves calmed, they found a small but new water treatment facility with cameras mounted on the exterior eaves of the building, and that posed a problem. However, the men reasoned that the facility looked vacant and the cameras were probably not actively monitored after hours. They simply donned ski masks and proceeded to unlock the door, exchanged the barrels, and were back in the van within ten minutes.

The next three locations, Butte, Bozeman, and Livingston, were unmanned, and the two men were in and out of each facility in a matter of minutes.

The next destination, Billings, was just over an hour and a half away and proved to be their most difficult location of the night. When they arrived, they found an antiquated set of buildings. They knocked and were greeted by a young man, who Habir quickly put down. Inside the building, they had to pass by an office with two other employees concentrating on a control console. Rabbel opened the door.

Without turning around, one of the men asked, "Who was at the door, Kevin?"

Rabbel shot both workers in the back of the head before either of them knew what had happened. But they had another problem: there was blood splattered all over the console, and it was very difficult to clean adequately.

Habir grabbed the dolly Rabbel had abandoned to shoot the two workers and quickly rolled it into the treatment center. As he changed the barrels out, yet another man approached him and asked who he was and what he was doing. Habir pulled his gun out, and the man began retreating, but not fast enough. Habir shot him, adding one more mess to clean and another body to haul out to the van. By the time they covered their tracks and were able to get back on the road, they'd spent almost an hour in Billings and were running out of time before workers showed up at their last location two hours away.

It was eight o'clock when they arrived in Miles City, their final destination. The gates were open, and they were able to drive right up to the building where they needed to install the last barrel. The door was unlocked, and they walked right in. As they rolled the poison toward the treatment area, they met a man.

"We have a delivery for you," Habir said, thinking on his feet.

"What are you talking about?" the man asked. "We already have our supplies for the month."

"Maybe someone else here ordered it."

"I'm the only one here."

"Good." Habir pulled out his gun and shot him in the forehead before the man had a chance to react.

Habir and Rabbel were out of there fifteen minutes later and had successfully completed their mission. In less than twenty-four hours, they would become the most prolific mass murderers in the history of the United States. They had poisoned the water supply of over three hundred and fifty thousand unsuspecting people in one of the most sparsely populated states in the continental US. Most of the other crews would be targeting much denser populations and could expect to exponentially kill many more people. Habir and Rabbel drove their van back to Billings, parked in the long-term parking area of Logan International Airport, and flew back to their home cities.

* * *

By mid-afternoon, the authorities in ten cities in Montana were being alerted at alarming rates of numerous sudden deaths. One agency contacted the Center for Disease Control after receiving more than one thousand reports of deaths within a two-hour period. In several of the areas, the personnel responsible for reporting such things to federal government agencies had become victims themselves and died before they could make the call. In all, more than two hundred thousand people died that day.

The CDC contacted the Department of Homeland Security, the Department of Defense, the FBI, and the CIA about the mysterious deaths in Montana. Johnathan Rosenthal had anticipated such a tragedy thanks to Duke's briefing and immediately sent out an urgent warning to all law enforcement agencies in the United States. Within minutes, the public address system was activated, and sirens blared throughout the country to gain the citizens' attention. Radio and television stations began issuing warnings for people to stay in their homes. Highway patrol departments in each state closed down highways, and city police departments closed down main roads and thoroughfares and immediately dispatched officers to each water treatment facility to safeguard the public water systems. Public waterworks personnel began examining their systems for anything that shouldn't have been there, and a nationwide boil order went into effect due to the efforts of the Syndicate and Quon.

Over the next few hours, numerous emergency response teams arrived in Montana to examine the water treatment facilities in the affected cities to determine exactly how the coronacyde had been injected into the water systems. Within hours of arriving on the scene, the emergency responders found a correlation: mysterious barrels had been discovered at several water treatment facilities in Montana, and an alert was sent out to all the facilities in the US, Canada, Mexico, and the rest of the world to check their chlorine barrels to make sure they contained liquid chlorine, not coronacyde. All of that happened within an eight-hour period from when the CDC was first contacted, after which no new deaths were reported. The world was stunned by what had happened in the United States and even more shocked by the rapid response the federal and local governments were able to organize.

Despite the two hundred thousand dead American citizens in Montana, numerous groups organized in the same short period of time to protest the temporary government restrictions across the country. They claimed it was a conspiracy by President Robinson to limit the American people of their freedom.

Rasheen was right—the day would live in infamy and become known as the greatest tragedy in American history.

At 1900 hours, many of the terrorists attempted to complete their missions in other states despite the added security. Many of them were killed, and many more were arrested. One common denominator that allowed the government to identify them was that they were all driving brand-new white Ford Transit cargo vans with temporary tags. An all-points bulletin went out, and every van that met the description was pulled over and searched. Every law enforcement agency in every jurisdiction in the country conducted traffic stops and roadblocks to examine any new white Ford van on the road. It was the first time every agency cooperated, and all law enforcement employees worked in unison to search for the suspicious vehicles.

The people searching outnumbered the official vehicles available, and many used their personal vehicles to assist in the search. All in all, seventy-nine of the eighty-two vans were recovered, seventy-eight of them still carrying ten barrels of coronacyde each. One empty and abandoned van was found in the long-term parking area at Logan International Airport in Billings with eight dead bodies in the back covered by a tarp. The two vans used to breach the border had been driven back to Canada and discarded in an abandoned warehouse and wouldn't be discovered for several months after the incident.

The national emergency was over, and millions of lives were saved. The Department of Homeland Security had pieced together the plan from the information they'd received from law enforcement authorities around the country after the apprehension of seventy-eight vans full of coronacyde and the testimonies of the arrested terrorists. They determined that the plan was to kill approximately 51 percent of each state's population, striking the most populous cities in each state. They'd found nine vans in California, six vans each in Florida and Texas, five in New York, three in Pennsylvania and Illinois, and two in Ohio, Georgia, North Carolina, and Michigan, but only one van in each of the other continental states—except for Nevada.

One van was unaccounted for and had eluded the authorities. The Department of Homeland Security speculated and feared that 550 gallons of coronacyde had been left in the hands of two terrorists somewhere in Nevada. A massive search was put together, and every highway in the state was set up with roadblocks to locate the last white Ford van. All Nevada police departments were on alert to pull over and search any cargo van they encountered. The Department of Homeland Security, FBI, and CIA all concentrated on the state of Nevada and were determined to find the coronacyde before any more deaths occurred.

* * *

Zikri and Mohammad didn't know what to do when the broadcasts began. There was no way any person in America wouldn't hear of what was going on. Instead of staying at a hotel, the men had stayed at Zikri's house in Carson City to save the money they'd gotten to pay for their lodgings. They'd parked the van in Zikri's garage and waited for the appointed time to start their route before the chaos ensued. There was no way Zikri and Mohammad could move the van—the police were driving through every neighborhood, and if they tried to go anywhere, even to ditch the van, they'd be caught. There was no one to contact because the only phone number they'd been given when they were recruited wasn't working anymore; they were on their own.

"What are we going to do? There is no way we can carry out our mission now. We'll be arrested or killed if we try," Mohammad feared.

"We can't move the van out of the garage. But I have another vehicle, a Mazda SUV that I left at the airport when I flew to Canada. I think a barrel will fit in the back of it," Zikri told him.

"You think we should get rid of the coronacyde one barrel at a time?"

"We have to get rid of it somehow. Eventually, when

things calm down, I can paint the van and ditch it someplace," Zikri told him.

"Where are we going to dump the coronacyde?" Mohammad asked.

"One of my favorite things to do is drive around Lake Tahoe and look at the water and the mountains. It's a beautiful area, and it isn't too far from here. There's a wooded area I know of where the road goes near the water, and there aren't any houses close to it. We could easily roll the barrel out of my SUV and dump it into the lake without being seen," Zikri assured him.

"How far away is it?"

"It's less than thirty minutes from here. We can go in the middle of the night when there aren't many people out and take the back roads. I don't think anyone will ever notice us," Zikri schemed.

"That sounds like a good idea. Let's map our route to make sure we avoid anywhere we might get stopped by one of the roadblocks," Mohammad urged.

"Okay, look here," Zikri said as he held out his tablet with Google Maps pulled up. "We can take this road through my subdivision to this road. It's a mostly abandoned old highway, which was replaced with a much better highway a few years ago. Hardly anyone uses it. It leads to a short stretch of new highway that is only about a half mile long before we can exit onto this old road. There are so many potholes on this road that nobody ever drives on it. My SUV can handle it, though, if we don't drive too fast. It'll take us right to the spot where we can dump the barrels."

"Are you sure we won't see any other cars?"

"I'd be surprised to see any other cars along the way," Zikri tried to reassure him.

The two men agreed on the plan, and Zikri took an Uber to the airport to retrieve his vehicle and parked it in the empty side of his two-car garage when he returned. Later, Zikri and Mohammad went out to tackle the first barrel.

"It's too heavy!" Zikri exclaimed.

"How much do you think it weighs?" Mohammad asked.

Zikri pulled out his smart phone and said, "Water weighs about eight pounds according to Google. So, a fifty-five-gallon barrel should weigh about four hundred and fifty-nine pounds—plus whatever the barrel itself weighs."

"You've got to be kidding! We're going to end up with three testicles each!" Mohammad complained.

"Well, let's try to rock a barrel out of the van," Zikri suggested since they couldn't open the garage door to give them enough space to slide the barrel out of the van and onto the dolly as they would have done delivering them.

They both grabbed the top of the barrel and began to rock it and ever so slowly worked it to the edge of the van, where it eventually slid out and onto the garage floor with a loud thud.

"I can't believe that didn't break the barrel!" Mohammad bellowed.

"Me too," Zikri replied. "There's no way the two of us can lift that barrel into the back of my SUV."

"We need a ramp."

Zikri started rummaging through some boards stacked in the corner of the garage. "I got it! Let's use these two-by-fours and roll the barrel into the back."

They tipped the barrel up on its edge and worked the dolly under it. Once it was in place, they were able to wheel it past the edge of the van and to the back of the SUV, where they pushed it over onto its side. The shorter SUV had more room between the garage door and the vehicle, so they could use the two-by-fours and roll the barrel up and into Zikri's vehicle.

"Push!" Mohammad shouted.

"I am!" Zikri retorted.

"We need to figure out a better way," Mohammad stated.

"What do you suggest?"

"I don't know, but this is going to kill us!"

"I have a ratchet strap. Maybe that will work?" Zikri said.

"Okay. We can wrap it around the seat here and make a loop," Mohammad devised.

They began ratcheting the strap and moved the barrel about eight inches up the makeshift ramp when they realized the ratchet had reached its maximum strapping capacity.

"Darn it! What are we going to do now?" Mohammad asked.

"We're going to have to release the ratchet strap and figure something else out."

"Okay, let it out slow," Mohammad said as he stood between the barrel and garage door to guide it down the slope.

Zikri moved the ratchet lever to reduce the tension and released the sprocket. The strap spun in the ratchet, and the barrel slammed into Mohammad and pinned him against the garage door, his head hitting the door hard.

"I'm sorry!" Zikri yelled. "Are you okay?"

"No! I'm not okay! I think you broke my legs!"

"Help me push it off of you."

"I can't!"

"Hold on. I'll get another board to pry it off of you."

"Yeah, I'll stay right here," Mohammad said as sarcastically as he possibly could.

Zikri returned with another two-by-four and placed it under the barrel and tried to lever the barrel up so Mohammad could escape. "Can you get out?"

"Not yet. Lift it just a little more. Okay, hold it. I can get out now."

Once Mohammad was free, Zikri looked at the garage door and exclaimed, "You left a dent! What are we going to do if it won't open?"

"Let's worry about that after we get the barrel in your car. I'm going in the house until my legs quit hurting," Mohammad said, and the two men went inside to recuperate and revise their plan.

As Mohammad and Zikri sat in Zikri's living room drinking a beer, Zikri thought he had the solution. "Why don't we move the barrel to the back of my SUV and tip it up so that the top is resting on my vehicle, then we both pick up the other end and wrestle it into the back? Once we get most of the barrel in, we should be able to maneuver it the rest of the way."

"I don't know if we can, but it's worth a try. We have to do something with this stuff, and we can't get anyone else to help."

The two men went back out to the garage and tried Zikri's idea. It took all they could muster to get the barrel to stand up so they could tip it up against the back of the SUV. "Okay, lift!" Zikri shouted.

They strained and strained until they had the barrel almost horizontal and worked it back and forth until over half the barrel was in the back of the vehicle and the two men didn't have to support its weight anymore.

"Let's take a break," Mohammad barely uttered.

"Okay, we can finish getting it in after we rest," Zikri agreed.

After a rest, the two men went back out to finish wrestling the barrel into the back of the SUV. "We did it!" Zikri exclaimed as he closed the hatch.

"I don't think I can do another one today," a fatigued Mohammad said.

They were exhausted; there was no way they could lift another one for a while, let alone take all of the barrels in one night. The first one had just about killed them. They waited until the wee hours of the morning, when most people would be sleeping, and began their task.

They arrived at the dark and lonely lake without incident. Thanks to the two-by-fours, the barrel rolled out of the SUV much more easily than it had gone in. It rolled down the ramp out of control, and the two men panicked as they tried to catch up to the barrel and steer it down the bank to the shoreline. Out of breath and panting, Zikri used his pliers to unscrew the plug on the top of the barrel and rolled it so the liquid spilled out steadily until it had to be rotated and tipped to get the last bit out. They knew the liquid was harmless unless ingested, so they didn't worry about it splashing up on them.

The barrel weighed almost nothing when it was empty, so they were able to carry it back to the SUV and load it easily. They got back into the vehicle and looked at one another triumphantly. The first barrel was done.

"That went really well!" Mohammad congratulated his partner.

"Yes, it did! I think we have this figured out. Do you want to try to empty another one tonight?"

"Sure, let's do it. The sooner we get rid of this stuff, the sooner we can get back to our normal lives," Mohammad said, exhilarated by their accomplishment.

After another struggle to get the second barrel into the SUV, they rested their muscles as they drove back to the lake and repeated the process. They did that one more time and called it quits for the night. They did the same thing the next night, only they started a little earlier and tried to move four barrels. Then, on the third night, they moved the last three. With their job complete, the van could sit in the garage indefinitely if it had to and Mohammad could go home to his own house in Bakersfield, California.

Lake Tahoe, one of the deepest and clearest lakes in the world, was a popular destination for recreation, tourism, and home ownership. Together, Tahoe Water Suppliers Association consisted of twelve municipal water agencies in Nevada and California that supplied up to one hundred thousand customers with what was considered the best-tasting drinking water in America.

A few days after Zikri and Mohammad had emptied their last barrel, authorities received sixty-four reports of sudden deaths within four hours of one another. In four more hours, over sixteen thousand more people had died. Authorities from Cave Rock were the first to contact the

CDC, but several other communities also contacted them within a few hours, and all of them were supplied by water treatment plants that drew water from Lake Tahoe. The CDC contacted the federal government, and within hours, several teams that were familiar with the Montana incident swarmed the twelve water treatment plants supplying the residents in and around the Lake Tahoe hydrographic basin.

They found nothing out of place at the plants—no coronacyde barrels had been injected into the system—yet the water still tested positive for coronacyde. When the actual lake water was tested shortly thereafter, trace amounts of coronacyde were discovered. No amount of filtering or chemical treatments could remove the poison, so a permanent boil order was issued. All aquatic creatures from Lake Tahoe were banned from human consumption, and all recreational water activities were prohibited, rendering one of the most beautiful lakes in the world useless.

Zikri and Mohammad had unintentionally become two of the four most prolific serial killers in the history of the United States and had caused billions of dollars in lost revenue to the states of Nevada and California.

As irony would have it, one of the communities supplied with water from Lake Tahoe was Carson City. Zikri didn't think twice about drinking tap water because he hadn't placed the barrels at the water treatment plants on his list and didn't suspect that the coronacyde he'd dumped into the lake would eventually end up in his drinking glass. But it did.

When the police showed up to do a wellness check on Zikri because the neighbor hadn't seen any movement at his house in weeks and had smelled a foul odor when he'd gone to his door, they found Zikri decomposing in his easy chair with the television on. But their biggest find was a white Ford van in the garage with temporary tags and ten empty fifty-five-gallon barrels inside. They'd discovered the last van—and the last of the coronacyde.

CHAPTER 23

If Johnathan Rosenthal hadn't been tipped off by the Syndicate, it would've taken days, weeks, or longer before anyone figured out what had killed the people in Montana. And by that time, the terrorists would've completed their missions in every state. Rosenthal and his team estimated that over 50 percent of the country's population would've perished if the Syndicate hadn't notified Mr. Rosenthal so he could put a plan of action into place. Within three days, over one hundred seventy million people would've died if the terrorists had been successful. Indiscriminately killing all classes of people of every occupation and age group could've completely destroyed the US. If a recovery from such a disaster was possible, it may have taken many generations.

Only President Robinson knew who'd really saved the country. Neither Mr. Rosenthal nor the Syndicate were ever mentioned for the roles they'd played in saving almost two hundred million lives. But that was okay with Johnathan and Duke; they liked being behind the scenes and didn't crave the recognition or the limelight. They were simple, honest men doing what they could to protect the world and the country they loved so much.

* * *

Just before news of the Montana water poisoning broke, Mr. Wu was stripped naked and taken into a room where a man with a rubber apron was waiting for him. The man stood with a table in front of him containing an array of medical tools and other devices. Mr. Wu was led past the table to a metal chair, where his wrists were bound to the arms and his ankles were bound to the legs. Mr. Wu tried to squirm, but his restraints were too tight, and the chair was anchored to the floor and wouldn't budge.

"I understand you don't want to cooperate," the man in the apron said. "Would you like to dispense with the torture by telling me what I need to know, or shall we get right into some pain and suffering? Either way, you'll tell me the truth."

Mr. Wu was an old man and a fairly smart one at that, and he knew he was going to have to talk one way or the other. So, he cooperated and told the man everything from the time he'd had Mingli develop the virus, the vaccine, and finally the coronacyde, to the plan to disperse it in the United States. But he assured the man it was only intended to be used in the US and only enough had been produced to accomplish the undertaking. Mr. Wu explained the plan to kill as many people as possible in the US, how he'd used Rasheen to organize things abroad so nothing could be traced back to him, and how he had imagined taking over as many businesses as he possibly could when the US economy tanked. He was honest for the first time in his life in every regard because he knew he couldn't cheat his way out of the situation. Unfortunately, his confession came too late.

When he was done with his confession, President Bo Xiong appeared out of the darkness. "I knew you were a deceitful man capable of much badness, but I underestimated you. You've far exceeded my contempt for you from when we were young. You've brought great shame and humiliation to our country, and you must pay for what you've done. It seems unfair that you've killed so many, but you only have one life to give. I must know though, why have you killed so many people with the coronavirus?"

"It was all about the money. With the entire world affected, I knew the vaccine would make Wu International very, very rich and the most respected company in the world," Wu said.

"Why kill the Americans?"

"It wasn't about killing Americans. It was about removing the corporate structure of the greatest conglomerates in the world. With their leadership decimated and their workforces crippled, Wu International could be poised to amass the greatest empire in the history of mankind. My son and I would have been the most powerful men in the world, and China would be the supreme superpower. Even you would have had to bow down to me."

President Xiong turned to the man in the rubber apron and said, "He's been through enough... for now. Give him a bottle of water."

Mr. Wu hadn't had anything to drink for almost a whole day and was very thirsty. The man unleashed one of his wrists and handed him the bottle of water, which Mr. Wu gulped down. A minute later, he had severe stomach pains. His body began to convulse and shake violently—he was choking—and then his eyes rolled back into his head, and he became still.

"Justice has been served," President Xiong said as he turned and walked out of the room.

* * *

Days after the Montana incident, international news agencies televised a broadcast from China's President Xiong. He'd called President Robinson the day before to offer his condolences for the men, women, and children killed at the hands of the terrorists. He'd also told President Robinson his men had recovered evidence that proved Mr. Wu was the mastermind behind the virus and the deployment of the coronacyde. Xiong had told Robinson he would announce to the world that Mr. Wu was in custody, had been found guilty of the heinous crimes, and would suffer the consequences for his actions. He'd wanted President Robinson to hear the news from him first.

* * *

On the *Charaka*, the Syndicate gathered around the large monitors in the superstructure's dining hall to watch a special news announcement with their visitors.

President Xiong began, "First, I'd like to offer my deepest and most sincere sympathy to the people of the United States for the loss of their beloved citizens due to the diabolical ideals of terrorists who carried out an unthinkable crime. Secondly, I'm happy to announce that we have apprehended the person who devised this scheme. We've analyzed the evidence and found him guilty of committing these atrocious crimes. He'll suffer the consequence for his actions and be put to death. The man is Hui fang Wu, the founder of Wu International. Many in the world have falsely regarded Wu International as the company that had saved the world from the deadly virus. We found that Mr. Wu had set up a secret laboratory to create a prolific virus that became known to the rest of the world as the coronavirus. Before introducing it into the world, Mr. Wu had already developed a vaccine that could have been widely distributed throughout the entire world to save many lives, but he didn't release it until the coronavirus had killed almost one million people. Then, Mr. Wu had another substance developed in his secret lab, which he called coronacyde. He used that poison to kill the good people of the United States, with the intention of killing many more. But thanks to the cooperation between the

United States and China, we were able to thwart the plan to distribute the remaining coronacyde, which could have potentially killed over half of the United States' population. This threat is now neutralized, and all of the people who willingly participated in it have either been killed or incarcerated. The rest of the world doesn't have anything to fear. Once again, on behalf of the nation of China, I offer our most sincere condolences to the United States and the people of that great nation. Thank you. There will be no questions."

Cheers and congratulations spread throughout the *Charaka* by those in the dining area and the main part of the ship. Steve and Bubba, along with the pilot and the *WU*'s crew members, watched the broadcast from the *WU,* which was anchored in Bohia Bay.

"Well, I don't think your boss is going to be needing a ride after all," Steve said, and the pilot just shrugged.

Steve called the *Charaka* to see what they wanted him to do with the *WU.* Duke told him to leave it and have its pilot fly the helicopter to the *Charaka.* Louis and Diego would decide which one they liked best. After they were through with the extra helicopter, they'd leave it on the *WU* and let the legal system sort out the estate.

When everyone was finally back on board, they sailed into Bohai Bay and found a secluded anchorage. Duke had Diego and Louis each take a helicopter to fly all of the guests back home. Duke had Ali book flights for the four scientists from Beijing to Minsk and returned them to their homes. He also had Ali book a flight for Larissa from Tokyo to Minsk. Once everyone was safe, Duke kept his word to Minzhe and flew him home too.

Mingli had named Minzhe his next of kin in case anything ever happened to him and his father was no longer alive. After Mr. Wu's death, Minzhe became the new head of Wu International, which was well on its way to bankruptcy after paying hundreds of billions of dollars in damages around the world. Even so, Minzhe had inherited enough assets that he wouldn't ever have to worry about money for the rest of his life.

Minzhe thought the best thing for him would be to sell his brother's house and enjoy life on the sea aboard the *WU*, the one asset he was able to keep. After closing on his brother's house, he drove to Tianjin from Beijing one night on his way to the dock where the *WU* was kept. He was ready to start his new life away from the stigma of Wu International and the Wu family. The first thing he was going to do was change the name of the *WU* to something else, but he wasn't sure what. He thought his mother and sisters could help him decide. They were waiting for him on the ship—his mother was going to live with him there, and his sisters and their families were going to vacation with him for a while. His stepfather had died a few years before, and his mother was all alone. There was plenty of room for everyone on the extravagant yacht.

As those thoughts went through Minzhe's head, he noticed a pair of headlights approaching him from behind. The vehicle was obviously going to pass him, and he didn't mind—he wasn't in a hurry. As the SUV began to go around Minzhe's Qiantu K50 electric sports car, all of a sudden, it turned into the back corner of Minzhe's car, spinning him around. Minzhe tried to correct the spin by turning into it, but his car was traveling sideways down the highway when the SUV slammed into the driver's side of Minzhe's car, causing it to flip up on its side. It began to roll over and over until it came to a rest with its roof on the pavement.

The SUV stopped with its headlights beaming on Minzhe's car, blinding him. Or was that the blood pouring down his face? He wasn't certain. He couldn't move at all and hurt all over. If he hadn't been wearing his seatbelt, he probably would have died. He wiped the blood from his eyes but still couldn't see anything except the bright light. But then he saw some shoes, then legs. Someone was coming to help him. He looked up to see a tall thin, bald White man approaching.

"Minzhe," the man said, "do you remember Grigori Shirokov? He called me as he was dying and told me that you and your brother had poisoned him. He gave me an account number and told me that I could have all of his fortune if I repaid you and your brother for what you did to him. I'm sorry your brother died without my assistance. But I'm happy to say that I'll be fulfilling my obligation to my late employer in regard to you." The man raised the tire iron he was holding and brought it down onto Minzhe's head.

* * *

Wu International ceased to exist. The empire Hui fang and Mingli Wu had controlled was sold off piece by piece to help defray the billions of dollars of claims against the company. The Wu name, known and hated throughout the world, was tantamount to the virus that had killed so many people, and it came to be associated with other infamous terrorist names. Many people believed the Chinese government was somehow complicit in the tragedy and that President Xiong had only crucified Hui fang to cover his government's involvement. China's reputation around the world had been disgraced, and the Chinese economy suffered tremendously because of their culpability in the pandemic.

The state of Montana was devastated by the loss of so much of its population. It took years for the state to recover. Many people saw the economic opportunity there and relocated to Montana, taking advantage of the business opportunities and temporarily cheaper land prices. But some of the new residents soon learned that the state's weather was extreme in the winter, and not everyone was suited to live in such a hostile environment. Over time, the population began to rebuild but never matched the numbers it once had.

One of the most pristine lakes in the world was still contaminated, and all water consumed from it had to be boiled until further notice. Lake Tahoe's population steadily dwindled after the mass exodus that had occurred right after the contamination. The lake's diluted solution of coronacyde had diminished each year, but the number of parts per million of coronacyde contamination still exceeded safe levels. Experts predicted the lake wouldn't be completely free of coronacyde for one hundred years or more.

Grigori Shirokov had given Yuri the account number to his largest bank account from his deathbed as soon as he'd realized that Mingli and Minzhe had poisoned him. After Yuri completed the second half of Grigori's last request when he'd killed Minzhe, the other half carried out by the Syndicate when they'd killed Mingli, Yuri decided to escape the frigid climate of Minsk and, with the fortune Grigori had left him, retired to the tropical island of Moorea in French Polynesia. He had a lavish house built on the east side of the island, with a view of Tahiti in the distance, and married a Polynesian woman. They had two children. The rest of Grigori's assets went to his three children and the Minsk government. The only mention of Grigori's involvement with the virus was during Mr. Wu's interrogation, but President Xiong never disclosed that information, and Grigori's character was never questioned.

The family members of those killed on Flight 818 finally learned what had happened to their loved ones, giving them a sense of closure. The aircraft was found by a remotely piloted submersible vehicle, which verified Quon's story. Meanwhile, Quon was one of the recipients of the claims against Wu International, and he moved to a province outside of Shanghai with the rest of his family, where he lived comfortably teaching physics on the main campus at Shanghai University.

The rest of Mingli's captives from the lab had been returned home, where they happily reunited with their families and were content to get back to their normal lives. Although they were compensated very well for their pain and suffering as part of the settlement from Wu International, they'd live with the emotional scars of their ordeal for the rest of their lives. Larissa went back to her home in Minsk and eventually met a very caring man who married and completed her.

Minzhe's mother had been through a lot in her lifetime. She'd lost the love of her life—her first true love—when she was a young woman. Alone and desperate, she'd had her oldest child taken from her out of the necessity to support herself and her other three children. Then, later in life, she'd watched her second husband slowly succumb to cancer. On top of that, both of her boys had met untimely deaths within less than a month of each other. Despite the nest egg that would comfortably carry her through the rest of her life, living with the pain of losing those loved ones made each day a challenge, and she clung ever tighter to her two daughters and her grandchildren, fearful that she might someday suffer the traumatic loss of another member of her family.

A small consolation in her life was the yacht her son, Minzhe, had left to her. Minzhe's mother and two sisters were his only surviving relatives, and his only asset remaining at the time of his death was the *WU*. Biyu, like so many other people around the world, regarded the name Wu as synonymous with the death of her loved ones, so the first thing she did was change the name of the *WU* to *我的孩子*, which translates to *My Boys*. She had a full staff that catered to her every need, and she planned to cruise around the world for the rest of her life, with her daughters' families aboard as often as they could manage. When she passed on, the hundred-million-dollar yacht would ensure her daughters and their families lived comfortably for the rest of their years too.

EPILOGUE

The *Charaka* had just finished provisioning in Nagasaki after modifications had been made to accommodate their new Sikorsky S-76C++ helicopter, and the ship was sailing south through the Philippine Sea when Ali alerted Duke that he'd picked up a distress signal from a catamaran twenty-six miles due east. He'd talked to a woman who'd stated she was alone on the boat and believed she was about to be attacked by pirates.

"Can we take them out with the GLGP?" Duke asked.

"No," Ali responded. "They're too close to the catamaran. The explosion might injure the woman."

"Tell Diego to get the copter ready, and let her know we'll be there shortly," Duke told Ali. "Steve, you and Kabir come with me. We'll get Diego to drop us off."

Diego heard the command over his earpiece and began raising the Sikorsky onto the platform, readying it for takeoff. The men boarded the helicopter, and Diego had them over the catamaran in minutes.

"What's she doing?" Steve asked.

"It looks like she's fending them off," Duke replied. "Drop us in."

The pirates couldn't get close to the catamaran because

a beautiful blonde woman was shooting at them with a power washer. Every time either of the two boats got within ten feet of the catamaran, the woman would squeeze the trigger and start blasting the men with a jet of high-pressure water. The pirates didn't make any attempts to shoot the woman, maybe because they had other intentions with her once they finally boarded. Either way, despite being pelted with a jet of water that could cut their skin to the bone, they weren't giving up and kept trying to get closer. Finally, one of the two boats went to the bow of the catamaran while the other stayed at the transom.

Diego lowered the Sikorsky just feet above the waves, and the three men dropped into the water like frogmen from a coast guard rescue helicopter.

The woman was busy concentrating on the pirates badgering her from the stern and didn't notice two of the four pirates on the other boat had moved to the bow and boarded her vessel. She kept the boat at the stern far enough away, giving Duke enough room to shoot up out of the water and onto the port-side sugar scoop like a missile launched from a submarine. He was on the boat in seconds while Steve and Kabir made the same entrance on the starboard sugar scoop.

Just before the pirates who'd boarded from the bow could grab the woman, Duke hit the man closest to her with his fist square in the nose, effectively breaking it and dropping the man to the deck while Steve did the same to the other pirate coming around the starboard side of the vessel. Duke turned, whipped out his Sig, and shot two of the five aft-boat pirates in their knees in an attempt to discourage them from any further shenanigans. One of the pirates on the boat picked up a rusty AK-47 and lifted it to shoot Duke.

Maybe I should let him try to shoot me to see if that old gun will blow up in his face, Duke thought but then decided, *why take the chance?* and shot the man in the forehead.

The only uninjured man remaining grabbed the tiller,

steered his boat away from the catamaran, and fled at full throttle. The two remaining pirates at the bow of the boat revved the outboard and followed their friend, abandoning their two associates who were writhing in pain on the deck.

Ragtag pirates were just no match for ex-Navy SEALs, and Steve and Kabir made short work of tying their arms and legs together behind their backs with zip ties.

"You killed that guy!" the woman exclaimed.

"In self-defense. He was getting ready to shoot me," Duke said.

"But you killed him!"

"I'm pretty sure he was already brain-dead," Duke joked.

"That's not funny. You killed him. You could have shot him in the arm or leg like you did those other two guys," the woman said.

"Or I could've let them have their way with you and take your boat."

"I can't believe you!"

"You know, I was kind of expecting a thank you or something," Duke said.

"I ought to shoot you." The woman pointed the power sprayer nozzle at him as he ducked backwards, raising his hands in surrender.

"Hey, I never shot anyone who didn't deserve it," Duke said.

"Who are you, John Wayne or something?"

"The Duke?" Duke smirked. "Well, ma'am, you're closer than you think," he said in his best John Wayne impersonation.

Steve chimed in and said, "Hey, Duke. I'm going to tell Diego to go back. We can have someone pick us up in a RIB."

"Okay," Duke said. Kabir just stood there watching with a big grin on his face, shaking his head back and forth.

Steve waved off Diego, signaling for him to fly back to the *Charaka*. Duke reached down and dragged the two pirates onto one of the sugar scoops. A few minutes later, they spotted an RIB on the horizon, and Kabir said, "Here comes our ride."

Duke turned to the woman and asked, "What are you doing out here all alone?"

"I'm heading into the Pacific to do research on some atolls," the beautiful lady said. "What are you guys doing out here?"

"We just finished with some boat repairs in Japan and are waiting for our next assignment," Duke answered. "What kind of research are you doing?"

"Oh, just looking for archeological artifacts," she responded. "What kind of boat do you have that there's a helicopter at your disposal?"

"We work on a cargo ship, usually transporting iron ore around the world. What's your name?"

"Dulcie," she replied, "but you can call me Ms. Flitter. What's yours?"

"I thought we already established that? You can call me Duke."

"How about I just call you smart-ass?"

"You wouldn't be the first person to call me that," Duke said with a grin.

"What are you going to do with those two guys?"

"We'll turn them over to the authorities."

Duke couldn't believe that the beautiful woman, perhaps the best-looking woman he'd ever seen in his life, didn't divert her attention away from him and try to strike up a conversation with Steve like just about every other woman would have. Instead, she was totally focused on Duke.

Maybe she's worried I'm going to shoot her? he asked himself. *No, that can't be. I just saved her. Well, I'm not going to let an opportunity like this slip by without taking a shot.*

"Do you have any time to spare, or do you have a schedule to follow?" Duke asked her.

"I make my own schedule, so I have a little time," she said. "What do you have in mind?"

"Well, we have an excellent chef on our boat. Perhaps

you'd like to join me for dinner tonight?"

"I've been alone for quite some time. Some company would be nice, and I'm not the kind of girl to pass up a good meal," Dulcie said.

"Great! I'll meet you back here in a few hours, and we'll pick you up," Duke said, then thought, *I hope I wasn't too enthusiastic.*

The men tossed the two pirates into the RIB and boarded the boat. Just like that, the encounter was over, and they were headed back to the *Charaka* with Ms. Dulcie Flitter etched into Duke's mind.

"What's that look?" Steve asked Duke. "I believe you're twitterpated!"

Duke just grinned.

* * *

A couple hours later, Dulcie saw a large ship on the horizon. As it approached, she wondered how she would tie her catamaran to the ship—the water there was too deep to anchor in. But as the ship got closer, she noticed two huge straps dangling from a large metal frame attached to one of the cranes.

Duke spoke over the loudspeaker. "Stay where you are. We'll maneuver around to pick you up."

As the *Charaka* was turning to a parallel position beside the catamaran, Dulcie saw two divers pop up beside her boat and guide the straps to either side of her vessel. When they were in place, one of the divers signaled to the bridge, and the catamaran began to rise out of the water. Dulcie didn't know what to think. Duke really did pick her up— literally!

With the catamaran safely secured, Duke rolled a ladder over to one of the sugar scoops at the stern of the boat so Dulcie could climb down to the *Charaka*'s deck.

"Looks like you haven't scrubbed the hulls for a while," Duke said as he examined the exterior of Dulcie's boat.

"I didn't realize you were going to see my private parts!" Dulcie teased.

"Well, I have to admit, I do like a nice bottom," Duke countered. "I'm sure I can coerce one of my colleagues to clean the hulls while we dine." Then, he escorted her into the superstructure and up to the dining area.

Ethan had already set a tray of hors d'oeuvres on the table. As Duke and Dulcie sat down, Duke asked what she wanted to drink.

"Do you have any Smirnoff Ice?" Dulcie requested.

"I doubt it. Perhaps you could try a lemon drop martini?" Duke proposed.

"I only drink Smirnoff Ice."

"It's time for you to broaden your horizons, ma'am," Duke told her, then asked Rodney to bring the lady one of Ethan's lemon drops. He ordered his usual: an Aberlour A'bunadh.

Rodney went into the galley and came back ten minutes later with a serving tray holding two drinks. Duke took the martini glass and handed it to Dulcie, then took the scotch glass and lifted it to his lips.

"Oh my!" Dulcie exclaimed. "This is amazing! It's the best drink I've ever had."

"Well, take it slow. Those are lethal. We should probably eat before you have another one." Duke took a sip of his drink and asked, "So, what do you do? I mean, for a living."

"I'm a researcher. Some would call me a glorified treasure hunter, but I call myself an oceanic archeologist," she told him. "You?"

"I'm just a cargo ship captain," Duke told her.

"Hmmm. A captain with a chef and a butler?"

"Well, those guys are mainly here to spy on me so they can report back to the rest of the crew. I've never really had, well, a lady friend on board before, and they're finding all of this amusing," Duke said.

"Is that what I am? A lady friend?" she asked.

"Ask me in a couple of hours," Duke taunted.

Just then, Rodney walked in carrying a serving tray of sushi and other appetizers and set the tray on the table.

"I don't eat sushi," Dulcie announced.

"It's not all sushi. Try this. It's smoked salmon in a spicy ponzu sauce," Duke persuaded as he prepared a small bowl of soy sauce with wasabi for dipping the roll in.

"Mmm, that's good!" Dulcie said. "What is that?" she asked, pointing at another concoction.

"That's seared tuna. Dip it in this sauce—it's a spicy Japanese mayo with masago," Duke informed her as he dipped a slice of his roll into the soy-sauce mixture.

"I can't believe I'm enjoying this stuff. I've never eaten anything like it before," she said.

"Trust me. Our chef is one of the best chefs in the world, and everything he serves will be excellent," Duke reassured her.

"I've noticed that everyone on this ship seems to be the best in the world at whatever they do," Dulcie stated questioningly.

"We tend to have some talented individuals working here," Duke said.

Rodney returned with two plates. "This is A5 Wagyu beef with a red wine reduction, twice-baked potatoes, and slightly charred brussels sprouts with a spicy agave glaze," Rodney announced as he placed the plates on the table—one in front of Dulcie and the other in front of Duke.

"Can I have some Lea and Perrins sauce for my steak?" Dulcie asked.

Rodney's jaw dropped.

Duke quickly spoke up, "She's just joking, Rodney. Don't say anything to Ethan. It's fine just the way he prepared it."

"But I like steak sauce," she said. "And I'll need a steak knife too."

Duke spoke up again. "Rodney, don't you dare!" he warned. Rodney grinned and went back into the galley.

Duke began to explain to Dulcie that Ethan had

prepared a dish once that Duke had really liked. But he'd thought it would've been even better with a little extra chili pepper. He'd told Rodney to ask Ethan to add a little spice to it the next time he prepared it. The next time Ethan had prepared the dish, he'd served it himself and stood by as Duke sampled it. Duke had taken one bite and his whole mouth was on fire, and it'd burned all night long. When he'd thought the pain had finally subsided, other body parts suffered the next day.

When Duke finished his story, the galley door burst open, and a red-faced Ethan Bernier stormed over to the table. He slammed down a plate with a piece of cardboard on it and a bottle of ketchup. "Perhaps madam would prefer this for dinner?" he sneered.

"She was just kidding, Ethan. She's going to love the steak exactly as you prepared it," Duke said, trying to calm Ethan down.

The chef glared at Dulcie for a few seconds and finally calmed enough to say, "Okay." He picked up the plate he'd brought and walked back toward the galley.

"Hey, Ethan. Would you please bring me a steak knife? All I have is a butter knife," Dulcie called after him.

Ethan turned and marched back to the table as Duke stood and held his hands up to intervene but to no avail. "Madam, if you need a steak knife to cut your meat, I will throw it overboard and fix you a hamburger," Ethan growled. He turned and stormed back into the galley, murmuring under his breath as he went.

"Well, isn't he just a little hothouse orchid?" Dulcie asked rhetorically.

"Please," Duke pleaded. "Whatever he serves for dessert, don't say a word. Just eat it."

To Dulcie's surprise, the steak cut so easily that she only needed her fork. It was the most delicious piece of meat she'd ever eaten. She loved twice-baked potatoes, but Ethan's surpassed anything she'd ever had. She admitted to Duke that she didn't like brussels sprouts, but when she tried one, she found that it too was remarkable. The entire meal surpassed her expectations, and she doubted she'd ever taste anything so good again. Duke breathed a sigh of relief when Dulcie devoured the chocolate soufflé Rodney served them for dessert.

As they sat there chatting and bantering, the night passed too quickly, and when Rodney asked if there was anything else they wanted before he retired for the evening, they realized it was extremely late.

"It's too late for you to leave tonight. Why don't you stay here in one of our guest rooms? It's nice and very comfortable too," Duke told her.

"I can just stay on my boat," Dulcie replied.

"You can take a long shower in the guest room. How long has it been since you had a long, hot shower?" Duke asked.

"That does sound good. I'll just get a change of clothes from my cabin."

"Okay, I'll walk with you."

"I do have one question I have to ask," Dulcie said as they walked. "Why is your ship called the *Charaka*?"

"'Charaka' is a Hindu boy's name meaning 'wanderer.' And that's basically what we are—a group of wanderers," Duke explained.

After showing Dulcie to her room, Duke went to his own room below deck and reminisced about the evening until he finally fell asleep. When he awoke, he showered, dressed, and headed up to Dulcie's room. She came to the door after Duke knocked, dressed and ready to go.

"What's for breakfast?" she asked.

"I don't know, but whatever it is, it'll be good," Duke answered. "But please try not to rile Ethan up. He's cranky first thing in the morning."

When Duke and Dulcie arrived in the dining room, half the crew was already waiting for them. All of them were curious about how the couple was getting along. The crew members didn't usually have visitors, let alone dates, and everyone found it almost as entertaining as reality television.

"How'd you sleep?" Steve asked.

"Very well," Dulcie responded. "The bed's very comfortable."

"I heard Ethan is trying to make something extra special this morning. He doesn't want to upset you again," Kabir said, and the whole table erupted in laughter.

"I wasn't the one who got upset," Dulcie defended herself.

"No worries," Bubba said. "We've all upset Ethan one time or another. I just wish we had a video of it."

They all laughed again because they *did* have a video of it and had watched it in the control room numerous times already. Rodney came strolling in with a large serving tray and walked around the table as everyone removed a plate from it until it was empty, prompting him to return for the rest. After another round, Rodney had served everyone and kept the last plate for himself, joining the group.

To Dulcie's dismay, their plates had eggs Benedict, smoked sausage, bacon, toast, and hash browns. Everything looked good to her except the eggs Benedict, a dish she'd never had before, but she knew she was going to have to try it. With all eyes on her, she cut a slice of her egg tower and took a bite, expecting the worst. But it turned out to be really good.

"What do you think?" Rodney smirked.

"It'll do," Dulcie said, inciting another response of tremendous laughter.

They all liked her, and they could tell that their good friend Duke did too.

After breakfast, they all went down to the catamaran to see Dulcie off. She was pleased with her hulls—they looked practically new after Bubba had power-washed them clean. She boarded her boat, and Valerie set it back into the water. Duke waved goodbye as she motored away and eventually raised her sails.

Steve sauntered up next to Duke, put his arm around

him, and said, "Catch and release, my dear friend. Catch and release. That's the sporting thing to do."

But in Duke's mind, he was determined to somehow, somewhere, some way, find that incredible woman again.

ABOUT THE AUTHORS

Louis grew up in the Midwest and worked at a factory for fourteen years after high school before returning to college and earning a degree in engineering. This led to a successful career in Construction Management. Never much of a reader himself, he met a beautiful girl who grew up on farm in the South. Despite living within a five-mile radius her entire life, Mandy was a traveler and had been to many places around the world. However, what Mandy loved most was reading, which allowed her to travel and enjoy adventures in many more places around the world through the stories she read. Mandy eventually talked Louis into listening to an audio book since he refused to read, and he discovered Clive Cussler and the Oregon Files—he was hooked.

When Clive Cussler died, Louis feared his favorite series of books had come to an end. Not finding anything else that interested him to read, he decided to embark on writing a similar book to the Oregon Files and voilà—The Charaka Adventures were born. Soon after Louis started writing the book, his son Brian, passed away suddenly at just thirty years old. The book was therapeutic in keeping his mind occupied during that traumatic period of time in his life.

Despite being confined to the house due to the pandemic, Louis' imagination took him around the world on action packed adventures with the Syndicate. After finishing the novel, Louis thought it was entertaining, but it was far from publishable. That's when Mandy took over—correcting grammar, re-wording sentences, and making the book much better than Louis ever could on his own. As with everything else in life, Louis and Mandy's potential as a team was much greater together than as individuals. L&M Payton, although not really writers, were now authors.